50

DEATH IN DELFT

Master Mercurius Mysteries
Book One

Graham Brack

SAPERE
BOOKS

DEATH IN DELFT

Published by Sapere Books.

20 Windermere Drive, Leeds, England, LS17 7UZ,
United Kingdom

saperebooks.com

ISBN: 978-1-913518-47-9

PROLOGUE

Now that I have arrived at the final chapter of my life, it occurs to me that everything in my head will be lost unless I write it down. I am vain enough to believe that at least some of my activities will be of interest to my fellow men, and if I have not glowed as brightly as others at least I have reflected some brilliant lights.

It is possible that in these pages I have been indiscreet to some extent. I would ask your pardon if that is the case, except that I don't give a fig.

I have enjoyed a long life. I have never gone hungry, I have avoided torture and imprisonment, and I have been of some service to others. What more can a man want? And if my homeland is less glorious now than it was when I first dropped into it in the Year of Our Lord 1638, well, it is still a desirable place to live. I once went to France and everywhere else has seemed much better since then.

I have done some things I ought not to have done, and I have left undone some things that I ought to have done. So be it. It's too late to cry over spilt milk. I have confessed and I carry some private griefs, but that's how they're going to stay — private.

Sometimes I wonder what happened to some of the people I describe in these journals. Oh, we all know about the famous ones. But it's the maids and the serving wenches, the boot-boys and the working men who fascinate me. Nobody puts up marble monuments to honest men who tramp the world looking for work to keep their family fed, but perhaps they should. And there are worse legacies for a woman than to have a tidy, well-swept house and some grandchildren to play with.

This story begins in 1671. I was three-and-thirty years old, just making my way in the world. I ask myself sometimes if things might have been different if I hadn't been so predictable that the boy knew where to find me.

You've got a brain. Judge for yourself.

CHAPTER ONE

When the boy found me, I was in an inn along the Langebrug, reading a book and drinking beer. The painter Jan Steen bought the inn shortly afterwards, which was no surprise, given that he contributed substantially to its income when he was a customer, but it was a prosperous enough place even without his money. Nobody in Leiden drinks water. If you saw what the woolworkers throw into it, you would understand why. Drinking water is a sure way to shorten your life.

I could have stayed in the university hall after supper; beer was available, and someone else would be paying for the fire and the candles, and I would have done, were it not for Master Cornelius. He is a fellow lecturer in the university, who has for some reason decided that I am best placed to discuss the infinitely tedious theories regarding the population of the world that he has expounded in an execrable and thankfully unpublished pamphlet, *De Generatione Populi*.

Each time he discusses this pamphlet with me, I find a new objection to his logic, which he then works upon for some time before pressing a revised version on me. I had, at supper, spotted him hastily reading through a few leaves and instantly decided that the inn was the place for me to pass the evening, knowing that Master Cornelius thought it a low place, much favoured by women of the commercial class. That is true, but they do not bother me for three reasons. First, because we are all sinners, and who is to say which sin God abhors most? Second, because I am a cleric. Third, because I work for the university and I cannot afford to pay for their services anyway.

The boy pushed the door open and saw me. I usually sit under the wall candles on the left side, the best light for reading being there. He marched boldly in and stood before me.

'The Rector wants you.'

Kitchen lads are rarely respectful, and were I not opposed to violence in all its forms I could cheerfully have clipped his ear. Of course, he knows which lecturers are clerics, and therefore which he can irritate with impunity.

'Me? Why?'

'He won't tell the likes of me that, will he?' said the impudent scallywag.

I finished my tankard with one draught and followed him back to the Academy Building. It was dark and the cobbles were slippery. A man could easily tumble into a canal, and many do, though this possibility seemed lost on the boy, who skipped happily along at speed. It took only a few minutes to walk to the Academy, where the Rector's candles shone from an upper window.

The boy insolently tapped the door with his hand. 'This is the place,' he said.

'I know,' I told him. 'I work here.'

The boy shrugged. 'Rector's upstairs. He said I could have a piece of pie if I brought you inside half an hour, so I'm off to the kitchens.'

I made my way up the stairs to the Rector's chambers. He seemed pleased to see me and invited me to sit by the fire, abandoning the work on his desk to come and stand beside me.

The Rector was a slight man, old-fashioned in his appearance and usually dressed in severe black with a small skullcap of black wool. His beard was white, trim, pointed, and his eyes were a bright blue. In this light they appeared even brighter than usual. He rested an arm on the mantelpiece and poked a log with his toe.

'You will, no doubt, wonder why I have summoned you by night, and chose to use a butcher's lad instead of my servant to do so. You may also wonder why it could not have waited until the morning.'

I judged that the question was rhetorical and made no effort to answer.

'I have received a letter from the mayor of Delft. They have urgent need of an educated man and so, naturally, they sought one from Leiden — more specifically, from me. They ask for someone with "a quick wit, a knowledge of God's law and abundant energy". I see all these in you, and more beside.'

'May I ask why someone is needed?'

He rubbed his chin. 'You may, but I won't answer. I want you to travel with a blank mind, a *tabula rasa* upon which anything may be written by God's grace. I know very little anyway, so I will leave it to the mayor to explain. There is a meeting of the leading citizens of Delft at three o'clock tomorrow afternoon in the town hall. Please be there.'

He returned to his desk and handed me a pouch. 'A letter of introduction and commendation, and some expenses towards the journey. Keep an account and any shortfall will be defrayed on your return. The mayor may offer you some too, which you may accept but must record and receipt. A barge will leave at six tomorrow morning from the fish market. The skipper will take you along the Vliet to Delft.'

I nodded. I would prefer not to rise so early, but it ill becomes a religious man to say so, since he would miss the first prayers of the day.

'I am at your service, Rector,' I replied, with a formal bow, and walked towards the door. I have never mastered the combination of walking backwards and bowing at the same time, and fortunately the Rector does not expect it, though I think he prefers his members of staff to be able to manoeuvre their backsides between the doorposts without banging a hip on the open door, as I managed to do.

'One last thing,' he said, so I stopped retreating and stood up straight. The Rector was sitting at his desk and declined to look me in the eye, preferring to sign papers as he spoke.

'Sir?'

'I have no influence in Delft. If you find yourself in difficulty, I will not be able to help you. Therefore, Master, I bid you be discreet.'

I knew what he meant, but not how he knew it needed saying, and that worried me rather more. I had a secret, which he must have known or guessed, which is the cause of certain difficulties. In a Reformed land, I am a Catholic. If this were generally known, a lot of doors would be closed to me. When I was ordained a few years ago in France, the bishop bade me to keep my ordination secret for the time being. His reasoning was simple. From time to time the Protestants rounded up all the priests they could find and burned them, and while this had never been great sport in Holland, he saw fit not to take the chance. It is my belief that His Grace had it in mind to create a church in reserve that could be activated if the original were paralysed. In fact, the position in Holland today for Catholics is tolerable. We can build churches provided they do not front a main road. We must not gather outside to talk, and must leave services in small numbers. We must not advertise anything happening in our church, and we must not upset the neighbours.

This would be a minor awkwardness were it not the case that I was also ordained as a Protestant minister. I never intended to act as one, but it was a condition of the stipend that kept me at the university and, at the time I accepted it, I had not yet been ordained a Catholic priest. I admitted it to but one man, the French bishop I mentioned earlier, who simply smiled and said it was very ecumenical of me. He then observed that if the Protestants were prepared to pay for my keep, that meant he could support someone else instead, and that therefore I should not trouble myself over it. But I confess that I do. Obviously the Rector must know of the Protestant ordination and, if he has discovered that I am a Catholic, it must puzzle him, but he has said nothing.

CHAPTER TWO

It was a bitingly cold morning as I walked to the Vliet shortly before six o'clock. There was no snow, but there was a keen frost that crunched underfoot. The fish market was busy even at that hour, the sailors unloading their catch and the buyers calling out incomprehensible numbers and waving their arms to indicate offers made and bargains accepted. A small number of serving women picked their way through the barrels, early shoppers hoping to get the best of the catch. They were mainly older women; the young ones prefer to snatch a few more minutes in a warm bed.

'Master Mercurius!' a cheery voice announced.

'Good morning, Katja,' I replied, having identified the pink pig-like face of the Langebrug inn's cook swathed in a woollen scarf inside the hood of her cloak.

'Good morning to you, sir. There'll be some fine haddock for supper tonight, if it pleases you.'

'I wish I could,' I answered honestly, 'but I'm bound for Delft for a few days.'

'Delft? Then you'll be the gentleman old Marten is waiting for.' She indicated a barge a little to one side of us. 'He's taking his catch to Delft in the hope of a better price, I bet.'

Katja nodded a farewell, and soon I was sitting in the bow of the barge, as far as possible from the oily fish that old Marten apparently specialised in. The north wind was keen and bore an icy sleet that left me in a quandary. Either I braved the sting on my face, or I turned my back on my host. I could — conceivably — avoid both by retreating to the stern and sitting amongst the fish but I decided to stay as I was and accept reddened cheeks as a mortification of the flesh.

The distance from Leiden to Delft is not quite five leagues, and in good weather a man might walk it in a morning, but the icy ground and the difficulty of seeing the path when it is overlaid with snow made the barge a better choice. I have known too many men take an involuntary plunge when they mistook the route.

In the early afternoon I arrived at Delft, walked to the Town Hall and presented my credentials, before being ushered into a spacious chamber to await the meeting.

You could tell that the two men didn't really like each other. Respect, yes, of course, but not like. They tried to hide it for obvious reasons, but even an outsider like me could see it within a few minutes. Perhaps only an outsider could see it?

Mijnheer Van Leeuwenhoek stood at the window, his cane planted by his foot and its top held out in his left hand like the bowsprit of a ship so the sail of his cloak opened to its full extent. He was a tall, lean man, with straight hair parted in the middle, a narrow, long, pinched nose — and a narrow, long, pinched mind. He was not a man you would warm to, but I imagined that if you made the effort, it would be rewarded with loyalty on his part, though without much affection. I was surprised to learn later that he was not yet forty years old; his gravity placed him in his middle years.

Mijnheer Vermeer, on the other hand, was a friendly, open fellow. He breezed in, slightly surprised that we had not started without him, largely because — for once — he was not late. You could not call Vermeer boisterous. In fact, he became very quiet as the meeting progressed, but when the subject was something he knew about, he held tenaciously to his view.

Van Leeuwenhoek was a plain dresser, a Calvinist in every sense, happiest in blacks and browns. Vermeer also dressed plainly, largely as a result of economy, but a bright sash or a feather in his hat drew your eye. On our first meeting he wore a buff coloured coat with a broad blue sash which he kept adjusting as he sat listening. In a room of men in severe black with white collars, he brought a small spark of colour.

The clock in the Nieuwe Kerk struck three with its fine peal, and the mayor invited us to sit. Everyone in the room knew why they were there — except, needless to say, me.

The mayor began by explaining that three young girls had been abducted from their homes. 'The first was Gertruyd Lievens, who disappeared on the eighteenth day of January. Her body was found last week in a shallow grave to the north of the town. She had not been molested, so far as our surgeon could determine.'

'May I ask the cause of her death?' I asked.

The mayor turned to a portly man to his left, who must have been the surgeon in question.

'I believe that she had been made insensible with wine and smothered, sir.'

Vermeer produced a piece of paper from his sleeve. 'I made a sketch of the scene,' he said diffidently. 'It's not too good — the light was poor and I had to work quickly.'

I unfolded the sheet. It was as if I were there. A path of some sort ran along a dyke, and the field was a little lower. The body had been laid to rest in the corner of the field. Vermeer had depicted the scene in several ways on the same page. In the top left corner was a view of the grave after the surface soil had been removed. I was puzzled to see a crude cross at her head.

'Was the cross placed there by the discoverer?'

'No, we think the murderer did so,' the mayor answered.

'That is most unusual.'

'Murder itself is unusual in Delft,' said the mayor.

To the right of the view of the grave, there was a version made from the field, showing the grave's setting hard against the bank. Below that there was a picture of the young girl's face, and to the left of that, a second version showing Gertruyd as she might have been in life.

'Is this from memory, mijnheer?'

Vermeer shook his head. 'I asked her father to tell me what was different about my first drawing from the living girl. He vouches for the accuracy of the second image.'

To my surprise, Van Leeuwenhoek spoke sharply. 'This is fancy,' he said. 'You will not find the murderer by examination of the fruit of an artist's imagination.'

'I draw what I see,' Vermeer retorted.

Van Leeuwenhoek tapped the page with the top of his cane. 'This snowflake — was it here, or perhaps a hand's-breadth to the left? Were there exactly six snowflakes falling when she was found?'

'Obviously not. I convey only that it was snowing.'

'But it is exactly that precision of detail that is needed to trap this villain! A man is condemned by facts, not fantasies. And facts are the basis of all science.'

The mayor sighed. No doubt he had heard all this before. 'But, mijnheer, the surgeon has made an inspection, distressing as that was to the family. What more could your science add?'

Van Leeuwenhoek spoke urgently. 'The cross — of what wood was it made? Where did it come from? There are no trees nearby to furnish it, so the murderer must have brought it. How did he transport the body without discovery, since the road atop the dyke can be seen from a distance? Why did he choose this place to bury her? Above all, *why* did he kill her, since he appears not to have slaked his lust upon her?'

His passion spent, Van Leeuwenhoek returned to the window and turned his back on us. I feared that he had already discounted the prospect of any help from me. There was a cough that appeared to have been forced.

'Sergeant?'

'If we are to view the sites today, sir, we should go now before darkness falls.'

'Indeed. We may resume here later. Let us take our cloaks and follow the sergeant, who will show us the relevant places.'

We stepped out into the sharp wind, treading gingerly on the icy cobbles. The sergeant led us over the Boterbrug, past, I was later to discover, Van Leeuwenhoek's old house, and along Oude Delft to the Armamentarium. There we crossed to the west side of the canal and proceeded into a maze of courtyards and small alleys connecting them. The houses were two storeys tall for the most part, and women sat at the upper windows leading me, I confess, to an incorrect assumption about their trade. As if reading my thoughts, Vermeer dipped his head and muttered an explanation.

'Weavers, sir. We are in one of the weaving quarters. They work upstairs where the light is better. They're paid much less for their labours if there is a mistake in the weave.'

I nodded my understanding. 'It is a hard life, mijnheer Vermeer.'

'It is for most of God's creatures,' he replied.

We skirted a well, passed through a short alley and found ourselves in another courtyard where the sergeant stopped. He pointed at a house to his left using his staff. 'The house where

Gertruyd Lievens lived, sirs. She was sent to the well that we have just passed and did not return.'

'To the well? On the morning of the Lord's Day?' said one of our party.

'They must work when they can, mijnheer Van Ruijven. The previous day had been stormy and dark, so it would have been difficult to work.'

A woman appeared in the open doorway of the Lievens' house. She was around thirty years of age, but stray hairs tinged with grey escaped from her cap. She was pale, drawn, with purple rings under her eyes. When she saw us, she dropped a listless curtsy. The mayor doffed his hat and withdrew to speak a few words to her. I heard nothing of it, but her tears flowed once more, and he awkwardly patted her shoulder and squeezed her upper arm as if enjoining her to fortitude.

The sergeant began retracing our steps and I turned to follow, only to bump into Vermeer who was staring at the woman. His eyes were glistening and I think his teeth gripped his lower lip.

'Poor, poor creatures,' he mumbled. 'And she the poorest of all.'

The sergeant now led us along the Zuidwal, under the Bastion and on towards the Oostpoort, the eastern gate to the city. There we turned along the water's edge and crossed by the first bridge to a serried row of sheds with turfed roofs. Many appeared derelict, though men and women scurried between them. There was a greyness about the scene, bleak in the dim light of a late winter's day, the griminess of their clothing and the lack of any flowers or other colour oppressing the eye.

We drew to a halt once more, and the sergeant again raised his staff to indicate one of the sheds. 'The home of Magdalena Kuijper, the second victim. She has not yet been found.'

'But you speak of her as a victim. How can you be sure that she is dead?' I asked.

'The coldness of the weather, mijnheer. If she is not in a house she will not have survived this chill. She disappeared on the twenty-seventh day of January, about three weeks ago.'

I was standing beside the mayor at this point. 'Forgive me,' I said, 'I had mistaken these low buildings for sheds. Why do they turf the roofs?'

'The wind here strips slates or tiles off, to the danger of those walking past. And turf is warm and cheap.'

'What is her father's trade?'

'That would be easier to answer if we knew who her father was, sir. But most here work at unloading the barges and portering their wares. The women gut and clean fish. Magdalena worked with shellfish, rinsing them and dividing them into pails to be taken to the city's kitchens.'

'How old is she?'

'Eight years or thereabouts. But, I hear, a big, strong girl for her age. The families here have the fish trimmings and can buy the old catch quite cheaply. And there are always things in the net that are not wanted by those with finer palates.'

We continued along the waterside and crossed towards the market square once more. The sergeant led us along another canal, lined on either side with fine houses of three or four storeys, and stopped a third time.

'The home of Wilhelmus van Setten, whose daughter Anna was abducted two days ago.'

Plainly Van Setten was a very different man to the fathers of the first two girls. One could understand why the burghers of Delft had decided to seek help, now that the higher classes of society were being threatened.

'May I know something of mijnheer Van Setten?' I asked.

There was an awkward pause, as if I had asked who John the Baptist was. Finally the mayor spoke. 'The Van Settens are an old Delft family. One of their women married into the Van Dussen family.'

If this was meant to enlighten me, it failed.

'Wilhelmus is a tobacco merchant, though he also has interests in pepper. He is a wealthy man, though his many business interests demand all his time and prevent his playing a full role in city life.'

I believe Van Leeuwenhoek snorted, but when I looked at him he had turned away and was studying the buildings opposite.

'Anna is, alas, their only child. Mevrouw Van Setten is not of an age ... well, they have not been blessed.'

'Was the child in the house?' I asked.

'She was not, sir,' the sergeant replied. 'She had been allowed outside to feed the ducks. She and a friend walked up the street to the little bridge you see, perhaps fifty paces away. A maid was sent to collect the friend, and together they walked through the Turfmarkt, which runs to the right as you look westwards now.'

'And Anna then came straight home?'

'We do not know. The maid and the girl did not look back, and tell us that Anna was standing on the bridge looking towards us here, facing her own house, when they left her.'

'I trust the maid has been soundly thrashed,' growled Van Ruijven. 'She must have taken leave of her senses, abandoning a child in the street like that. She should have walked Anna home, then taken her own charge with her.'

'Perhaps, but she did not,' said the mayor with a sigh, 'and that is all there is to it.'

The thought crossed my mind, not for the last time, that I would not wish to be a maid in Van Ruijven's house. There was overmuch relish in his voice when he spoke of thrashing her.

'And what time was this?' I asked.

'About two o'clock. The cook says that she gave Anna some stale bread for the ducks after lunch. It is the custom of the household to dine after the evening service on Sundays, you understand.'

I tried to understand what this implied, and was helped by Vermeer, whose eyes were fixed firmly on mine. He had an intensity of gaze I found unsettling, as if he really saw all there was to see, open or concealed.

'Your brow is furrowed, Master Mercurius. What puzzles you?'

'It's curious,' I began. 'Presumably Anna was dressed as befits her station. Unless she was abducted into a closed carriage, she must therefore have walked happily with her abductor, because this is a busy area. On Sunday afternoon the streets must have been filled with people taking the air or walking to or from church.'

Van Leeuwenhoek's grey eyes brightened. 'And you think therefore that her abductor must be known to her? But what manner of man is known to the Lievens girl and that fishwife's daughter?'

'Those who trade in cloth and fish, presumably,' I replied. 'Though any man who frequents the barges might have seen Magdalena Kuijper. But there is more to this. First, gentlemen, we must not presume the kidnapper to be a man. A woman, after all, would be more readily trusted by any girl.'

I thought Van Ruijven was about to die of apoplexy. (Actually, he did, later; but that is another story.)

'A woman? Monstrous! What woman would smother a young girl and bury her in a field? It is unthinkable.'

'Nevertheless, Van Ruijven, it must be thought,' Van Leeuwenhoek boomed. 'There is no evidence to exclude it, so we must consider it. Pray, sir, continue.'

'Whether a man or a woman, I say again, they walked with the child, either through the streets or to a waiting carriage. But I presume, sergeant, that you have asked and no-one saw such a carriage?'

'No, sir, no-one.'

'And I further presume that the child was old enough not to enter a carriage willingly?'

'She is as yet an innocent, sir,' the mayor replied. 'Barely eight years old. One hopes that children will have discretion, but...'

'But no cries were heard, no screams, no attempts to pull away; and if passers-by saw nothing, it is because there was nothing unusual to see.'

'Nothing that they recognised as unusual,' Van Leeuwenhoek corrected me.

'Indeed. They saw a normal Sunday afternoon scene. Therefore, it seems to me, they did not see Anna and her captor as mismatched. That suggests to me that he was dressed as she was.'

'It is the fashion for drabness,' Vermeer remarked. 'When all wear black and white, there is no distinction to be made. A man dressed so may be a pauper or a prince.'

'I would hope, mijnheer, that the cleanness of my collar and hose separates me from a bargemaster,' Van Leeuwenhoek replied. 'In superficialities we may be much the same, but the penetrating eye sees the differences. I grant, however, that not all men possess such an eye.'

'Do we have a likeness of Anna?' I asked.

'Her father has lent us a miniature of her which is being copied by one of the sergeant's men. Fortunately the city is not lacking in good artists. There will be a copy in every church porch by tonight.'

'And where was Gertruyd's body found?'

The sergeant led us to the east end of the road and pointed to the north-east. 'If you walk for ten minutes in that direction and leave the city, you will come to a lane with a pair of small windmills. She was found about a hundred and fifty paces along that lane, on the north side.'

'If you have nothing more to show me, sergeant, I should like to see the site.'

'It is almost dark, mijnheer,' the mayor protested.

'Indeed, sir, and I ask none other to accompany me, if someone will just show me the place.'

'I'll take you,' Vermeer offered. 'If the mayor is done with us.'

The mayor consented, and reminded us that he had arranged a meal for us all within an hour. There was a deal of bowing, and we went our ways.

With the company dispersed, Vermeer was much more voluble.

'What did you make of them?' he asked.

'I must not form impressions on such short acquaintance, mijnheer.'

'Call me Johannes, if you will. And you have already formed impressions — they showed on your face.'

'Nevertheless, I may be wrong.'

'You may. But let me help you. The mayor is a good man. And I can't complain about Van Ruijven — he buys most of my paintings and without him my family would probably starve.'

'What family do you have?'

'Wife, mother-in-law, nine children living — did I mention my mother-in-law? My Gertruyd is about the same age as these three girls. Did you notice that — all of them are eight or nine years old?'

'Yes, I did. An odd age for abduction.'

'Meaning?'

'Some men are depraved enough to lust after small children, and some attack girls on the point of becoming women, but these are neither. But we have no reason to suppose that one man carried out all three attacks.'

'Or woman. Do you really think a woman could have done this?'

'Probably not,' I replied. 'But I just wanted to open their minds to the possibility.' Vermeer sniggered. I tried to suppress a smirk and failed dismally. 'It was worth it to see the beetroot complexion on Van Ruijven's face.'

'You won't say it, but he is the most pompous prig,' Vermeer added.

'I wouldn't wish to be a maid in his house,' I remarked.

Vermeer's face hardened. 'What have you heard?' he asked, gripping me by the arm. Taken aback, I said nothing, and he released his grip. 'I'm sorry,' he said, 'but there have been rumours.'

'Rumours? What rumours?'

'Unworthy, no doubt. But some say that Van Ruijven makes very free with his maids.'

'And other people's?'

'It is said so. Though most maids need little leading astray. And he is a rich and generous man. He would never pay a girl for her favours, but he would take the favours and make her a present of some trinket or a couple of yards of cloth afterwards, I think.'

An elderly man emerged from the doorway of a tumbledown cottage beside the road and hailed Vermeer, who paused to exchange a few words before we marched on.

'Old Cobus knew my father,' he explained. 'They were of an age.'

'Are you from Delft, then?'

'Yes, born and bred. My father kept an inn here and dealt in paintings.'

'So didn't everyone know him? There's no better occupation for becoming known than innkeeper, surely?'

'True,' said Vermeer. 'I've done it myself. But my mother-in-law thinks it unbecoming to a gentleman. Quite all right to accept the rent from one, of course. I should have been clearer. I meant that Cobus knew my father when they both lived in Amsterdam.'

'If you were born here, that must be some time ago.'

'Above fifty years. Cobus speaks of it as if it were yesterday. It's nineteen years now since Father died.'

'And your mother?'

'Died last year.'

'I'm sorry.'

'She was seventy-five. It's a good age. She rarely visited us. I think she found the children a bit overwhelming.'

'If there are nine in your house, that's understandable.'

'Yes,' Vermeer conceded, 'though she always said she loved children. Old Cobus is remarkable, isn't he? Almost blind, and yet he recognised me at once.'

'Men say the blind develop their hearing to compensate.'

Vermeer pondered over the proposition. 'Perhaps, and Cobus may have heard me talking to you, but his keenest sense is his smell. He was a cook in an inn my father particularly liked. We turn here.'

Sunset was drawn out in those winter months and the sky still had a pale ribbon of blue resting on the horizon to the west. Unfortunately we were headed east, and little could be seen, though we could make out the shapes of the two windmills that gave the lane its name.

'You see ——' Vermeer indicated with his walking stick —— 'although it is very gloomy a man can stay on the road if he keeps the two mills lined up to his left. I wonder if that is why the murderer brought her here. I just can't imagine that he took her body through our town given how busy it is at all hours of the day and night. Even walking out to the suburbs he risked being seen, unless he could somehow do it at night.'

I nodded. 'Indeed, but I suppose that it is no unusual sight to see a man pushing a cart or barrow in the direction of the mills. Nobody checks what is in a farmer's sacks.'

'But surely he can't have dug the grave by day, when he might have been seen at any time? Anyone climbing to the upper floor of these mills would have seen him clearly.'

'One would think so, but we must check for ourselves in daylight. The dyke may have obscured him from view. After all, it doesn't matter if people see him digging —— there are plenty of people digging in fields every day —— but they must not see what he is digging for.'

We arrived at a field not far from the second windmill. The dyke was actually quite low here, about halfway up my thigh. A man digging the grave would have been more than half revealed.

'Maybe he dug it before he brought the body?' I said, intending it for my ears only, but Vermeer heard it.

'It could be! He might well have dug the hole by day and come back with the body later. But anybody could have discovered the hole between the two visits.'

I shrugged. 'A man may dig a hole in his own field without explanation. But whose field is it?'

'A man called Jan Pieterszoon. He grows turnips here, but there isn't much to do in the field in January. He might not have come here for a while.'

'Did he discover the body?'

'I'm not sure. His neighbour Harmen was the one who brought the news to the town hall.'

'Perhaps we could speak to them.'

'The light is fading, Master Mercurius. We ought to complete our inspection and return to the town centre before it grows much darker. Here is the corner. The earth is still disturbed where the sergeant's men dug up the body.'

It was exactly as Vermeer had drawn it, though why that surprised me is difficult to say. Could it be that I was impressed by the detail that he had recorded in a quick sketch, made in poor winter light with cold hands?

'When was she found, mijnheer?'

'Johannes, please. Let's see. Today is Tuesday. It would have been last Wednesday, late in the afternoon. I would not have been near the town hall normally, but there was a meeting to discuss building more almshouses.'

'In a prosperous city like Delft? There must be less poverty here than in most towns.'

'I can't say, but you can have plenty of poverty without an almshouse. What causes almshouses to be built is not poverty, but having men willing to pay for them, and the rich men of the town are keen to show off their generosity by donating a cottage or two. In fact, if you will permit me the unworthy thought, you might almost say that they were in competition to relieve the deserving poor.'

'Do they have some secret gift that enables them to distinguish the deserving and undeserving poor?' I asked, not entirely innocently.

'No, they're as bad at it as anyone else. They just try more often and tell each other how well they've done.' Vermeer smiled. He had a gentle, friendly smile with eyes that could not quite match the fun in his lips. There was always a little residual sadness in his gaze as if things were never perfectly right in his world.

I climbed onto the dyke to gain a better view. 'Do you know what happened to the cross?'

'It was taken with the body, I believe.'

'And has the body been buried?'

'Not yet. It is planned for Saturday. The mayor has asked for contributions towards the funeral costs but I don't think enough has been forthcoming. They're a poor family, Master. They ought to be enabled to bury their daughter decently. I wish I could help more myself, but...' He spread his hands eloquently.

No doubt having twelve mouths to feed strained his resources considerably. I found myself wondering whether he was as open as this with all new acquaintances, or whether there was something special about our relationship: it seemed that there was something about me that opened his heart.

Dutch towns are often small and claustrophobic. Everyone knows everyone else's business and I can imagine that may be uncongenial to those whose business is not going well. Vermeer was plainly a painter of great skill, and I had some slight recollection that his name had reached me in Leiden, but there are a lot of fine painters around and they cannot all make a good living. The cuffs of his jacket were a little frayed, and while it was possible that he simply took little interest in his appearance such a conclusion jarred somewhat with the care that he took in adjusting his sash or his hat.

'I'm sorry?'

'I asked, Master, whether you were ready for me to conduct you back to the town hall? There will be food ready soon and if I know the mayor he will not allow anyone to eat until we return.'

'That would make me unpopular,' I grinned.

'No, it would make *me* unpopular,' Vermeer grimaced. 'Though I wouldn't be popular in some circles if I brought Our Lord himself to sup.'

The meal was quite lavish. I was invited to sit at the mayor's right hand, next to an old man called Lieftingh who proved to be an apothecary. He had an irritating habit of hinting that he knew all the secrets of the town and then declining to provide any succulent titbit of gossip. No doubt he knows the diseases that people have and can guess how they came by them, and some of it may not be creditable. Since he was providing no information I decided to ask him for it.

'Do you know the Van Setten girl?'

'No,' he replied, shaking his loose grey locks vigorously. 'Too healthy to know me! Her mother, on the other hand...'

'Yes?'

'Inclined to hysteria, I suspect. There is an imbalance in the humours. She leans towards melancholy.'

'A woman is entitled to be melancholic if her daughter disappears.'

'Yes, but before that. She is easily put out of countenance.'

'Not being married, I am the last person to discuss household arrangements, but I can imagine that a young married woman in a house full of servants and with a husband much occupied in business might be rather bored and lonely.'

'Ah, that I cannot say. She lacks company, that's true enough. She made up for it by doting on her daughter. But, if I may be indiscreet for a moment, mevrouw Van Setten is not a young woman. I think she must be above forty years old. She does not consult me, of course. The family employs a surgeon in The Hague. I believe he is a specialist in diseases of the rich.'

Despite myself, I chuckled. If mevrouw Van Setten was a hypochondriac, she had plenty of company among the well-off, bored wives of famous men, I am sure. And mijnheer Lieftingh was quite entertaining in his waspishness.

'I was fortunate enough to be shown the place where the first girl's body was found by mijnheer Vermeer.'

'Johannes? He's a good sort. Wife's a complete monster, of course, and as for his mother-in-law...' Lieftingh's dismissive gesture conveyed his feelings clearly.

'What's wrong with his mother-in-law?'

'Airs and graces. Goes around with her nose in the air looking down on the rest of us. The thing is, young Vermeer is smitten with his wife. He would put up with any conditions to get her and almost as much to keep her.'

'Conditions? What sort of conditions?'

'Vermeer's wife is a Catholic. His mother-in-law would not allow them to marry unless he converted, so he did. And now they trip along each Sunday morning to Mass trying to look inconspicuous so as not to draw attention to the secret church. Bit difficult when there are a dozen of you.' Lieftingh lowered his voice. 'He has money troubles, you know.'

'Is that so?'

'Keeps the children fed and his mother-in-law helps out, though I'll wager she keeps reminding him of the fact. His home life must be hell. She lives in, you see.'

'His mother-in-law?'

'That's right. Maria Thins is the name. Mind, but she's had a hard life herself. Her husband was one of the great wife-beaters of our age and she has a son who is feeble-minded. Last I heard he was in an asylum.'

'An asylum?'

'You know, a madhouse. Place where they put the insane.'

'I know what one *is*,' I said. 'I just wondered what he did to be imprisoned in one.'

'I'm not sure. Some say he threatened to kill his mother, but you don't get put away for doing people a service. Others say he pulled a knife on Vermeer. I'm not even sure he's still alive. That's Willem Bolnes, obviously — Vermeer's still alive, he's over there.' Lieftingh gave a little cackle and busied himself with a chicken leg, so I turned to the mayor.

'We've booked you a room in the inn behind the hall,' he said. 'I thought you'd want to come and go as you please and might find being billeted on one of us a shade constricting. I do hope that's acceptable?'

30

He seemed genuinely concerned so I hurried to assure him that I would be very happy with that arrangement.

'The reckoning will come to us, of course,' he continued. 'You're welcome to take your meals there, although frankly I wouldn't recommend it. If you're agreeable, I've arranged that you should dine with each of us in turn.'

'I would be honoured,' I replied, though inwardly I was cringing. The idea of having to make small talk sent shivers down my spine. And you must understand that as an unmarried man I found that a family setting could be difficult. Women seemed to believe that they and only they had a duty to find me a wife, so inevitably my unmarried state would be raised. I know my bishop was accommodating about the compromises I was obliged to make to keep my place at the university, but I think if I married he might find that to be an accommodation too far.

'Excellent. I'll have my clerk give you a list.' The mayor dipped his head towards my ear. 'Frankly, it's a great help to me. At least this way none of them can complain that they don't know what's going on. Oh, there might be a difficulty on Friday. There is a meeting of the Civic Guard for drill and I would imagine a man of the cloth would not feel comfortable wielding a pike.'

'I don't know how I'd feel. I've never done it.'

'Perhaps that would be a good day to pay your compliments to the sisters at the Convent, if you have no qualms about mixing with Catholics.'

'No, sir, none. It is important that I meet as many people as possible while I'm in Delft.'

'Very good, very good. You never know, you may grow to like the place, despite the circumstances that bring you here. It's good to have a learned young man amongst us.' I was just composing a suitably bland reply when he added guilelessly: 'The minister of our Nieuwe Kerk will be retiring before long, I expect.'

One of the benefits of clergy is that they can travel light, because nobody minds if they wear the same clothes every day, the dictates of hygiene being observed, of course. The porter at the inn was therefore pleasantly surprised when he asked if he could help with my bags and found how small it was. This did not prevent his loitering by the doorway in case I felt like giving him a tip. Instead I offered him a blessing and turned to setting out my things.

I laid out a clean shirt on the top of the chest and waited for the maid to bring me some water to wash myself. She took me by surprise when she asked if I was ready to go to bed and then blushed prettily as she explained that she was charged with bringing me a warming-pan for the bed. I said I would be happy to have it as soon as she could prepare it, and she bobbed in something resembling a curtsy, albeit one made by a newborn foal, and returned after a few minutes with a copper pan whose handle she held in two thick cloths. Peeling back the blankets she thrust the pan well down the bed.

'Do you need me to remove it for you later, my Lord?' she asked.

'Thank you, I can do it myself. And I'm not a Lord, just an ordinary mijnheer. Men call me Master or Magister, if they're being formal. What is your name?'

'Lucie, if it please you, sir.'

'Lucie, would you stay just a minute?'

She clutched the neck of her blouse as if she expected me to spring upon her. 'The mistress will expect me back in the kitchen, sir, and I ought not…' She stumbled as if unable to name exactly what she ought not to do, but with a slight reproof in her eyes as if she ought not to have to tell a minister what she ought not to do.

'I mean you no harm. I will sit on the stool by the window and you may sit on the chair or the edge of the bed, as you please.'

'You should have the chair, sir, and I will take the stool.'

'As you please, Lucie.'

We took our places.

'How old are you, Lucie?'

'Sixteen years old, sir. I was born in October 1654. My father named me Lucie, although no woman in our family has the name, because I came into the world just after the explosion.'

She did not need to expand on which particular explosion she had in mind. In October 1654 a gunpowder magazine in Delft had detonated and destroyed a third part of the city. No doubt there had indeed been a great light that day.

'Your family must have been in Delft some years, then,' I said, but it was obvious that Lucie lived in a world in which people stayed where God first placed them. The idea that anyone might travel far seemed not to have occurred to her.

'I don't know that they were ever anywhere else, sir,' she replied simply.

'Do you know why I am here, Lucie?'

'No, sir. Except that the mayor sent for you. And you've come all the way from Leiden.'

'It's not that far, Lucie. I'm here to help discover what has happened to the girls who have gone missing. Did you know any of them?'

'They're much younger than me, sir.'

'I thought perhaps they might have sisters.'

Lucie thought hard. 'Gertruyd's mother is quite young. I think she may have a younger daughter but Gertruyd was the oldest. The girl who sold shellfish was born when her mother was very young.' She cast her eyes downward before continuing. 'She is not married, sir.'

'No, I know. And I suppose that Anna van Setten would not mix with other children.'

'No, sir. She was allowed out sometimes, and you would see her in the street sometimes, but she wouldn't speak to us.'

'And I hear she has no brothers or sisters?'

'I'm sure I don't know, sir. The likes of me don't go in those houses.'

'Have you heard any stories about what might have happened to the girls?'

'A customer said he thinks the Devil has spirited them away. The other girls here think someone has taken them to use as his wives. They think we'll never see them again because they are on a ship to Batavia. They say the great men of those parts will pay a good price for white girls.'

'You know that one has been found dead?'

Lucie shook her head and clasped her hands in prayer. 'I heard nothing of that, sir.'

'And what do you think, Lucie?'

'I think they would have escaped if they could, sir, so it's my opinion that they've had their throats cut.'

I had hoped something in the gossip of the town might have given me a line to follow, but it was clear that Lucie did not know of it.

'Thank you, Lucie.'

'Sir, may I ask you something?'

'Of course.'

'They say that the bad men or spirits are only interested in pure girls, sir, who have not been with men.'

I did not want to commit myself until I knew what the question was, and it proved to be just as well.

'Sir, I swear I haven't been with a man. But perhaps I should, then the wicked ones won't come for me.'

'Lucie, that's scandalous! No, keep your virtue. Say your prayers, and I shall say one for you too, and you will be safe from the demons, I promise you.'

She appeared doubtful, but nodded slightly and curtsied once more as she left the room, leaving me to consider why I had made a promise I had no means of keeping.

CHAPTER THREE

I think that night in Delft may have been the coldest I ever knew. Leiden can be bitterly cold in February, but the university buildings are kept warm with fires which are never quite allowed to die out. I had expected that the upper floor of a wooden inn would be warmer than a brick building, but my room was not above the kitchen, and there was a split in the wood beneath the window that seemed to face directly towards the North Pole. When I came to splash my face in the morning the water in my bowl was frozen.

I threw my cloak about me and ventured downstairs. Lucie was setting the fire while two other girls brought bread and cheese to the table.

'Will you break your fast now, sir?' asked the innkeeper's wife.

She was as short a woman as I had ever seen who was not a dwarf, but nearly as broad as she was tall. It was as if her Maker had used the normal amount of flesh but had erected it on soft foundations.

'Thank you, mevrouw,' I replied, and sat at the long table.

'I'll send Lucie up presently with some shaving water, sir. We didn't think you'd be up so early, but of course as a religious gent I expect you're up for the early service.'

I smiled weakly. If this were expected of me, I had better go so as not to forfeit their good opinion, but I confess that I view the services before nine o'clock as a penance rather than a joy. 'What time is it?' I asked.

'Bless you, sir, the clock will soon strike seven. I doubt you'll have time to eat and shave and still make it to the service.'

'Oh, dear,' I said, and feigned disappointment.

'I'll warm some beer for you, sir, to keep out the cold.'

'That would be kind.'

'It's of our own brewing, and you'll find none like it this side of Amsterdam.'

Having tasted it, I wished sincerely that she was right. It had the smack of physic. The bread was fresh and warm, though, and the butter and cheese were good. Lucie brought me some more bread and nudged it aside to reveal a slice of beef. I assume that its position beneath the bread indicated that it was not supposed to have been offered.

'You did say a prayer for me, sir?' she whispered urgently.

'I did, Lucie,' I replied, and I was telling the truth. Well, I could think of nothing else that I could do for her.

The mayor's clerk had a list ready for me when I arrived.

'If it please, mijnheer, you dine tonight with Master Ranck.'

'And who is he, pray?'

'Why, sir, he is a notary. A man of business and discretion.'

Discretion seemed to be a quality that the clerk valued, though I have always preferred indiscretion myself. Not on my part, of course, because I must observe the sanctity of the confessional, or at least I would have to do so if I ever heard confession, but as a secret priest that duty is not laid upon me.

I was going to spend a lot of time with the clerk and thought it would be as well to befriend him and try to engage on terms of confidence with him.

'Forgive me, I don't know your name,' I began.

'People call me "Clerk",' the clerk replied.

'But you must have a name,' I persisted.

'Claes, mijnheer. Claes Claessz.'

'Your father was also Claes?'

'Is, sir. He lives yet, by the grace of God.'

'God be praised for it.'

If this were not my private journal I would be slow to admit it, but I do not share the willingness of many of my fellows to attribute every good thing to God. Of course, He gives us many blessings, and I give thanks for them, but I do not think He wants the credit for everything. After all, if I give thanks to God for letting my mother live two years longer than my father, should I then complain because He took my father two years earlier than my mother? Both responses seem to me to be equally valid.

Claes looked acutely awkward. 'Was there something more, mijnheer?'

I indicated the chair. 'May I?'

Claes opened his palm to gesture that I should sit, and I did so.

'It would make my job easier, mijnheer Claessz, if I had some background on the city and its leading men.'

'It is not my place to gossip on my betters, sir,' said Claes.

'Ah, gossip, no, indeed,' I hurriedly added, 'but the opinion of a man who has lived amongst them would help me, a mere visitor. Especially that of a man of … discretion.'

The magic word seemed to mollify him.

'I am eager to assist in any way I may, of course.'

'Thank you. And I need not add that you are under no obligation to make any comment if it would cause you discomfiture.'

He made no reply. Conversation with this Delphic oracle was going to be difficult.

'I wanted to ask…' I began, but at that moment the door opened. The mayor entered, Claes leapt to his feet, and all hope of a confidential exchange was lost for the moment.

The mayor invited me into his chamber and made some polite conversation for a little while, which would have been entertaining to any man who wanted to enlarge his knowledge of peas. The mayor was keen to plant his crop, but the ground was too cold, even for the new strain he had imported from Denmark. This seemed to exhaust the conversation, and he fell quiet for a moment, before a glance at the paper on his desk seemed to remind him of the business of the day.

'You may not be aware that we hope to bury the Lievens girl on Saturday, but it may be that something remains to be found from an examination of her, if you have the stomach for it.'

'I conceive it my duty, mijnheer, whatever my own feelings.'

'It does you credit, sir. My surgeon will be happy to show you the body. Claes will take you there.'

The mayor called for his clerk. Is it fanciful to imagine that the speed with which Claes appeared at this signal indicated that he had been listening at the door?

We walked together across the Markt and towards the Armamentarium.

'Why keep her in an armoury?' I asked.

'There is plenty of ice nearby, mijnheer, to keep the girl fresh. And there is no more secure place in the city.'

I was unprepared for the sight that was revealed to me in the small cellar where Gertruyd lay. She had been laid on a silver cloth and covered with a similar one on which a posy of herbs was balanced to freshen the air. It was undoubtedly cool, but it was also too dark to work, so a couple of soldiers helped us to bring her up to a bright chamber with large windows.

The surgeon was in attendance but there was another man with him, a younger man with a fine head of hair, clean shaven, square-jawed and vigorous. He was introduced to us as Dr

Reinier de Graaf, who had studied at Utrecht, Leiden and Angers and was a man of some reputation, as we were told.

'My friend Van Leeuwenhoek told me that you hoped to view the girl's corpse,' announced De Graaf, 'so I offered my services, such as they are.'

'We are honoured, sir,' said the surgeon, though I detected an undertone in his voice that strongly suggested that this might be a barefaced lie.

The surgeon removed the upper cloth and exposed the naked girl. I may have forgotten, but I think Gertruyd Lievens was the first naked girl I ever saw, and I was surprised by one or two features that we need not discuss here. I can only hope that I did not reveal this by any facial expression.

He reached forward to turn the girl over and was immediately checked by a sharp command from De Graaf.

'Mijnheer! Let us not touch until we have seen. When a body is soft it may retain the marks of our handling, and I must be sure that any we find are of the killer's making. Perhaps you would be kind enough to indicate the points of interest, without touching her.'

The last words were spoken in the manner of a schoolmaster addressing a particularly doltish pupil, and the surgeon was clearly upset by them. I felt the need to placate him.

'I regret very much that my presence here may have disturbed your careful practice,' I said.

The surgeon inclined his head slightly to accept my apology as if it explained his complete incompetence, but continued to eye Dr De Graaf with suspicion. As for the young expert, he was examining the girl's upper arms intently.

'These are interesting,' he remarked. 'What do you make of them?'

The surgeon crossed to the other side of the body and indicated the livid marks on the biceps. 'A man's hand at each side. No doubt he has pressed down upon her in the act of smothering her so that she should not escape.'

De Graaf pursed his lips. 'Pray continue,' he said.

'You will observe, gentlemen, that the lips are blue and the nose is bruised. This is the reason for my belief that she has been smothered.'

'I believe that you suggested yesterday that she had been made insensible with wine,' I commented.

'I did, mijnheer.'

'How did you arrive at that conclusion?' asked De Graaf.

The surgeon produced a dull blue dress and a canvas apron. 'Here you may see wine upon the clothes. If you will smell the stains, I think you will concur.'

We sniffed obediently, and I was prepared to be convinced. There was an extensive stain on the apron. To my surprise, De Graaf was sniffing the girl's hair.

'We must remove her cap to let her hair fall free,' he said.

'Is that entirely necessary?' I asked. 'She has been subjected to some indignities already.'

'Master Mercurius, we must use such skills as God gave us to find this girl's killer. My gift is to read the body and deduce what a mute cadaver can tell us. I would not ask if I did not believe that it would further our efforts to find her murderer.'

The surgeon made as if to lift the body, but De Graaf was already rolling the silver cloth that had shrouded her until it formed a sort of bolster which he pushed gently under her head until it nestled at the nape of her neck. He then slid the lower cloth gently up the table until her head began to drop off the end, when he tugged at the ribbon and delicately lifted off the cap before pulling the cloth from the feet end to return her to her previous position. Even the surgeon must have been impressed with the dexterity of the operation.

De Graaf then took a good handful of the hair about her neck and sniffed it.

'You have learned something, doctor?' the surgeon asked.

'I believe I may have done,' De Graaf replied, 'but it is a mistake to speak before concluding the examination. Have we seen all the marks you wished to show us?'

'Yes, we have,' the surgeon agreed.

'Thank you,' De Graaf said, and stood for a while with his hands clamped together as if in prayer, the tips of his index fingers brushing his lips. 'I wonder if I might have some water to wash my hands?'

One of the soldiers brought a pitcher of water and a basin, and Dr De Graaf rinsed his hands carefully. He removed a large ring from his right hand and tucked it in the pocket of his waistcoat. Having stood perfectly still for a few more seconds, he strode to the girl's feet, opened her legs and spread her privy parts.

'*Virgo intacta*,' he declared. 'Let us be grateful for that.' He turned to me, his brown eyes enlivened by an inner flame. 'Magister, you accept the necessity for some enquiry into the way in which this girl met her death?'

'Of course,' I answered.

'I realise that to open her would distress the family, but I believe that I can advance our cause without major damage to her if you will allow some small and discreet damage.'

I was doubtful, but he seemed to interpret my muteness as acquiescence, and opened his bag to produce a fine knife, a silver tube and a small dish made of the finest white porcelain.

He carefully probed about the girl's ribcage with his fingers, and traced the line of one of her ribs with a thumb, before

42

using the knife to make a small but deep cut in her white skin. There was no bleeding.

'The dead do not bleed,' De Graaf remarked, as if we were students at his anatomy lectures. 'With a needle and thread I can draw the skin together again when we are done here.'

He parted the skin on either side of the cut using his thumb and forefinger, then inserted the silver tube. It entered to the depth of an inch or so, but would go no further, so De Graaf withdrew it and searched in his bag once more. He then produced the smallest dagger that ever I saw, equipped with a fine point which he used to deepen the hole that he had made. This time the tube entered further, and De Graaf applied his lips to the tube and sucked gently.

After a moment he placed a finger over the end of the tube, extracted it from the hole, and reached for the dish. As he removed his finger the contents of the tube dribbled into the dish, and De Graaf took them to the window to examine. He also lifted the dish to his nose to inhale the scent from it.

'Gentlemen, I ask you to note whether this dish contains any taint of wine.'

It smelled rank, but I could detect no wine there, and said so.

'I believe that I can now explain what we see here,' De Graaf continued. 'I regret, mijnheer, that I disagree with you in some respects, but I will make my case and leave you to judge.'

The surgeon reddened but said nothing, so De Graaf kept talking.

'You will observe that there are finger marks made by a man's hands on each of her arms. That is undoubtedly true, and I note that the man has all ten of his digits so we may exclude anyone whose hands have been mutilated. However, if he were pressing down to smother her, his palms would have been pressing on the upper surface of her arms, whereas we clearly see the palms were at the outer surfaces as shown by the way the fingers extend right around the back of the arm. Now,' he said, turning to Claes, 'you have the smallest arms here, so I beg you will allow me to demonstrate my point. The murderer gripped her arms so, from the sides, and held them tightly, but what purpose would this serve? I can think of only one circumstance in which a man would grip a girl so firmly, and that is to shake her.'

He released Claes and lifted up the girl's clothes.

'There is indeed wine upon the apron and dress, but there is none in her stomach, so I conclude that she did not swallow much, if any at all. By the way, her last meal was probably a fish soup. There is so much wine on her apron because she could not swallow it. I think that she was already dead, a circumstance confirmed by the wine in her hair. It dribbled down her cheek and lodged there because she was horizontal when it was poured on her lips. And if I consider when a man might do that, I come to the conclusion that he shook her and gave her wine because he was trying to revive her.'

I gasped. In a few minutes De Graaf had changed my understanding of the events that led to Gertruyd Lievens's death.

The surgeon departed, somewhat mollified, following a discussion with De Graaf about the latest medical discoveries, in the course of which De Graaf was careful to lavish praise on the surgeon's treatment of toothache and shared his technique for replacing parts of diseased teeth with porcelain counterfeits. I confess I doubted the efficacy of this method but then I still have all my teeth. Perhaps I will be a willing candidate for tooth replacement when I have a few gaps.

Claes and I sat on small barrels outside an inn and gazed across the water.

'Have you seen mijnheer Vermeer's *View of Delft?*' Claes enquired.

I admitted that I had not.

'It is very fine,' Claes opined. 'I have seen no painting like it. It shows a view of the city from that bank opposite us, or somewhere very near to it.' He leaned towards me as if about to impart a great secret. 'In the foreground there are two women. My mother was one.'

Since I saw no reason to doubt that his mother was a member of the general class of "women", I take it that he meant that she was one of the particular women depicted, and I would still believe that were it not that above fifty men must have told me since that their own mothers or sisters were shown in the painting.

He sipped his warm ale. We chose to sit in the cold air to freshen our senses after the gloom of the Armamentarium and to escape the smoky interior of the inn, where a servant had put some green wood upon the fire which was now filling the room with a horrible stink.

'I ought to get back, Master. The mayor will be wondering where I am,' said Claes, but made no effort to move. I formed the impression that he thought sitting with me was preferable to doing the mayor's paperwork.

'Whenever you wish, Claes. I can see myself back to the inn later.'

Claes nodded. 'Do not forget dinner with Notary Ranck,' he said, and gave me directions to the house. 'He will dine at five o'clock if that suits you.'

'Thank you, it will do very well. It will be too dark to do any work outside at that hour.'

Claes wrapped his cloak about him and bade me goodbye, leaving me with my thoughts and the first palatable ale I had found in Delft. I do not have a head for strong drink, as will appear later in this tale.

I finished my drink and gave the potboy his coppers. My original plan to find my own way had involved a measure of bravado on my part and it seemed prudent to get some directions from him, which he willingly gave.

I pulled my hat down over my face because a fierce sleet had started, and was very glad I had left my clerical hat in Leiden. It covers the ears but has no brim, and a little protection from the weather was very necessary on this February morning.

Following the lad's directions I looked for a small sluice-gate and turned there, finding myself entering the court with the well from the south side. I turned to the west and stepped carefully over the uneven cobbles. A man could easily break an ankle on those treacherous setts.

I glanced about me and recognised the window I was looking for. A familiar face was turned in profile, the white cap not quite able to capture all the stray hairs. Hearing my feet, mevrouw Lievens glanced down at me and raised a hand to cover her mouth as if uncertain or surprised. I raised my hat a little and gestured to the door, and a few moments later it swung open at her touch.

'Good day, mevrouw,' I said.

'Good day to you, Master,' she replied.

'My name is Mercurius. I have been summoned from Leiden to help the council here to find whoever was responsible for your daughter's death.'

'Gertruyd,' she muttered. 'Her name was Gertruyd.'

'Yes, of course, I'm sorry. I'd like to talk to you about her if it isn't too painful.'

She shook her head. 'They will bury my girl on Saturday and then she will be forgotten by all but this family,' she said. 'Let us talk about her while we may.' She stepped aside to let me in. 'Pray forgive the state of the house,' she said, though this must have been a formal greeting only because I saw nothing out of place. If she had seen my student lodgings she would have swooned at the disorder there. 'I'm afraid I have nothing to give you,' she stammered.

'I have just taken some refreshment,' I said, then, fearing she would think it just a tactful untruth I corroborated it a little. 'At the inn across the canal from the Armamentarium.'

'Jos's inn. I know it,' she said.

'A potboy directed me here.'

'A dark-haired lad about fifteen? That would be the son of the household across the court. A good, hard-working boy, they say. The sort my Gertruyd should have married.' She rolled a cloth into a ball and clutched it to her mouth to stifle her sobs.

'Do not distress yourself, mevrouw,' I pleaded. 'There is enough sadness without wishing more upon yourself by thinking of what might have been.'

'*Ought* to have been,' she corrected me. 'Children die, it's true, but not at the hands of villains. Tell me, learned sir, will the murderer really burn in Hell for all eternity?'

'So we are taught,' I began.

'Good,' she said, 'for I feared that God might be tender-hearted and forgive him.'

'God is just,' I answered, 'and we must trust in His justice. All of us rely also on His mercy, because we are all sinners worthy of condemnation.'

'I'm not,' she replied. 'Not big sins, anyway. I've always kept the commandments. I am true to my husband and he to me, and I sweep the house clean to keep the devil out. Why then should the Lord visit this horror on me?'

I opened my hands. 'I don't know, mevrouw. I will not offer easy answers for your comfort. But I am assured that on the last day His purpose will be made plain to us all. I cannot believe that God is responsible for any harm to a child. That is the work of men, not of the Almighty.'

'But tell me, Master,' she continued, 'if I see a man about to stab another, and I make no cry, the magistrates will call me his accomplice, for they will say that by refusing to act I have allowed his evil to prosper as surely as if my own hand were on the hilt. And so I ask you, if God, who is all-powerful, saw my child in danger and did not raise His hand to help her, may I not hold Him guilty of her death as if He had struck the blow himself?'

I reached out and took her hands in mine. She did not withdraw them, but fixed me steadily with her pale blue eyes.

'Think, mevrouw, of when Gertruyd was very small, maybe a year old, and she showed signs of wanting to walk. At first you walk with her. You support her and hold her hands. You stand ready to catch her if she should fall. Wherever she goes, you are no more than a pace away. But in time you know that she must walk unaided, and you know also that in doing so she may fall, and perhaps she may be hurt. You could insist on holding her hand all her life, but a loving mother knows that she must let her child go and risk a mishap. So it is with God. He must let us make our own way upon the earth, and when we fall, He feels it keenly. He must weep when He sees what we do with our freedom. But a loving father can do no other. You must see that, I hope?'

She bit her lip doubtfully. 'I cannot forgive the killer. If he is caught, I hope to watch him hang.'

'It is my job to see that he is caught, mevrouw.'

I said nothing about hanging. I accept that a man pays for his crime with his life and thereby expiates his sin, but I prefer not to reflect on my work leading a man to his death, particularly a public one.

'How can I help you then, Master?'

'If — when — we catch this man, he will be taken before the magistrates and have to answer to them. They will want you to tell what you know. I need to write that down now while it is fresh in your mind in case you forget anything.'

'You think I can ever forget what has happened to my girl?'

'Maybe not, mevrouw. But the magistrates are used to working this way. Can you write?'

'Only my name,' she answered.

'Then if you tell me what you want to say, I will write it down and you can sign it.'

She agreed and offered me a stool at the table, placing herself on the bench on the other side.

'These things have a form,' I explained, 'so we must begin with explaining who you are and why you are giving a deposition.'

'Depos—?'

'Deposition. Telling them what you know. The paper is called a deposition. Now, let's begin with your name.'

'Jannetje Dircks.'

I wrote it down. She concurred with my spelling, but she would probably have agreed to a dozen variants.

'So, you are the daughter of Dirck. Which Dirck?'

'Dirck Aelbrechtszoon.'

'What trade does your husband follow, mevrouw?'

'Why, he works in the brickyard,' she answered, as if I were a child. Many men in Delft follow that trade.

'And can you tell me when and where you were born or baptized?'

'I was born on the third day before St Luke's Day, in the year of Our Lord 1642.'

If I was surprised that this greying woman was only twenty-eight years old, I hope I did not show it.

'Here in Delft?' I asked.

'In Rijswijk.'

'How did you meet your husband?'

'I came to the goose fair at Michaelmas.'

I noted the use of Michaelmas to date an event.

'Are you a Catholic, mevrouw?' I asked.

'No, mijnheer!' she replied indignantly. 'We are Reformed.'

'I beg your pardon,' I quickly responded, thinking how curious it was that so many had become nominally Protestant while maintaining some Catholic customs; but then, I had done that myself, had I not?

'You're not writing that down,' she reproved me.

'I asked only to understand,' I said. 'On reflection, the court will not need to know that. I have written that you are Jannetje Dircks, of the village of Rijswijk, born in the year of Our Lord 1642 and married to mijnheer Lievens since...?'

'1661, sir. I was not quite nineteen.'

'And your daughter Gertruyd was born — when?'

'On Easter Sunday, 1662, sir. But we had been married a full ten months,' she quickly added.

I made a note to check the date of Easter in 1662. It has long been the custom in these parts for the first female child to take her mother's mother's name, and so it proved here. Jannetje's mother had been called Gertruyd.

'Have you other children?' I enquired.

'A younger daughter, Clara. She is six years old, sir.'

'And where is she now?'

'With my mother. I have sent her away to Rijswijk to be safe. It pains me, but I dare not keep her here.'

'Let us hope that soon she can return and all the children of Delft will play safely out of doors. Now, Jannetje, tell me about the day Gertruyd disappeared.'

I realised just too late that I had used Jannetje's Christian name without permission, and I saw her start with surprise at being thus addressed by someone outside her family, but she did not make any complaint. She closed her eyes as if to order her thoughts, and then continued.

'The day before being stormy, I did little work. The windows had to be shut against the rain and wind and the clouds were black and heavy, so I busied myself in baking bread. Then the Lord's Day being brighter, we set to work as soon as we woke. My husband helped me by feeding the spun wool to my loom and Gertruyd gave him his breakfast. Thus I did not have to stop and was doing well in recapturing the lost time. We had used our water to wash for, being Sunday, we have to wash thoroughly.'

I knew what she meant. Amongst some of the more traditional folk it is customary to wash every inch of the body before church. I know that some doctors hold that too much washing is injurious to the health, being a cause of chills and ill humours, but the poorer sort have done it for many years and will not go to church except they be clean inside and out. It is idle to tell them how dangerous the practice of bathing may be. Yet I confess that I wash myself on Saturday night without fail, my grandmother's injunctions being engraved on my brain.

'And so Gertruyd went again to the well to draw water to clean the kitchen. She told us she was going.' Jannetje faltered in her story, and tears formed once more in her eyes. 'Sir, I wish with all my heart I had forbidden her! Or at least that I had taken one last hug from her, or spoken a tender word!'

I acknowledged her regret with a mute nod. There are moments when no words will serve, and when I wonder what good I am as a priest when I can find nothing to say to the afflicted.

She collected herself once more, and carried on. 'I cannot say how long it was before I realised she had not returned. In my head it is but a few minutes, and yet I was so busy in my work it may have been longer. I called for Gertruyd to ask her to look at the church clock so that we might know when to prepare for Divine Service, but no answer came. So I called again — "Gertruyd! Gertruyd!" — but there was no reply. And then I called Clara and asked where her sister was, and she told me Gertruyd was gone to the well. "And not back yet?" said I. "No, Mummy," said Clara, so I put down my spindle and went to seek her out. I could not see her, so I came in to fetch my husband, and together we wandered the neighbourhood, joined by many good people who heard our cries. But we could not find her.'

'Were there any signs of a struggle?'

'No, sir. The man next door, one Adriaan, called us to notice that the path gate was latched.'

This was the gate through which I had passed that led to the sluice-gate and the high road, though it was open when I arrived.

'Should it have been closed, mevrouw?'

'It is kept closed so the little children will not fall in the canal, sir. But Adriaan thought that if Gertruyd had passed that way she would not have shut it, because he has reminded her several times before.'

'Were there any other children about?'

'We cannot be sure, sir. Little Nico who lives nearest the well may have been sitting in his doorway, but he is not yet two years old and does not speak well. Sir, being the Lord's Day many of us keep our children indoors so that they should not dirty themselves playing outside.'

There was a deal of truth in this. If I were thinking of snatching a child it would be done most easily on Sunday morning when there would be few witnesses, if any.

'Think carefully, mevrouw. Were there any of your neighbours who did not run to help in your search?'

She considered at length before venturing an answer. 'Trijntje's father who lives with her, an old sailor, but he cannot run, having only one leg. And even he went to the window to look out for her, because Trijntje's house backs onto this court but it has a window to the high road too. I know of no other, sir. I think they were all there.'

'Thank you.'

'Frans!' she suddenly cried.

'Frans?'

'Frans would not have been there. He is a deputy verger at the church and goes there to prepare the church for the services. He was not here.'

'By what name is he known?' I asked.

'Frans Deputy-Verger,' she answered, reverting to the tone of a schoolmistress faced with an especially stupid child.

'Do you believe that Frans is the sort of man who might have taken Gertruyd?'

'I don't know what sort of man would take my Gertruyd,' she answered, 'for if I did he would have been kept far from her. And I would have stabbed his black heart though it cost me my own life.'

53

CHAPTER FOUR

With the signed statement in my pouch I set off along the road in pensive mood. I needed to see if Jannetje's husband could add to her statement, but he would be at work all day and I dare not cost the family earnings. In leaving Jannetje I had placed two coins on the table to compensate her for the work she had lost in talking to me, but she pushed them back towards me.

'I cannot take blood money for speaking about my daughter's murderer,' she explained.

'The mayor has empowered me to pay anyone who has lost work so that no-one is deterred from helping us,' I explained, semi-truthfully, for I knew he would allow me to include the money in my account of expenses. She looked uncertain, but picked up the money and dropped it in her apron.

Where now? In all truth I could not think of anything I could usefully do, but the idea came upon me to visit Magdalena Kuijper's mother near the Oostpoort. I set off along the road, this time with hailstones spattering my back.

I had underestimated the number of low cottages near the Oostpoort and it took me some time to find the correct row of them. Magdalena's mother was sitting in front of her little home gutting herring and cutting off their heads.

I introduced myself. She said her name was Liese.

'I am charged with finding your daughter, mevrouw.'

She gave a coarse laugh. 'Mevrouw? Nobody mevrouws me! Don't you know, fine sir, that I'm a bastard's mother?'

'Yes, I know it,' I told her, 'but all I see is a woman who has lost her daughter and wants to know what has become of her.

God has a care for bastards just as for the children of the most pious couple.'

She inspected me slowly, head to foot. 'I'll wager mevrouw Van Setten has seven of you for every one that I have searching for her child. If you seek Magdalena it's only because the Van Setten girl may be with her.'

'I have not spoken to mevrouw Van Setten. I am speaking to each mother in the order that their child vanished. I need to hear what you can tell me so that I can report to the mayor.'

'Me? An illiterate fishwife? The slut who had a girl out of wedlock? The one who isn't welcome in your churches because I won't name the father?'

I doffed my hat and shook the hailstones from it. It was pointless but it gave me some time to think what I might say next. 'Won't, or can't, mevrouw?'

She paused in the act of slicing a herring's belly, and slowly began to laugh. 'Can't. I don't know exactly who the father was. I was barely sixteen and someone plied me with genever, so as I knew nothing of my deflowering. And my Magdalena was the result, so I cannot regret what happened, however much I fret about the way of it. The finer sort of woman is bedded with silk sheets, French wine and sweet-scented flowers. Me, I get a tiled doorway, cheap gin and someone's spew on my skirts.'

Slut or no, I warmed to this woman, who had a quick wit despite her lack of learning. 'Have you any other children?' I asked.

'No!' she growled scornfully. 'What man will look at a woman with a bastard?'

'You are young yet, mevrouw. You must not give up hope of a good marriage.'

I thought she was about to throw the knife.

'Are you telling me it would be good if my Magdalena is lying dead because then a man might wed me?' she snarled.

'No, no!' I protested. 'I mean that as a man I see no difference between marrying a widow with a child and marrying an unmarried woman with a child. If you love the woman you will love the child who has issued from her.'

'But you're not a man,' she countered. 'You're a minister, a domino.'

'Dominie,' I corrected her.

'Whatever you are, you're not a man who has to worry about his wife's reputation. I'm spoiled goods, mijnheer dominie. There's no price for the likes of me.'

'Our Lady was an unwed mother,' I answered.

She eyed me keenly again. 'How so?'

'The bible tells us she was betrothed to Joseph. But if she were married, it would have said so. Ergo, when she gave birth to Our Lord she was unmarried.'

'But she made it right later by marrying Joseph.'

'But the bible tells us that he was not Our Lord's father.'

'No, dominie, but Our Lord's real father wasn't the marrying kind, was he?'

I smiled despite myself, and she reached behind her and handed me a tiny stool.

'If you will talk, then talk in comfort,' she said, though how any man above a yard tall could have been in comfort on such a stool I cannot tell. 'That was Magdalena's stool,' she said. 'She doesn't need it now.'

'But pray God she will return to reclaim it soon.'

'Aye, pray God, but I doubt it. This cold will do for her even if her throat isn't cut.'

'Can you write, mevrouw?'

'Can I write? There's not a woman in this row can write. What need have we of writing? Fish don't read.'

'If you could read you could read the bible,' I offered.

'Aye, if I had one,' she agreed, 'but do you think I'd give you so small a stool if I had money to spare on a bible?'

'Since you cannot write, I will take down what you say, then I will read it back to you, and if you are content that I have written what you said, you will please make your mark upon the page at the bottom.'

She indicated assent to my plan.

'I understand your daughter disappeared on the twenty-seventh day of January.'

'I don't know about that,' she said. 'It was a Tuesday.'

'What sort of day was it?'

'I just said, a Tuesday.'

'I mean, was it cold? Sunny? Wet?'

'A day much like this. A biting wind, but then it always bites hereabouts in the winter. A low sun, and it was tardy in rising. Magdalena and I walked to the fish quay to collect our work for the day.'

'And what exactly do you do, mevrouw?'

'Call me Liese, if it please you. I can't take all this mevrouw stuff. We get the small catch, the herring if there's plenty. I gut herring for pickling and smoking, and Magdalena sorted shellfish into pails and washed them in fresh water. Then we'd take them to the fine kitchens and the smokeries and sell what we could. Mevrouw Van Setten's cook never bought from us, yet we could sell to the inns on the Markt.'

I mentioned the inn where I was lodging.

'Bought two dozen herring of me only yesterday. They can buy them whole, of course, but this way it saves them work and any that don't sell can be swiftly soused before they go off.'

Having smelled the cooking the night before, I was not quite so sure that the herring were not allowed to rot, but I left the point unchallenged.

'So Magdalena must have been a strong girl, to carry pails of shellfish so far?'

'A good strong girl indeed, sir, and she only just eight years old. She grew well as a child, for I had plenty of milk, and she had a great fondness for fish, which we can get quite cheap at the end of the day, so she grew well. She could take a yoke across her shoulders with a pail on each side and walk to the Markt and back without complaint.'

'And did she go to school?'

'No school would have her, being a bastard. As if that's the child's fault. Since I cannot go to church, the Sunday School won't teach her. I ask you, sir, what's Christian about that? Didn't Our Lord say "Let the little children come to me"?'

'The evangelists Matthew, Mark and Luke all say that He did.'

'Then write that on a scrap of your paper, Master dominie, and I'll take it to the church and shame them with it.'

I hesitated, but I saw that she was in the right, so I wrote out the verse as I recalled it: Jesus said "Let the little children come to me. Do not forbid them, for of such as these is the Kingdom of Heaven." I added "Matthew 19:14" to the text, hoping that I had that right then, just to be sure, I pulled my Testament from my pouch and checked it.

'Is that little book a bible?' she asked.

'The New Testament only,' I replied.

'Won't they give you a whole one?' she asked, and I marvelled at her innocence until I saw her suppressing a smile as she worked on the fish.

'Liese, tell me when you saw Magdalena last.'

She laid her knife in her lap and stared straight ahead. 'It was around the middle of the day. She had finished her first pails so I gave her a cup of buttermilk and a hunk of bread.' She showed me a piece that she had in a dish beside her. It was coarse, brown-black, gritty and thoroughly unappetizing. 'She ate it all,' said Liese. 'She had a good appetite. Then she wanted to play, but there was still work to do, and I cannot do it all. We sang a song or two together and made play of our work, and so she was amused a while. We heard the church bell strike twelve o'clock then, as I recall. Then, sir, she went to fetch fresh water to cook our supper, for she did not choose to go in the dark. And I never saw her again.'

'She must have taken a bucket or jug?'

'A fine earthenware jug, found by the pump.'

'There's a pump here?'

'Aye, and I send her to it or the little imp will take water from the horse trough and save herself the work of pumping.'

'How far is it to the pump?'

Liese calculated. 'You may see for yourself. Just walk to the corner there and it's twice as far along the road after you turn.'

It was my turn to calculate. 'Perhaps a hundred paces?'

'For you perhaps, but I have shorter legs, and Magdalena's were shorter still.'

'How long was it before you realised she would not return?'

'Half an hour, maybe. I thought she had stopped to gossip with the other girls. They're told not to talk to her, but at the pump their mothers can't see them. So of course they all say they never saw her there, but that's because they were asked in front of their parents. She must have been there, or my jug would not have been found next to the pump. That's the very jug behind you,' she added.

I turned and saw a red earthenware jug, unpainted and coarsely glazed, resting on the cobbles a yard behind my stool. 'It's intact,' I exclaimed.

'Of course it is,' answered Liese. 'Surely even a dominie has sense enough to know a jug in pieces is no good for carrying water?'

'But it wasn't smashed when she dropped it?'

'Why would she drop it?'

'Well, when she was grabbed. If I grabbed you, wouldn't you drop whatever you were holding so you could use your hands to fight me off?'

'No,' she replied, 'I'd stick this knife in your belly and gut you like a herring. But I see what you mean.'

'This pump,' I asked her, 'is it overlooked?'

'It's a narrow street,' Liese replied. 'The houses aren't far away.'

'And surely the women sit outside like you do?'

'Yes, they do.'

'But they didn't hear her cry out? And nobody saw what befell her?'

'The bitches wouldn't say if they did.'

I confess my anger rose up within me. 'They may keep quiet to you, but I have the mayor's backing. Let them try to obstruct me!'

And with those foolhardy words I set off to find the pump.

I may be an academic, but I know something of life in small towns, and therefore I did not immediately bang on doors when I found the pump, but took a turn about it a couple of times, and then sat on the granite block that supported the pump. As I expected, the inquisitive housewives peeked out to see who was there.

'I am Master Mercurius of the University of Leiden,' I proclaimed loudly, 'and I have the mayor's commission to investigate the disappearance of Magdalena Kuijper of this district. I will ask questions and you will answer truthfully or you will be dragged in shame to the town hall to answer in the great chamber there.'

To be honest, I was not sure that there was a great chamber there, but most town halls have them and I gambled on the fact that these women would not know any better.

'Who here has daughters?'

Women emerged from their narrow doorways to admit their parenthood of girls.

'Are you not concerned that this man could return to seize your own children?'

It was injudicious, but my dander was up.

'The Kuijper girl is a bastard,' one woman protested, to general support from the other women.

'Do you think the murderer knew that? Is there some badge that bastards wear that allows a killer to pick them out? How then can you think that your children are safe just because you are married?'

'But our children would not go off willingly with a strange man,' said one.

'And how do you know she went willingly?'

'The unbroken jug. But also because we saw a man loitering.'

My heart raced. Why had these stupid creatures not said this before, when the trail was still warm and we might have tracked the man to his lair?

'What man?'

'A man passed by earlier in the day. He seemed to be looking for something or someone. He came along the street and then turned towards the Kuijpers' house.'

'And why do you think he took Magdalena?'

'Why, because just before she came to the pump, he came back this way. He stopped at the pump and asked her if she would draw some water into her jug so he could drink from it.'

'Describe him to me.'

'We saw so little, mijnheer. He had a large cloak or cape about him.'

'Was he grand or poor? Well-dressed? Tall or short?'

'Not well-dressed. The cloak was old. And his hat was without a brim, but the collar of his cloak was turned up to shield his cheeks from the wind.'

'So he talked to Magdalena and she gave him a drink. What then?'

'He set the jug down by the pump and talked some more to her in a low voice.'

'How do you know it was low?'

'Because I couldn't hear what they said. Anyway, after a minute or two he walked off and she followed.'

'Be precise. Did she go with him, or just follow him?'

'She ran after him and then he offered his hand and she took it.'

I threw my hat to the ground in anger. 'And none of you thought to say anything about this to the mayor's men when they came? None of you was prepared to say something that could perhaps have saved this young girl's life? If we find her body, and we discover that she lived a while, you may be sure that I will return with the Civic Guard and arrest you all!'

I was on surer ground here. Every town of any standing boasts a civic guard. Of course, they do not arrest people, but I am sure that they would if they were given the chance. The Civic Guard in Leiden like nothing better than to march back and forth in the sun showing off their polished cutlasses and demonstrating that their hours of drill have not been entirely wasted. The opportunity to march through town and round up a streetful of women before marching them back again would send many into raptures.

The women had obviously decided that attack was the best form of defence, for one of them boldly stepped forward. 'We are all good, God-fearing women here, mijnheer. We have nothing to fear from being summoned to tell the truth.'

I could not allow this woman to have the last word if I wanted to retain the hold over them that the dread of authority lends. It was possible that they had told me all they could and that I would never speak to them again, but if their help was needed in future I needed to know I could coerce it out of them if need be, so I resolved to take a firm line.

'Very well,' I said, 'you will come with me now to face the mayor. The rest of you may go about your business.'

I was pleased to see the shock on the woman's face when her friends meekly returned to their work and left her alone before me. So much for solidarity and companionship, I thought.

'My husband will be expecting his dinner...' she began.

'You may want to take a warm cloak,' I told her. 'The town dungeons are exceptionally bleak at this time of year.'

I need hardly add that this was pure supposition on my part, but a safe conclusion. I have never seen a dungeon where a man would choose to spend a night.

'Dungeons? Why should I go to the dungeons? I've done nothing.'

'Precisely, mevrouw. A young girl was abducted in your sight and you did nothing. Explain that to the mayor; I'm sure he'll be understanding.'

'I wasn't the only one,' she argued.

'I'm sure you're right, and they will have their day behind bars too. But perhaps when you do not return home tonight it will cause them to think more carefully about how they can help me. I hope so anyway. The dungeons are unpleasant enough without adding overcrowding to their qualities.'

There are times when I can clearly discern the hand of Providence before my eyes. We arrived at the town hall and I marched Henriëtte — I now knew her name — into the large chamber at its heart and made her stand in the centre of the room.

'Stay there,' I ordered. 'I will go to bring the mayor.'

I instructed Claes to guard her. He stationed himself by the door. This was as much to ensure that he could escape if she became violent as to prevent her escape. I found the mayor in the private office where he was in animated discussion with Van Leeuwenhoek. I do not know what they were arguing about, but it was clear that Van Leeuwenhoek thought the mayor was wavering in his resolve to deal with the matter.

I came to discover that this was a regular difference of opinion. As Vermeer had claimed, the mayor was a good man, and, being a good man, he could see the good in others. He found it difficult to take a firm line about anything because he could always see both sides of the argument. Van Leeuwenhoek, on the other hand, was a man of stern values who would discount any sentiment that opposed the inevitable conclusion that he had already reached. They paused in their dispute when I entered. In the awkward silence I bowed politely, and they followed suit.

'I beg your pardon for disturbing you,' I said, 'but I hoped for your assistance. I have found a woman who saw the second girl being abducted but has withheld the information.'

The shock could be seen on their faces.

'Withheld information?' Van Leeuwenhoek snapped. 'What possible excuse could she have?'

'I have not questioned her on that point yet. I informed her that I represented the mayor, and I regret to say that she was defiant. I thought that she might be more compliant if she were confronted with the mayor in all his dignity.'

The mayor may have been flattered by this assumption, but he accepted it as a natural conclusion. 'Of course. Let us speak with the wretched woman.'

Whether Van Leeuwenhoek had thus been invited to participate was not clear, but he had no intention of being excluded. As the mayor's chief chamberlain he had a baton of office, allegedly to protect himself against physical attack, but unless he were battered by a small child or a midget the short staff would have little effect. Nevertheless, he took it in hand and followed the mayor who had donned his chain over a fur mantle. There was no denying that they made an impressive pair and Henriëtte was sure to be cowed.

They entered the chamber and the mayor stood at the end, some distance from Henriëtte. Van Leeuwenhoek, a tall, angular man clad in black, stood at the mayor's right shoulder, remaining a respectful half a yard behind him.

I walked to Henriëtte's side and turned to face the mayor.

'Mijnheer Mayor, mijnheer Chamberlain, I bring before you one Henriëtte Maertens, who lives near the Oostpoort and the home of Magdalena Kuijper.'

'The learned master tells me that you saw the abduction of Magdalena Kuijper and yet you did not inform my sergeant when he investigated the incident. Explain yourself!' said the mayor.

'I saw no such thing,' Henriëtte answered.

'Are you calling the master a liar?' Van Leeuwenhoek blazed.

'No, mijnheer. I mean that I saw a man with the child, but she went willingly, so how was I to know she was being abducted? For all I knew he could have been her father.'

'Her father?' said the mayor.

'Well, no man knows who that was, but a daughter knows her own blood. Even a bastard, I suppose.'

'And you think a bastard is not worthy of your notice, mevrouw?'

'A child is worthy of any mother's attention. But if her mother did not take care of her, how can we be expected to do so?'

The mayor took a couple of paces forward. 'She is a child of a citizen of Delft, and therefore entitled to our care.'

Van Leeuwenhoek's voice boomed across the room. 'The woman should be flogged in the Markt. It would encourage others to tell what they know. And it would remind these ignorant people of the honour due to your office and your officers.'

If Henriëtte felt any concern at the prospect of a flogging, she concealed it well. Indeed, she shrugged her shoulders as if to say that she expected no less and a flogging was a regular occurrence for her kind. 'You may flog me as you like, but I have no more to tell you,' she cried. 'You won't be threatening to flog mevrouw Van Setten, I'll wager.'

I thought Van Leeuwenhoek was going to slap her. He strode forward and raised his arm, but instead he grabbed her chin and lifted it so her head fell back and her eyes met his.

'If mevrouw Van Setten is as insolent as you, she'll get a flogging. We are determined to keep the children of this town safe from harm, and we need the help and support of every citizen to do that. That is why we are severe with you, mevrouw!'

He released his grip and stepped back. Henriëtte was as defiant as previously, as I could see in her eyes, but she said nothing.

The mayor would have conducted the questioning himself, but he had no idea what to ask, so he settled for addressing her firmly. 'The Master will ask you some questions. He is acting on my behalf and in answering him you are speaking to the mayor of Delft, mevrouw. I do not demand any respect in my own right, but the office I have the honour to hold has a dignity that demands respect, and therefore I charge you to answer him fully and truthfully. Is that clear?'

Henriëtte gave a subdued nod.

'Continue, Master Mercurius!' said the mayor.

'You told us this man met Magdalena at the pump. If he was the man who abducted Gertuyd Lievens he snatched her at the well. This suggests that the place is important to him. That perhaps he loiters there in wait for unaccompanied young girls. If so, he may have been there before or been there for some time. Had you seen him before that day?'

'No, sir. At least, I think not. But his collar was turned up and his face was difficult to see. He wasn't a black man, I can tell you that.'

'Did you see his hair?'

She thought for a moment, chewing her thumb as if this would help her recall. 'It was under his hat and cloak. Perhaps it was blond, but I couldn't really tell. It could have been any colour.'

'Well, then, was it neat, tied back perhaps?'

'I don't think so.'

'His height — he can't have disguised that with a cloak?'

'Above middle height. And not a fat man. He looked strong.'

'A young man, then?'

'He didn't walk like an old man, if that's what you mean.'

'And how does an old man walk?' barked Van Leeuwenhoek.

'I mean he was nimble, not jerky. He bent down to her quickly and easily.' Henriëtte's eyes brightened with the spark of recollection. 'He wasn't wearing gloves. He had big hands — rough hands, not handsome. He must work with his hands. He offered her his hand and she took it, though her hands were tiny next to his.'

'And where did he lead her?'

'To the east, out of the city, as I thought.'

'I am a stranger to Delft. How long would it take to walk to the Oostpoort from the pump?'

'With a child, ten minutes at the most. It's not very far.'

Now that Henriëtte had started answering questions without complaint I wanted to keep her answering. The only difficulty was that I had run out of things to ask. Fortunately Van Leeuwenhoek came to my rescue.

'With your leave, Master Mercurius, I'd like to ask how the child was dressed.'

'A drab black skirt, a white blouse, and an apron. I think the apron was dark blue.'

'On her feet?'

'I didn't see. She didn't make a lot of noise when she walked, so she can't have been wearing clogs.'

'And no coat or cloak?'

'No, mijnheer. I doubt she has one.'

Van Leeuwenhoek rubbed his chin in thought. I let him continue, because I had no idea where it was leading.

'Mevrouw, if you were this man, where could he hide the child nearby? She was not dressed for cold weather, so he must have taken her somewhere near at hand.'

'There are lots of alleyways.'

I cursed myself, because I had forgotten to ask this question of Gertruyd's mother. When she was snatched at the well, where could he have taken her? There were no sightings of children struggling or fighting off men, so the girls seemed to have gone willingly, but they were probably not dressed for a winter day.

Sensing that our questions had come to an end, the mayor invited us to confer with him. 'Is there any reason not to let this woman go?' he asked.

'I can think of none,' I replied, 'so long as she promises not to leave Delft without your leave.'

'So be it,' said the mayor, and dismissed the woman before returning to me. He looked hesitant and uncomfortable, so I deduced that he had a message he would rather not convey. 'Mijnheer Van Setten presents his compliments, and asks why you delay in calling upon him.'

'I have been questioning the witnesses in the order in which the sergeant showed us the scenes, which corresponds to the order of the abductions, but having seen the first and second I am now ready to proceed to the third,' I replied with, I hope, no little dignity.

'Excellent,' the mayor beamed. 'Then I can tell him you will call soon?'

'I can call now,' I said, 'if someone will direct me on the way.'

Claes was deputed, though I noted that he had no intention of going anywhere near the front door, simply walking me to the street and indicating the large house. It sat on the canal in the Molslaan, distinguishable by its broader frontage. I had planned to go out to the grave site in daylight, but that was going to have to wait.

I knocked at the door, which was swiftly answered by a pretty young maid with the rosiest cheeks I had seen for a long time, who informed me that Van Setten was in his study and would be notified of my presence. As I expected, he kept me waiting a few minutes before opening the door and inviting me in.

'I wonder, Master, that you have not waited upon me sooner,' he began.

'I have been viewing the sites in the order of the abductions,' I responded. 'That seemed the most logical approach.'

'Did you learn anything?'

'I learned that the three girls seem to have gone willingly, or, at least, not to have drawn attention by any loud resistance.'

'It takes only a moment to bundle a girl into a closed carriage,' Van Setten snapped.

'Indeed, mijnheer, and if anyone could describe such a carriage to me I should be indebted to them. But the first girl was abducted from a place where no carriage could be near at hand, and the second was seen to walk away with a man.'

This was news to Van Setten, which was not surprising since I had only known it for a couple of hours myself, and he was startled. 'You have a description of this man?'

'Hardly an adequate one. He is above middle height, not well dressed, with coarse hands.'

'That is not much help,' Van Setten growled. 'I cannot imagine that my daughter would go willingly with such a man.'

'You will forgive me if I ask a question that may seem impertinent, mijnheer, but I assure you it bears upon my investigation. As a result of their station in life, the other girls are perhaps more worldly. Would it be true to say that your daughter has led a sheltered existence?'

Van Setten fidgeted with one of his buttonholes. Though he wore the same black suit and white lace as most men of his class, he had discreet black braiding and frogging on his coat. He could afford it, according to Claes, who had no doubt that a ransom demand was in the offing.

'She is schooled at home. Anna comes with us to church on Sundays. Occasionally she is allowed out to take the air in the street and play with her fellows. Our neighbours' children are suitable company for her. For the most part,' he added.

'Do you have doubts about any?'

Van Setten hesitated. He ached to cast suspicion but was very aware of the effect on his reputation if he were proved to be wrong. 'There is a boy in one of the houses in front of the Beestenmarkt. I should have judged him to be thirteen or fourteen years old. He is at an age when he has the attributes of a man without, perhaps, the judgement of one. I have had reported to me that he has made suggestions to girls that ought to shame him.'

'Reported, mijnheer? By whom?'

'Our maids have heard things as they go to market.'

'To be clear, mijnheer, have you any reason to think that he has made such suggestions to your daughter?'

'No. If I had, I would have acted. But that does not mean it hasn't happened now.'

'Indeed it does not. But you will understand that if I am to speak to the family I must be certain of my facts. Imagine how you would feel if a stranger were to cast aspersions on a child of yours, mijnheer.'

'But that is precisely what you have done in suggesting that Anna would willingly go with a man of the sort that you describe!' Van Setten protested.

'I apologise if that is how it appeared to you. I can only describe what others say. No doubt she has been deceived in some way, which is why I asked how worldly she is. May I ask what men you employ about the house that Anna may be familiar with?'

'You suspect one of them? It would explain why Anna was not suspicious. But she has very little to do with any of them. We have a manservant, a kitchen boy and a gardener. The manservant lives in. But he was here when she was abducted, and joined in the search for her.'

'As you said yourself, it takes only a moment to put a girl in a carriage. And he could then have returned to his duties. I think we can exclude the kitchen boy, because the witness to the abduction of Magdalena Kuijper describes a man rather than a boy.'

'She also described coarse hands, I think you said, which should exclude my manservant. Schuyler has been with the family for many years but he does not have coarse hands. In fact, he is quite a fine fiddle player.'

Had I then possessed the experience I now have, I might have challenged his assumption that musical skill exempts men from depravity. One of the most violent men I ever met was a skilled harpsichordist. But I let it pass.

'Your gardener, though, would have rough hands.'

'Verelst does, but he is old and stooped. He can barely carry out his duties, though I believe he employs his nephew to help him. Out of his own resources,' Van Setten added quickly, as if

72

I thought him enough of a fool to pay two men to do one man's work.

'And Verelst's nephew?'

'I never see the man. Ask Verelst. You'll find his house near the Oostpoort. There's an inn called The Fleece or something like that, and he lives behind it.'

The coincidence that Verelst lived near the Oostpoort was not lost on me. His home could only be a couple of minutes' walk from the pump where Magdalena Kuijper was abducted. And if he was not able to do it himself, yet his nephew could have enticed her away, if she had seen him before around the gardens. I made up my mind to pursue the enquiry at once.

'If you will excuse me, mijnheer, I will go there immediately.'

'Do so. And I trust you will keep me informed.'

My impression of Wilhelmus van Setten was not favourable, but since I am required to be charitable as befits my calling, I told myself he was probably under strain as a result of his daughter's disappearance. I have since learned that he was deeply unlikeable at all times. He bullied his inferiors and was unpopular with his peers because he did not choose to play his part in civic life. As I have recounted, Van Leeuwenhoek held office as a sort of chamberlain, and Vermeer was active in the Civic Guard, though I am told he was more enthusiastic than skilled in his wielding of a pike.

It took me very little time to walk along the Molslaan and find The Fleece. It seemed a good time to have some refreshment too, as I realised that I had taken no food or drink since breakfast, so I pushed open the door and went inside.

As one might have expected, a docks tavern is not a refined place. Some rough tables littered the room, and there were some stools and at least one long bench. The clientele eyed me suspiciously, since clergymen are not known for frequenting places where sailors congregate.

The innkeeper was ready enough to take my coin, though, and supplied me with a cup of beer and a hunk of rough bread, together with a piece of herring. There was no knife with it, so I laid the herring on the bread and bit them together.

'I'm trying to find out what happened to Magdalena Kuijper,' I explained to him.

'The bastard child who went missing? I'd have thought a fine gentleman like you would be more concerned about the rich folk's girl.'

'The mayor treats them equally,' I said evenly. 'They are inhabitants of Delft and therefore equally worthy of his concern. I am charged with finding them and discovering who killed the third one.'

The innkeeper paused as he dried the interior of a jug. 'One's been killed? I hadn't heard that.'

'Found last Wednesday in a grave near the lane leading to the two windmills.'

In a city ringed by windmills I was unsure whether this would suffice as a description, but everybody seemed to know where I meant.

'Would that be Lievens's daughter, then?'

'You know mijnheer Lievens?'

'We sometimes see him in the docks loading bricks on the barges. He doesn't come in here very often, but he stands out.'

'How so?'

The innkeeper chuckled. 'He's a giant of a man, over two yards tall and topped off with the reddest hair you ever saw. He's never short of work, because you only have to look at the breadth of his chest to see how strong he is.'

'I'll look out for him. I need to speak to mijnheer Lievens.'

A sailor at the table behind me interrupted. 'I hope for the murderer's sake you find him before Lievens does. He'd rip his heart from his body in a trice.'

There was general assent at this.

'Is Lievens a violent man, then?'

'No, he's as gentle as they come. Rarely in drink, and he dotes on his wife and children. But he's not a man to take liberties with. No man's docile when his blood is threatened. No real man, anyway.'

This was said with something of a sneer and, I thought, a disparaging glance at me. I will grant that the life of a university lecturer is not physically demanding, but it takes a certain manliness to engage in prolonged robust disputation. However, I thought that pausing to convince those present of this would distract me from my mission, so I did not bother.

I thanked them for the information and left, as I thought, a generous tip, in the hope that it might encourage them to forward any useful bits of knowledge that they might stumble upon.

Verelst's home was exactly where it was first described to me, behind the inn. In fact, you had to walk through the inn's back yard to get to it. It had at one time been the last cottage in the row, then the inn was built in front of it. In an orderly but compact city, men build wherever they can squeeze a house or shop on a piece of land. As a result, Verelst lived in permanent shadow.

He was a grey-haired man of about sixty, missing a front tooth and plainly crippled by arthritis in his knees. He walked stiffly and had difficulty rising from his chair.

'Isn't gardening hard work for you?' I asked.

'It is, Master, but it's work. I can do no other. But I have my sister's boy to help me.'

'So I understand. I would like to meet him. Does he live nearby?'

'He does, mijnheer. If you will kindly hand me my cape there we'll go together.'

I gave him a smelly oilcloth cape. I was unsure whether it had started out green and darkened with use, or begun its life as a black garment that had mouldered over time. Either way I wanted to handle it as little as possible.

Verelst's hovel may have been sparsely furnished, but he wanted to keep what he had, and spent quite a while securing his front door with a chain and lock. I did not like to suggest that any burglar worth the name could simply lift off the entire door and frame in one go and walk inside. Verelst had a stoop and walked with the aid of a stick, but he kept up a reasonable pace and it was not far to his sister's house which was in the third street along the main road.

Verelst's sister was a near copy of Verelst, allowing for some slightly feminine accoutrements, though more guarded than her brother. She eyed me suspiciously until Verelst spoke up. 'That's all right, Minnie. The gentleman wants to have a word with Frans.'

'I'll bring him out,' she said.

Frans loomed in the doorway. He was a big lad in his early twenties, but disfigured by a palsy that gripped his face. His right eye was wide and staring, and his mouth drooped on that side. By the way his mother spoke to him I grasped that he was slow-witted to some degree. He was undoubtedly strong enough to have seized the girls, but would a child have gone willingly with a man with such a distorted face? He might well have had a kindly heart, but children are wont to regard us externally rather than look for the good within. I could not imagine this man speaking soothingly to Magdalena Kuijper and receiving her trusting hand in return.

This impression was strengthened when he spoke. As a result of his affliction he could not clearly form some of his sounds. I also noticed that his shoulders were uneven, though he seemed able to use his arm on the affected side.

'I had a hard time delivering him,' said his mother. 'That's why he's as he is. He hasn't been marked out by the Almighty for some sin, as folk around here say.'

'I don't believe the Almighty does such things,' I replied, 'at least since the days of Cain and Abel. Why would a God of love punish the innocent?'

'Why indeed?' she said. 'But that's not what most people here think.'

'And your husband, mevrouw?'

'Killed in the explosion seventeen years since. He shouldn't have been anywhere near the gunpowder store. Out of the goodness of his heart he gave a mate a hand with a load of timber, and both of them lost their lives. So how does God explain that one, eh?'

'I don't know. I can't pretend I know everything God does and doesn't do. I try to help those left behind, as I'm doing for the families of the three young girls that have gone missing.'

The boy had removed his cap respectfully and was wringing it in his hands. 'I helped look for juffrouw Anna, mijnheer. Uncle looked too. We couldn't find her.'

'Were you there when she went missing, Frans?'

'No, mijnheer. It being the Lord's Day, I went to church with mother. They let me stand at the back if I'm quiet.'

Verelst butted in. 'I was at home when one of the maids came for me. They were looking for Anna and wanted all the help they could find. Anna has always got on well with me,

Master. She likes to watch me working in the garden. It's the only time she's allowed outside, poor thing.'

'And me,' Frans added. 'She watches me, too.'

'So did you also help in the search?'

Frans nodded vigorously. 'Uncle came for me. He said they needed as many as could go.'

'He got there before me,' Verelst added, 'on account of not being stiff in the knees like I am. He ran ahead and left the maid and me far behind.'

'Can you tell me where you searched?'

'Where didn't we!' Verelst replied. 'We walked all the streets, opened any gate we could, looked in the courts and yards. We started by walking towards the Markt, because we thought that's where she could be hidden in a crowd, but at that time of day, it was quite empty. I walked along the Turfmarkt, and Frans here looked in the canals.'

Frans agreed. 'I looked in the little one all the way to the city wall and then I came back and looked in the big one going to the South Gate. We had men with poles from the barges sticking them in the water to see if she'd sunk.' His eyes were watering, and if it were possible to discern any expression in that destroyed face, it was one of the deepest misery.

'It must have been very sad for you,' I sympathised.

Frans nodded again. 'The lady was wailing awful,' he said.

'Mevrouw Van Setten?'

'Anna's mum. She wasn't normal. The master had to hold her tight to stop her running up the street and he told her to be still.'

'Well, she must have been very sad too,' I began.

'She kept saying "I knew this would happen one day" and the master told her she was a silly woman and to hold her tongue.'

'Now, Frans,' said Verelst, 'you didn't ought to be talking about the family's business like that and spreading tittle-tattle.'

'One moment,' I answered, as the import of Frans's words struck me. 'She said exactly that? "I knew this would happen one day".'

Frans nodded. Reluctantly Verelst agreed. 'I heard it too.'

'What did you think she meant? She knew that her child would be kidnapped? Had there been threats or previous attempts?'

'I don't know what she meant,' Verelst told me, 'for I took it for the sort of thing women say when they're vexed.'

His sister concurred. 'It's every woman's nightmare. When your child goes missing, even for a moment, you lash out at those around you. You say stupid things. If she really knew it would happen, she'd do things to stop it, wouldn't she?'

'Yet you tell me she kept the child indoors most of the time.'

'That's the way of those people,' Verelst said. 'They don't want their child mixing with riff-raff so they keep them by them. Frightened of catching lice or the plague, probably. After all, Master, she was their only one, and the lady wasn't likely to have more at her age.'

'She's not that old!' protested his sister. 'Plenty of women have babies in their forties.'

Verelst was looking sideways at me as he addressed his sister, as if he did not want to discuss the matter in front of me, but neither did he want her to win the argument. 'Not when they've gone so long childless. Anna's above eight years old now, and they were married as long again before she came along.'

'Aye, barren for years and then along comes a gift from God. But she doesn't look like her father, does she? I'll warrant the fine lady got a man in to stand in her husband's place when he wasn't able. And if she did it once she can do it again,' the sister announced triumphantly.

Verelst's shock was transparent. His mouth dropped open and flapped wordlessly a couple of times. 'How dare you speak of the lady like that? If word gets back that you've said such things I'll lose my place.'

'Be calm, mijnheer Verelst,' I interposed, 'my lips are sealed. No-one will hear it from me.'

It occurs to me as I write this that I have now broken my promise, but if I do not give a full account you will not understand what follows. Anyway, my concentration was disturbed by the sound of a bell. It must have sounded every fifteen minutes but I suddenly became aware of it. 'What time is it?' I asked.

'That's half past four, Master,' said Verelst.

I blush to think of the words that entered my head as I realised I had only half an hour to find a house I did not know for my next appointment. I quickly thanked them for their assistance, assured them that I believed every word that they had told me, and hurried to find the home of Notary Ranck.

It was a great contrast with the evening before. Whereas Lieftingh was full of chirpy asides, gossip and inconsequential chaff, mijnheer Ranck was dull beyond my ability to express it. I doubt that I have ever passed an evening in such quiet, even when I was on my own. As befitted his profession, Ranck weighed all his words very carefully, so much so that an entire sentence could drag on for so long that by its end I had forgotten how it had started.

Ranck himself was a fairly nondescript man. He had a good practice, because he had a reputation for taking considerable pains over his work, and he kept copious notes. He had shelves of journals containing records of his cases, and so far as I could see everything was meticulously catalogued. After supper he took great delight — or, rather, the closest a dry stick like him was capable of to delight — in showing me his system and when I was imprudent enough to ask what he knew of the Van Setten family's antecedents he consulted a ledger and selected two volumes from his shelf.

'The present mijnheer Van Setten is the son of Balthasar van Setten who was himself the son, naturally enough, of another Wilhelmus. The family wealth — the extent of which I am not at liberty to discuss — was founded largely upon the overseas trade, first with the Americas and latterly with the East Indies. Balthasar van Setten drove a hard bargain. He expanded the business rapidly by taking shares in new ships rather than buying them outright. Then, when his partners needed ready cash, he would offer to buy their share. Not having to rely entirely on his own resources, he could grow his fortune much quicker. The younger Wilhelmus inherited a large sum and contracted an excellent marriage. I have a copy of the marriage contract here. I acted for his wife's family in the matter.'

I had just long enough to see that it was indeed a marriage contract before Ranck closed the volume.

'Do I understand that the lady is the only daughter of the house?' I asked.

'The only surviving child, alas. Her brothers and only sister all died before her marriage. Her dowry was quite exceptional,' he continued, licking his lips at the thought of the dowry's size.

'And I understand that Anna is their only child, which must make the thought of losing her even more painful.'

'I doubt the anguish would be diminished if they had ten children,' Ranck replied drily.

'Just so. I meant only...' I tailed off because I did not really know what I had meant. It was just one of those foolish things you say when conversation is difficult.

We sipped our wine in silence. Ranck would happily have let it continue all night, I think.

'I plan to visit the grave of the girl Lievens tomorrow morning,' I said eventually. 'Mijnheer Vermeer took me there last evening but the light was poor.'

'By the two windmills? That would be sensible.'

'I was surprised to see two windmills so close together.'

Ranck pursed his lips and considered this for some time. 'One was there many years ago, before the ring of mills on the city walls were all in place. It will fall down someday soon, no doubt.' He licked his lips again as if anticipating the fees from the compensation claims that he would lodge. Looking about his room it was clear that Ranck had accumulated a decent amount of money and that he had good taste.

'Vermeer has been very helpful,' I offered.

'I am pleased to hear it. I have known him a long time.'

'Oh?' I said. I grant that this ejaculation was capable of bearing many meanings, but to my delight Ranck took it as a request for further information.

'I was instrumental — in a small way — in his marriage.'

'Indeed? Can you tell me any more?'

Ranck seemed to be conducting an internal debate that would end in a terse yes or no, but finally produced whole sentences. 'I was admitted as a notary in 1652. In April 1653 I accompanied Leonaert Bramer, of whom you will have heard, and a sea-captain called Bartholomeus Melling, to the home of Vermeer's future mother-in-law, Maria Thins. I have to explain that the Thins family are adherents to the Roman church, and mevrouw Thins objected to the marriage of her daughter

Catharina to Vermeer because he was a Protestant. Bramer had already made his name as an artist then, and was a man of some influence but, more importantly, he was also a Roman Catholic. I was there to draw up a letter of consent that would permit the marriage vows to be published. I had, of course, drafted such a letter in advance to save time. Mevrouw Thins read it over and declared that she would not sign it. Bramer then said that Vermeer had undertaken to convert to Catholicism if that was necessary to win her daughter's hand. "Then let him come here when he has done so" was the reply. But at length, and moved much by her sister's urgings, Maria Thins said that while she would not consent, neither would she object, knowing her daughter's heart to be set upon the match.'

'I sense that it remains a happy marriage,' said I.

'As happy as any. Vermeer dotes on his wife and their many children and I have never heard him express even a moment of regret at his choice. Although, of course, his Catholicism is a barrier in some areas of life.'

'I am surprised that he is a member of the town council, then,' I remarked.

'He isn't,' Ranck answered. 'The mayor has a separate circle of advisers which allows him to bring in people who cannot serve officially. Men of influence and wealth like Van Ruijven, for example.'

'Van Ruijven is a Catholic?'

'No, much worse than that. He is a Remonstrant.' Ranck hissed the word with such venom that I judged it best to leave the subject.

Remonstrants still live among us today, but in those days they were a growing group. The conventional Protestant view was — still is — that God, being omniscient, knows which of us will enter Heaven and which are condemned to Hell. Our actions are foreknown too, so nothing we do can alter that fate which Providence has predestined for us. The Remonstrants, following the teachings of Arminius, hold that God intended that all men should be saved. It follows that God wills that all men should have that potential, so there cannot be a rigid predestination. By the grace of God, working through the faith that God places within us, men can be saved though they cannot themselves ever be good enough to win salvation for themselves. However, the ignorant man can ignore the promptings of faith and still fall from grace.

No, you're right, I do not really understand it myself. But Van Ruijven apparently did. His kind were thought impossibly lax by the standards of the day, dangerous people who believed that the elect of God could fail and the sinner could rise. It was very nearly a doctrine of revolution, an invitation to disorder. No wonder Ranck despised it so.

I thought I should change the subject. 'Is Leonaert Bramer still living?'

'Yes, he is an old man but he lives on the Koornmarkt.' I must have shown some puzzlement because he elucidated. 'When you face the Armamentarium from the south, it lies along the right side and runs up towards the Markt.'

'He is not one of the mayor's circle, though?'

'He would be, were it not for his age. He is past his seventieth year, but yet a sage man, one of sound judgement.'

'Perhaps I shall have the opportunity to wait upon him while I am here.'

Ranck drained his wine cup. 'I think you will be here a while yet. I am not sure that mijnheer Bramer will be.'

As I entered my chamber I recollected that I had neglected my devotions for two days. I fell to my knees and found myself reciting the words of the *Stabat Mater*.

Stabat mater dolorosa juxta Crucem lacrimosa, dum pendebat Filius.

I have no idea why they came into my head, since they are rarely sung these days, but as a meditation on the suffering of Jesus's mother Mary they seemed apposite. There were three other mothers grieving over the loss of a child, albeit in their own ways.

Quis est homo qui non fleret?

Which man would not weep indeed, to see those mothers so distressed? I must find out what had happened and bring the perpetrator to justice.

I said my prayers, climbed into bed, and blew out my candle.

CHAPTER FIVE

I woke in the early hours with an uneasy feeling. Apart from the desire to make water, I soon detected another reason for my unease. I could hear breathing.

The moon was not too bright that night, and although I lay still with my eyes open trying to accustom them to the dark, I could see very little. Slowly reaching for my pouch, I found my old penknife. If I were very lucky I might be able to jab it in my attacker's throat before he could reciprocate with his own weapon.

I slipped out of bed, and tiptoed towards the door, intending to go for help. A warlike spirit may become a man, but I believe in a healthy retreat whenever possible. I trailed my fingers along the bed to give me some direction, and then realised that the breathing was coming from the floor at the end of the bed. Reaching down, and with my knife poised, I slowly made out a human form. Moreover, my hands were telling me it was a female.

'What are you doing, mijnheer?' whispered Lucie.

'Never mind me, girl. What are *you* doing?' I asked.

'I thought I'd be safe sleeping here, Master. No evil spirit can torment a man of God.'

'Maybe,' I responded, 'but a man of God cannot sleep with a young girl in his room.'

'I won't snore!' she protested.

'That is not the point. It's not becoming.'

'I don't understand, Master.'

'If people find out that you have been in my room at night, they might think things.'

'But you're a godly man, mijnheer. They won't think ill of you for protecting me.'

'They may think I have … you have… we have…'

'Master?'

'I'm thinking of your reputation. They may think you are no longer a maid.'

'You mean I've been sacked?'

'No, but you will be if your master finds you've been in a guest's room.'

'He encourages it, Master. He says so long as he knows so he can add it to the bill…'

'Lucie! You haven't…'

'Oh, no, Master, not me. His wife mainly.'

'His wife?'

'And the cook. She's a widow, you see. And the other kitchen maid.'

'What kind of place is this? Does the mayor know?'

'I shouldn't think so, mijnheer. He never stays here, having a fine house just down the street.'

I hope I am a fairly broadminded man, but I was deeply shocked. That the innkeeper was prepared to offer his wife to other men was almost incredible; and that any man who had seen her would accept the offer was *completely* incredible.

I should have been firm, but I just wanted to get back to sleep.

'For tonight only, you may stay. But you can't sleep on the floor. You may have the bed, and I will sleep in the chair.'

If I expected her to demur as she had refused the chair on my arrival, I was mistaken. She leaped onto the bed and snuggled in, while I wrapped myself in my cloak and settled into the chair, thanking God that I had slept in my shirt. If it had been in the summer, Lucie might have had a terrible shock, if she knew as little of men as she claimed.

Then again, I know very little of women, but after that night I knew one thing more. Whatever women may tell you, they do suffer from wind.

When I awoke again, the bed was empty. I decided that I needed a shave but I would have to do it myself. There was nobody in Delft I trusted with a blade at my throat quite yet. I went downstairs to order some hot water and have some breakfast, which Lucie brought to me, studiously avoiding eye contact as she placed a basket of bread on the table, tilting it just a little so I would not miss the slice of ham concealed within.

Having attended to my chin, I decided to start the day by finding out whose dinner I was to eat that evening, and headed for the town hall. Claes appeared pleased to see me.

'What are we going to do today, Master?' he enquired.

We? When, I wondered, did we become a team? Though I admit that Claes was helpful and did not attempt to intrude his own thoughts.

'I thought I might walk out along the lane to the two windmills and look at the grave again.'

Claes looked disappointed, but he cannot have expected to examine a body every day. I was hoping that there would be no further bodies to examine.

'Tonight mijnheer Vermeer would be pleased to offer you dinner.'

That was a positive step. I could not imagine a silent night in the Vermeer household and I was rather intrigued at the prospect of meeting his wife and mother-in-law. A wife who inspired such love and devotion must be an exceptional creature, and his mother-in-law sounded like the nearest thing to a demon that I was ever likely to encounter on this earth.

'Excellent. Where does he live?'

'On Oude Langendijk, Master. It's very near.'

I thanked him and bade him good day before drawing my cloak close about me and setting off towards the grave. I was beginning to get my bearings and soon found myself retracing my route of Tuesday afternoon.

As I rounded the corner old Cobus was sitting outside, whittling a wedge from a piece of tree branch.

'Good day to you, mijnheer,' he called cheerfully.

'Good day, Cobus,' I replied. 'If you don't mind me calling you by your first name.'

'Of course not. Any friend of the Vermeers is a friend of mine.'

'Forgive me,' I asked, 'but I'm told you're nearly blind. How did you recognise me?'

'I see colours, size, shape. And your cloak smells of libraries and candles.'

Needless to say, I had not noticed. It is a smell that is always with me.

'Aren't you worried you'll slice your finger with that knife?'

Cobus laughed. 'Bless you, mijnheer, I could do this in the dark. Keep up a rhythm and don't change your grip, and you'll be safe.'

I walked on and reached the lane. I had not realised how muddy it was the other night. Fortunately the top surface was frosty, which reduced the mud spatters that splashed my clothes and shoes. The field was not hard to find, and I climbed up on the low bank to view it again.

It occurred to me that I had not seen the wooden cross that Vermeer believed had been taken with the body, but the drawing he had made reminded me of the peg I had just seen Cobus making. Was it possible that the murderer had whittled a cross here, calmly sitting by the grave as he did so?

I heard some noise and spotted a man in the next field who was dragging a tool through the cold earth to make a shallow furrow. I walked across and hailed him. 'I'm looking for a man called Harmen.'

'I'm Harmen.'

'Then you must be the one who reported finding the young girl. I am Master Mercurius, of the University of Leiden, and I am assisting the mayor in discovering what happened here.'

Harmen rested on his hoe and sucked his cheeks in expressively. 'From Leiden, eh? Is it as fine a city as they say?'

'Leiden? Yes, it's very fine.'

'Finer than Delft, would you say?'

The question stumped me. How can you compare two cities, one of which you know very well and the other you have spent less than two days in? 'No,' I said cautiously, 'I wouldn't say it was finer.'

The answer seemed to satisfy him. 'What can I tell you, Master?'

'Just explain to me in your own words what happened when you found the body.'

'Well, they're certain to be my own words, Master, for I know no other. I came out to this field after midday. I keep some chickens in a pen by the house and I'd passed that morning in making the fence sound. I was looking for the best way to lay out my beans this season, because the land tires if you don't move them after a few years, so I paced the field and then I spotted a patch of dark earth in the corner of Jan's field.

"Odd time of year to turn the soil over," I thought, and then I saw the little cross. So then I fell to wondering who had died, because Jan's children have moved away and his wife is frail, but I couldn't imagine that he would just up and bury her in a corner of the field without so much as a few flowers or a bit of a wreath if she'd died. There's only one thing to do, says I, I must go and ask him. So I walked up to Jan's cottage and told him what I'd seen. He said I was a fool and there was no grave there when he last looked, but I held to what I'd seen and, to cut a long story short, he came down with me and we viewed it together.'

'Do you know when Jan last visited the field?'

'It'll be a while. Jan doesn't come down here much in the winter, because there's not much can be done while the ground is hard and he suffers cruelly with the cold in his joints.'

'And when had you last been in your field?'

'Let's see, that was Wednesday, and I don't think I'd been down here since the Saturday before. Although I'd walked past on my way to church on Sunday.'

'Did Jan go to church too?'

'He went that Sunday — last Sunday before Lent. I have to know if he's coming, because it takes me longer to get there if I have to walk beside him. Now, when he's coming with me, I walk along the lane there, and he watches for me, so he doesn't stand around in the cold, because we both know if he sees me pass that part of the low wall and then leaves his house, we'll meet at his side gate. So usually he waves to me to show he has seen me, but on Sunday I paused just there because I didn't see him wave for a minute or two, and I reckon if the grave had been there I couldn't have missed it, because I would have looked straight across it.'

'But on the way back you wouldn't have stopped, presumably?'

'No, I leave him at his gate. He was struggling a bit but he badly wanted to go to ask the minister to call so his wife could get shrived before Lent.'

Aural confession is much more a Catholic practice, as I well knew, but old customs die hard, as they say, and I could well imagine an elderly couple wanting to enter Lent having made their confession. Some Calvinist ministers would have refused, saying it was unnecessary to receive absolution from any intermediary if a man or woman has made their peace with God, but either the local minister had given up that fight, or he was more tender-hearted than some. After all, even if you believe that confession to a priest is not necessary, that does not make it positively wrong.

It was then that an idea came to me. 'How long were you gone?'

'The best part of the morning, Master. It's half an hour or so each way and about two hours for Divine Service.'

'And do all the people around here go?'

'Except the infirm, yes.'

So that would allow the murderer time to dig the grave. He might even have buried the body then, but if not, he could have come back later. At worst, if the empty grave had been found, he would not have buried the body and tried again elsewhere. If he waited until everyone was in church, he would have ample time to dig a hole unobserved.

I suggested as much to Harmen, who leaned on his hoe and scratched his head.

'The digging of it isn't a puzzle, not if you're right. And this isn't a busy lane, so if he wasn't seen by me or Jan, he wouldn't be seen at all, likely as not. But while you're testing your brain, Master, answer me this. What's he done with Jan's soil?'

'Jan's soil?' I repeated.

'Aye, Jan's soil. He digs out the earth and makes a heap. Then he puts the girl in the hole. I know she's only a young thing but she takes up space, so when he fills it he either gets a hump or he has some soil left over. But the hump was quite shallow, if it was there at all, and there's no pile of earth. So what did he do with it?'

What indeed, I wondered. And why is it that when I answer one question, someone immediately gives me another to solve?

I suppose one pile of earth looks very much like another. There may be farmers and gardeners who can tell the difference, just as there are men who can identify the provenance of wine by taste and colour, but to my eyes earth is all one.

I had planned to speak to Jan Pieterszoon, but this conundrum vexed me. I find that I think better when I walk, so I began perambulating along the lane in an easterly direction, then I realised that I could not think and look for the earth at the same time, so I sat for a moment on a gate.

This is ridiculous, I told myself. I have one of the finest minds in Europe, or they would not employ me at the university. I have studied under some of the foremost logicians of the age. I ought to be able to think this through.

Then I remembered what Professor Heereboord told us when we first entered as students. Lay aside the circumstances, and think logically about the essence of the problem. It was probably the only sober thing I ever heard him say, poor man, for he died soon after I arrived. But I knew what he meant.

Very often a problem is presented in a jumbled way, with extraneous information that serves only to confuse or stir the emotions. For example, if we are told a story by a pretty young maid, and then the same story by a drunk sailor, we are more disposed to believe the maid, though the facts, the essence of the story, be the same.

Thus I sat myself down and asked myself what Adriaan Heereboord would have thought. First, he would probably have thought a drink might help, but fortunately I had none. Concentrate, Mercurius, concentrate!

Question: why would a man move the soil?

Possible answers: he wanted the soil — but then he could take it from anywhere, and what use could he have for it? Second answer: the soil would have betrayed him — but any stain could not have done so, because the girl was not killed there. Third answer: the soil would have drawn attention to the grave. That made sense.

A patch of turned earth in a ploughed field causes no comment, but a mound of earth looks at once like a grave. But then why erect the cross? Possible answers: he could not bear to leave the grave unmarked. Or maybe he wanted the body found — but then he could have left the earth. I scratched my head in perplexity.

It is my experience that sometimes the memory will intrude itself upon your thoughts in a thoroughly apposite way, and as I stood there I seemed to hear Van Leeuwenhoek's voice: 'There are no trees nearby to furnish it...'

Let us suppose that the murderer buried the girl and then thought that reverence demanded a headstone or grave marker. After all, if Dr De Graaf was to be believed, the killer had tried to revive the girl. He could simply have dumped her body in a canal. Goodness knows enough people found themselves dead in one each year in the Low Countries; one more might hardly have been noticed. But he gave her a reverent burial. He dug as good a grave as he could, he laid her tenderly in it, what more natural than that he would want her to be guarded by a cross?

That might tell us something about him. A Catholic would certainly want a cross. A Protestant might not, since many Protestant thinkers denounced crosses as symbols of idolatry. Yet for all that the common man, even if he espoused the Reformed faith, might still have a hankering for a cross. I had often noticed students in the chapel discreetly cross themselves during a Reformed service, especially if they were up from the country.

Let us then further suppose that having conceived the desire for a cross, he found nothing nearby to furnish one. He had no tools except a spade and, perhaps, his knife, but apart from the gate I was sitting on, there was little wood nearby. So, fearing discovery, he removed the earth, loading it into the cart in which he had brought Gertruyd, and took it away somewhere. He returned later having made the cross at his leisure. It would be the work of a minute to climb the squat bank and drive it into the ground with a mallet or the heel of his boot.

The question of the earth remained, but now I could see that all that mattered was that the earth should be moved from the field. It would not matter where it went, because the soil would mean nothing to anyone once it was moved. In the field, it discloses a grave; out of the field, it is only soil.

Seen in that light, my training instantly pointed to the application of the *lex parsimoniae* or Ockham's Razor, as the vulgar would have it. In any set of competing theories, favour that which requires fewest assumptions or, to put it in terms my readers will understand, choose the simplest. I had been looking for a pile of earth, which required me to devise a means of moving it, which led me to assume the cart had been used, which meant shovelling the earth at least twice, once into the cart and again out of it, and so on. Much simpler if the killer stood in the corner of the field and just spooned the earth into the road; and, retracing my steps, there on the hard surface of the icy lane were scattered clods of earth. It was not conclusive, of course, but it might answer that riddle.

Thus, buoyed by my success, I visited the home of Jan Pieterszoon and his wife, another Anna. Jan was a robust, ruddy and rather deaf old man whose hips gave him some trouble, so that he hobbled as he walked. Anna was a well-built woman who seemed to have problems with her breathing. She sat in a large chair surrounded by cushions and held a handkerchief to her mouth much of the time. Her cheeks were very red and the least activity seemed to be beyond her.

Recognising my dress as clerical costume, Jan asked me if I would pray with his wife, who had not been able to attend church for some months.

'Of course, the minister visits when he can,' Jan added.

'When he can,' echoed his wife.

'But that isn't very often with such a large congregation.'

'Large congregation,' Anna agreed.

This seemed to be their standard mode of conversation. He spoke the long sentences, and Anna repeated a word or two to show her accord with his remarks. Sometimes the echo was simultaneous with the original, when she could guess what he was going to say.

I explained my mission to them both.

'It's a horrible thought,' said Jan, 'that the poor girl's body was there on our land.'

'Our land!' Anna repeated.

'Unhallowed ground,' they chorused.

'At least she will be buried decently on Saturday,' I was able to tell them, in which the old couple took some comfort.

'No flowers,' said Anna.

'My wife means that there aren't many flowers for the grave at this time of year. I might see if there's a bit of greenery to make a posy or wreath.'

'Wreath,' Anna concurred. 'Greenery.'

'That would be very thoughtful,' I said.

'I'm sure they'll want a good crowd to show how we all feel about it. The family deserve that. I'll try to get into town myself, if Harmen will walk with me. He's a good man, Master. Very patient with us old folk.'

'Patient. With us.'

'It's good to know you have such a helpful neighbour.'

'Oh, yes,' Anna answered, and reinforced her comment with a nod and a bout of coughing.

It transpired that Jan had not visited his field since the Friday before, and he admitted that with his poor eyes he might not have seen the grave anyway, because he would have been more than sixty paces from it. In every other respect, he backed up Harmen's account.

I glanced out of the small window. 'Is the old windmill still active?'

'Well, Master, the wind still blows, and the sails go round, but I don't know anyone who takes grain there to grind now. It's sad to see the state it's been allowed to get into. There's the fine windmill further down the lane on the city boundary, and we have to use that. '

'How can they make you?'

'If you go anywhere else, they may not accept your grain another time, so unless you know the old mill can do your grinding, you go to the newer ones. And given the state of the old mill, who would trust it still to be standing come harvest, Master?'

I could see his point. The whole sail assembly looked like it was held in place with a couple of nails and a lot of prayer. I thanked them for their help, acceded to the request to pray for them both, and set off along the lane towards the town, deep in thought.

At the Town Hall Claes was quick to invite me to look at the portraits of Anna van Setten that had been copied from the miniature. She looked a frail, thin girl, with pale skin, blue eyes and a thin fringe of hair visible under her lace cap. A lace collar covered her shoulders so only the narrowest strip of dark velvet dress could be seen. If she had been ill-used I did not think she would have survived very long. There was not the robustness of form that I saw in the sketch of Gertruyd Lievens that Vermeer had given me. It occurred to me that if I were to find Magdalena Kuijper I needed a portrait of her too, but it was unlikely that she had ever sat for one.

'Can you draw, Claes?' I asked.

'Me? No, Master. Not so you'd know what it was, anyhow. But Delft is full of artists. And you're seeing mijnheer Vermeer tonight, don't forget. Maybe he would draw you.'

'It's not me I want to draw. It's Magdalena Kuijper.'

'That's going to be difficult,' said Claes, 'seeing as she's been kidnapped.'

Rather than contend with more of this idiocy I resolved to go at once to Vermeer's house to see if he would be willing to assist. If not, I would have to look elsewhere, but I was confident that he would if he could.

Arriving at Oude Langendijk I found the house and knocked. The maid seemed to be in some confusion at the sight of me.

'Bless me, Master, I don't think the master was expecting you until dinner.'

'That's quite all right. I just wanted to speak with him and ask a favour.'

I was invited in and asked to wait in the hall. There was a mirror near the door, presumably so the family could check their appearance before they left, and as I glanced in it I was fairly sure I caught the reflection of an old lady in a stiff black dress peeking from the room behind me, but as I turned she slipped behind the door and thus out of sight.

'The master says I'm to conduct you to his studio, if you will,' the returning maid announced, and led me up the stairs and into a room at the front of the house.

It was light and well-scrubbed, though I cannot say that Vermeer kept his atelier particularly tidy. The area where his subject sat was, of course, meticulously prepared, but behind the easel the floor was cluttered with the items that did not form part of the composition, including a large porcelain bowl, some pieces of fruit cunningly formed from wax, a sword, a broad-brimmed hat with a large feather, assorted other pieces of costume, a lute (missing several strings), and a tray of drinking glasses.

A young girl was sitting on a chair as Vermeer sketched her lightly with a stick of charcoal on a canvas that he seemed to have prepared with a grey ground. She was dressed in an ivory dress with a matching shawl and had a chaplet of flowers in her hair. I am no artist, but I could see that Vermeer was confident as he swept arcs of charcoal across the canvas, switching to a fine pencil to mark in the hairline, though he did not trouble to draw the face at this stage.

'One moment, if you don't mind,' he said. 'Master Mercurius, this is my daughter Beatrix. No, dearest, don't get up for the gentleman! There's a good girl. Let me just get your hands and then we can stop.' He drew in the hands which sat gently clasped on Beatrix's lap, declared himself satisfied and gave the child a kiss on the forehead. 'Now, run along. You've done well. Would you ask Tanneke to bring us something to drink?'

Beatrix bobbed prettily to me as her feet touched the floor and set about her errand, so very soon the maid reappeared with a pitcher of ale and two beakers.

'This is a pleasant surprise,' Vermeer said, offering me a seat where Beatrix had been sitting and bringing his own stool from its place behind the easel.

'I apologise for arriving unexpectedly. I'm afraid your maid thought I'd arrived early for dinner.'

Vermeer laughed as he was drinking and broke into a coughing fit. 'I can imagine how that would upset Tanneke,' he said, once the spluttering had stopped. 'She likes a life full of order. And therefore she despairs of me, I'm afraid.'

His good humour was infectious and I found myself laughing too.

'I haven't come early for dinner, by the way. I was hoping you might be able to use your gifts to help me.'

'Of course, my dear fellow. What do you need from me?'

'I have your sketch of Gertruyd Lievens, and I now have a copy of the miniature of Anna van Setten...'

'Do you have it with you? May I see?'

I retrieved the picture from my pouch and handed it to him. He studied it carefully for a few moments. 'Good heavens, when you think of all the artists we have in Delft, and then the mayor picks one like this!'

'It's not a good likeness?'

'It may be a good likeness — I barely know the girl — but it's not a good painting. I suppose the miniature may not be too good either, so I mustn't be too hard on him, but I doubt that Wilhelmus van Setten would have paid for a portrait that wasn't up to scratch. Still, we can check that. It's one of Leonaert's.'

'Mijnheer Bramer?'

'Yes, nothing but the best for mijnheer Van Setten.'

'Is Bramer a miniaturist, then?'

'I hadn't heard of it, but I remember his complaining that he was being pestered by Van Setten when he was already completing a fresco. Have you seen his frescoes? Utterly brilliant. He travelled to Italy to learn the technique and there's none like him.'

'You've never wanted to do likewise?'

'Go to Italy? Naturally, but I have responsibilities here now. Maybe when the children have all left us Catharina and I could go together.'

'That would be nice,' I suggested.

'Yes,' said Vermeer wistfully. 'Yes, it would. Well, drink up and let's go and see what Leonaert can tell us.'

'You haven't heard my request yet,' I protested.

'Oh, I thought that was it.'

'No, welcome though mijnheer Bramer's opinion would be. What I wanted was a drawing of Magdalena Kuijper. I realise it's asking a lot of you to draw a portrait of someone who can't sit for you, but I thought if anyone could do it, you could.'

'I'll be happy to try,' Vermeer said. 'It all depends on how good the mother's descriptive powers are. Maybe it would help if some of the neighbours contributed too.'

'I doubt you'll get much from the neighbours. The Kuijpers don't seem to have got on too well with at least some of them.'

'If they're Delft people I'll get round them. I'll just tell them someone from some other place is being considered for the job.'

As we walked to the Koornmarkt Vermeer pointed out the architecture of his native city. He seemed to have noticed every door and window. When we arrived at Koornmarkt 48 he rapped on the door and soon we were sitting in the parlour opposite mijnheer Bramer, who was a stocky man of around seventy years, with a high forehead and broad cheeks. With his brown hair hanging loose over his ears he looked a little like one of those small spaniels favoured by King Charles of England.

Vermeer invited me to show Bramer the portrait. The old man took it to the window to be able to see it better, but soon handed it to me again.

'Shocking! No depth, no feel! No sense of where the light falls. Well, where do I start? Mijnheer van Setten commissioned me to paint his daughter in the summer of 1669. She was about six years old, I think. I was busy at the time so it wasn't until August or September that we were able to organise a sitting. It was, of course, a standard portrait. Van Setten must have had a miniature painted from it.'

Bramer sniffed. 'I'd like to think it's lost something in the copying,' he said.

'Is it an adequate likeness for the searchers to show people while they look for her?' I enquired.

'It'll serve. She's no doubt a bit bigger. The likeness is there, but there's no life in the eyes. She looks dull, flat. She's a very docile child, not given to running around. I had no trouble getting her to stay on the chair while she was painted. I think she may be sickly, but at any event she kept up a lively conversation with me as I painted.'

'Can you recall anything she said that may give us a clue to her whereabouts?'

Bramer looked puzzled. 'You mean like "I'm going to run away to the East Indies" or "I've always wanted to live in Amsterdam", for example?'

'I had in mind that she might have expressed an idea that a wicked man could use to entice her to go with him. Something like owning a pony or a boat.'

Bramer gave the question reasonable attention before shaking his head. 'I think not.'

I was returning the picture to my pouch, having run out of questions to ask, when Vermeer interrupted. 'Leonaert, run your practised eyes over it! What's wrong with it? What precisely hasn't the copier captured?'

Bramer accepted the portrait again, and studied it at length. 'The fear.'

'Fear?' I echoed.

'That's what I'd call it. The girl was relaxed with me, but when her parents were with her, she was afraid. Maybe she wanted so much not to be a disappointment to them.'

I empathised with that. I'd felt the same way about my parents, particularly since I actually was a disappointment to them. They had hoped that I would become a warrior like my brother Laurentius, who was one of those irritating children who seem to be able to do anything. Except, unfortunately, keeping out of the way of an English bullet at the Battle of Lowestoft in 1665. Still, at least it was only a bullet. The commander was knocked off the quarterdeck by a cannonball.

'But why fear?' Vermeer persisted. 'I could understand it if you'd used a word like concern, but fear is such a strange feeling to have in the company of your parents.'

There was something that needed to be said, but I hesitated to say it. 'Is it possible that her fear had a more concrete cause?' I asked.

Vermeer was visibly shocked. 'You mean her parents may beat her?'

'Yes, or worse.'

'Worse?'

'I have heard of cases where a father behaves improperly with a daughter.'

Now Vermeer was really shocked. He looked both perplexed and anguished. 'But why? She's just a little girl. I can't imagine how any father ... words fail me.'

'I don't say that this is happening to Anna van Setten, but we cannot exclude it.'

'It would explain the tenseness she showed,' Bramer conceded.

'So would a poor report from her tutor,' replied Vermeer. 'We ought not to look for a more wicked explanation than is needed.'

'If that were the reason,' I ventured, 'it should have been temporary. I wonder whether she has continued in that vein. Who would be able to tell us?'

'She rarely leaves the house,' said Vermeer. 'Perhaps one of the maids. Or the minister of her church, perhaps?'

Bramer laid a heavy hand on my shoulder. 'And who better to speak to a minister privately than another minister?'

Vermeer and I found Liese Kuijper exactly where I had last seen her, sitting by her front door gutting and cleaning fish.

'That must be almost her entire life,' I muttered as we approached.

'Master,' said Vermeer, 'so many of us have no idea how our fellows live. It is a world of toil and trouble ending in pain.'

'*Qui habuerit substantiam mundi et vident fratrem suum necesse habere et clauserit viscera sua ab eo quomodo caritas Dei manet in eo?*' I murmured.

'Whoever has the world's plenty and sees a brother in need but shuts up his bowels of compassion from him, how can the love of God be within him?' translated Vermeer, fairly loosely. 'Indeed, Father.'

It was my turn to look surprised.

'You dress as a Protestant but you behave as a Catholic,' Vermeer explained. 'Don't worry, I won't say anything. No doubt you have your reasons for denying your faith.'

It was said with his usual good humour but I knew that I would have to explain my history to him later.

Liese looked up as we approached. 'Come to buy some fish, have you?' she asked.

'When we leave,' said Vermeer.

'I've asked mijnheer Vermeer to sit with you and draw me a likeness of your daughter so I will know who I am looking for.'

Liese paused, eyed us warily, then wiped her cheek with the back of her hand and indicated a stool. 'Then sit with me and let's get it done,' she said.

Vermeer produced some paper from his portfolio, pinned it to a piece of board, and selected a small stick of charcoal. 'Her build, mevrouw?'

'Call me Liese. She's a strong girl, broad in the shoulders.'

'And her head? Her cheekbones?'

'Higher than mine. She has a round head. Quite thin lips, pale blue eyes, high arched eyebrows.'

'Her chin? Pointed, square?'

'Squarer than mine. It comes slightly forward at the tip.'

Vermeer sketched quickly but confidently, pausing to listen for instructions and amending as he was directed. In about half an hour he had a working image, and by the time an hour had passed Liese declared herself satisfied.

A little crowd had gathered, and Vermeer showed his picture to them. There was general approbation and one or two requests for him to do the same for them.

'When Magdalena is found,' he announced, 'I will come here one Sunday and draw as many of your children as I can. But for now, good people, the Master and I must get this picture copied for the sergeant and his men.'

Liese gently tugged his sleeve. 'May I have a copy?' she asked. 'Just in case.'

We parted, I to go to the town hall, and Vermeer to return home with his fish and prepare for dinner. Claes received the drawing, and suggested that he knew someone who could make a good woodcut by the following evening, from which many copies might be made.

I was about to leave when Claes told me that the mayor had a plan.

'A plan? What manner of plan?'

'He says that until the villain is found, we must assume that all the young girls are at risk. Therefore he will send the sergeant's men around the city tomorrow to proclaim a warning to keep girls between six and ten years old within sight, and any such children found unaccompanied will be brought here and put in the guardroom for their own safety.'

I applauded the purpose, but I was by no means sure that we could announce that only girls, and only those between six and ten, were at risk.

'Whose idea was this?' I asked.

'I don't know,' Claes shrugged, 'but the mayor was talking with mijnheer Van Leeuwenhoek earlier.'

It had the taste of one of his ideas. It was coldly logical and in accordance with the evidence we had. It could not be argued against. And yet, it seemed to me, if we were wrong, it allowed the murderer to pursue his prey with impunity, because we would be protecting the wrong group. It was true that the victims so far had all been girls aged about eight, but given how slight Anna was, and how strong Magdalena was, how could a man who chanced upon them have known they were the same age? I had not yet found any other link between them, and so far as we knew the three girls barely knew each other. I resolved to see if Lucie could suggest any hypothesis that we might test, because she seemed to know most of the gossip of the town.

I returned to my room to wash and change my hose. I was rinsing the soiled ones in the water when Lucie tapped at the door.

107

'I would do that for you, Master,' she said.

'You don't need to, thank you. I'm quite capable of washing my own clothes.'

'I know, Master, but it's my job. If you give it to me I'll wash it and return it to you by the next morning.'

I stuttered an expression of gratitude, feeling rather unsure about the whole thing. No woman other than my mother had ever touched my underthings and I was not sure it was entirely proper. But then I reflected that at the university our shirts were taken to be laundered and no doubt women handled them then. It was just that I did not see it. That, in turn, made me think of Liese cleaning fish all day, every day, in order to be able to afford one for herself and her child. Vermeer was half right. The bible does indeed tell us that we should be ashamed if we see our brothers and sisters in need and do nothing about it — the third chapter of the first epistle of St John, if I remember correctly — but how much more should we be ashamed if we do not even see the need?

'Is something wrong, Master? You look upset.'

'Don't be silly, Lucie,' I said, turning away quickly and gazing out of the window for longer than the view warranted.

'Have I offended you?' she persisted. 'I'm sure you know how to wash things, but the mistress would be cross with me if I did not offer to do it.'

Somewhat chastened, and feeling I had been hard of heart with her, I turned back.

'Lucie, you have done nothing wrong. I would feel guilty if I lived a life of ease when you have to work so hard, that's all.'

'I must work, Master, for if I do not work then I do not eat,' she answered simply.

'You're young to be working so hard. And I was moved to realise that Magdalena Kuijper is only eight but already she works all day to earn her keep. Her mother works from dawn till dusk to earn the sort of money that many men will spend in an hour in this inn.'

'You may be right, Master, but when they spend that money in the inn, then they make work for the likes of me. If the minister has his way and nobody ever gets drunk again, I shall be out on the street, for the inn will close within the month.'

There was a lively spark within this girl, I thought. If Providence had caused her to be born in a different family, who knows what she might have achieved? But then, if she had a life of ease perhaps her wits would not have been sharpened so.

For once in my life, I made an impetuous decision. 'Lucie, I don't know anyone here, but you do. I want you to be my assistant for an hour. I will pay for your help.'

I held out a guilder. Lucie touched it, but then drew her hand back.

'I don't have change,' she said.

'Why should you need change?' I asked.

'That's nearly three days' pay,' she said. 'I get two of those a week, before they make me pay for my board and keep.'

'So how much is left?'

She shrugged. 'A few stuivers, mijnheer. But I'm fed well,' she quickly added.

I placed the coin in her hand and closed her fingers around it. 'Think, Lucie. What possible link is there between the three girls? Do they know each other? Do they go to the same church? Do they have sisters or brothers who know each other? I can't think what they have in common, but perhaps you can find out. Will you think for me?'

She nodded. 'I don't see how they can know each other, because Anna never leaves the house, and I don't expect the poorer girls go to school. Juffrouw Van Setten has no brothers or sisters, and if gossip be true then the shellfish girl has none either. And I have seen the rich girl in her family's pew in the Nieuwe Kerk, but I expect the other girls either go somewhere else or not at all.'

To be honest, I could not imagine what I was thinking when I gave her the guilder, because the chances that this young woman was going to think of something that I, who was a member of the faculty of the University of Leiden, had not must have been vanishingly slim. But I am the first to admit that I am not worldly. Well, now perhaps, a little; but not then. If I had been familiar with the ways of the world, I might have avoided the trouble that was coming.

CHAPTER SIX

I arrived at the house in Oude Langendijk a few minutes before five. I have an aversion to being late, though this does not apparently extend to church services, where I frequently have to slip in at the back. I was going to wait for the clock to strike, but Tanneke saw me outside and assumed that I had knocked.

'Beg your pardon, mijnheer. I didn't hear you knock, what with the children being excited.'

To say that the children were excited was an understatement. I could not count them, though I think there may have been nine, but since they refused to sit still it was difficult to be sure. I once gave a friend some help loading piglets on a cart and the effect was very similar.

Vermeer greeted me warmly and led me to the front room. 'I hope you don't mind, but we usually eat as a family. I'm afraid it won't be very quiet but it will pass quickly, I promise you, then we can have some more adult discourse.'

The children lined up at Vermeer's command, and I was introduced to each in turn. The older ones were all girls — Maria, Lijsbeth, Aleydis, Beatrix — then Johannes junior, Gertruyd and now it all gets a bit hazy. There was another boy, Franciscus, who was about six and appeared to be a species of comet, flying rapidly about the house and transiting the room at intervals before vanishing again for a while. I was also introduced to Vermeer's wife Catharina, who was not, perhaps, a conventional beauty, her nose being a little straighter and larger than the classic form would require, but who was plainly an object of adoration for Vermeer. She teased him in front of me, but he took it in good part, explaining that being a noted painter did not mean that he knew anything about whitewashing the parlour walls.

'They have needed repainting for some time, Master,' she told me, 'but Johannes is always too busy. Or so he says.'

After a few minutes the door opened and the elderly lady I had glimpsed earlier made a grand entrance, leaning on an ebony and silver stick because she was weak in one hip. Vermeer made a great fuss of her, leading her to her favourite chair and ensuring that she was well supplied with cushions.

'Mother-in-law, may I present Master Mercurius, of the University of Leiden, who has come to assist the mayor in finding the young girls who are missing. Master, my mother-in-law, Maria Thins.'

She held out a hand in the manner of an imperious bishop. I was unsure whether to take it, kiss it or genuflect before it, but as soon as I took it in mine she withdrew it.

Vermeer leaned towards her and said something that I did not catch, but which I learned later was that I was an adherent to the old faith. Immediately she seemed brighter and warmer towards me and insisted that I sit by her.

Mevrouw Thins spoke loudly, the result, as she claimed, of being hard of hearing, although if this were true she showed no signs of it and distinctly heard something that Lijsbeth whispered to Maria at the far end of the table. She was obviously an intelligent woman, the daughter of a prosperous family in Gouda, about as far from Delft to the east as Leiden was to the north, who made no bones about her failed marriage though, as she pointed out volubly, she did not hold with divorce and simply chose to live apart from her husband. At this point Catharina decided to call us to the table, much to the consternation of Tanneke, who was still laying plates.

Having arranged us to her liking, with Vermeer safely placed between mevrouw Thins and me, she invited me to say grace. I was a little wary, because one never knows what children may say, but since they appeared not to be paying much attention anyway I recited a benediction and we sat down.

It was not a grand meal, but it was a happy one. I had not previously seen much attraction in having a family, but it was clear that it was the pivot of Vermeer's existence, and he was so transparently happy in their company that I wondered if I might be missing something. The older girls, Maria and Lijsbeth, were vainly trying to maintain some order among their siblings so that their mother could attend to the smallest, little Catharina, who had somehow managed to sleep through the tumult and only woke as the first course was served.

Mevrouw Thins was very complimentary about her son-in-law, though whether that was because he was there, I cannot say. She explained her life history to me, glossing over her opposition to the marriage of which I had been told earlier, and describing her delight at having so many grandchildren though, she admitted, she found their energy wearying from time to time. It was a big house, but not always big enough. Fortunately she could retreat to her room which was sacrosanct, if I would permit the use of the word in a secular context. There was, I noted, an assumption in that aside that just because I am ordained I am particularly religious in outlook. I suppose I am, but I confess that I do not consider language that carefully. I try to avoid blasphemy in my speech, of course, and have the added handicap that some things that I might say in a Protestant milieu I could not say in a Catholic setting, and vice versa. Occasionally I think that my life might be easier if I became a Mohammedan, though I promptly reject the thought and look over my shoulder to check there is no avenging angel nearby to chastise me.

The meal ended in a vast pile of pancakes that Tanneke bore from the kitchen on a wooden platter. The children descended on them like rats attacking a dead chicken, but Vermeer insisted firmly that they wait until I had been served, and offered the plate to me. I at once held it for mevrouw Thins, who smiled graciously as she helped herself, and in that moment I gained the support of a forceful ally. As I helped myself and returned the platter to Vermeer I noticed him suppressing a smile, so I suspect that he had buttered up the old lady himself from time to time and recognised an act of flattery when he saw one.

After the meal the children withdrew and we were left at the table. Mevrouw Thins said she was comfortable in the taller, firmer chairs, and called for a cup of herbal tea. I recognise that some herbs have medicinal properties and that those which are most beneficial are frequently the foulest-smelling, in which case the tea she took must have been the healthiest decoction man's art can devise. If I had smelled it in my room I would have lifted the floorboards to search for something rotting. Mevrouw Thins explained that her drink contained valerian, which helped her to sleep; I do not doubt it, the only wonder being that she ever woke up again after imbibing so filthy a mixture.

We talked pleasantly enough, the ladies expressing some interest in the fashions of the Leiden womenfolk, though why they should expect a celibate priest to be an adequate expositor on the subject is beyond me. They asked if I enjoyed music, to which I replied that I treasured the music of others, but not my own. Mevrouw Thins commented that Vermeer had a very fine voice but could never be prevailed upon to sing, and that her daughter played on the virginals but had little leisure to practise. Vermeer looked as if he had been accused of black magic or high treason and quickly changed the subject before anyone suggested that this was a suitable occasion for a chorus or two.

'Master, if you wish to smoke a pipe, please do so, though I'm afraid my husband does not smoke,' said Catharina.

'Thank you, mevrouw, but I have never smoked either,' I answered.

'Johannes says that the smoke destroys the light,' she explained.

'I do not doubt it, mevrouw. Good light must be important to an artist. As must a good sitter, Johannes. I thought Beatrix was very patient today.'

'You're painting Beatrix?' Catharina said.

'Not exactly — well, yes, I suppose,' Vermeer said unenthusiastically.

'Why Beatrix?'

'Why not?' he said. 'I'll paint them all in time.'

'Your husband, mevrouw, has been assisting me greatly by drawing the young girls I am trying to find. He is a very public-spirited man.'

'Indeed he is,' she said proudly. 'I hope Delft will one day recognise the fact. He is head of the Guild of St Luke this year, did you know?'

'The Master won't be interested in our little local offices,' Vermeer protested, his cheeks reddening slightly as if he did not choose to be talked about.

'On the contrary, one of the comments that people keep making to me is that mijnheer Van Setten neglects his civic duties. Is it really that heinous?'

Vermeer might not have intended to say anything, but his wife and her mother certainly wanted to do so.

'A man of wealth and privilege has responsibilities to the common good,' said mevrouw Thins. 'He has benefited from the custom of others and all the leading men of this town have always undertaken civic duties, whether in the Civic Guard, as guardians of the almshouses, or members of the council. It is the consequence of wealth. As Our Lord Himself said, much is expected of those to whom much is given.'

Catharina joined in. 'The Van Settens do not mix much. They attend church but otherwise they stay within their own walls. Mevrouw Van Setten is a little older than me but only by a few months, I think, yet we could never be friends. She lacks maternal spirit, if you know what I mean. It is as if she had the child only because it was expected of her, and after birthing the infant wanted as little to do with her as possible.'

'I understand the Van Settens to be an ambitious family.'

Mevrouw Thins laughed bitterly. 'And so they are. They set great store by a cousin who married into the Van Dussens. A comely woman, I grant, and not unaccomplished, but her gifts are her own, not her family's. Van Setten himself worked a while at The Hague, though I think he was never as influential as he would like it to be thought. His wife went to live there for a short while; indeed, I believe Anna was born in the city.'

'They had been trying to conceive for a long time,' Catharina added, 'but they had not been blessed. No doubt living apart while he was in government service did not help, so she moved to be with him, and soon they were expecting a child. Not, I suppose, a particularly healthy child, but lively enough as I hear, and a dutiful daughter. Of which, you may be sure, I have several myself.'

'Maria and Lijsbeth look to me to be very fine young ladies,' I said, feeling that a compliment was being angled for, but then adding quickly, 'but perhaps the view of a confirmed bachelor is not to be relied upon.'

'Priest you may be,' said mevrouw Thins, 'but you are also a man, and therefore fit to judge of women. As a priest, of course, you will always judge kindly of them, I'm sure.'

She might have been sure. I wasn't.

'My daughter Aleydis entertains thoughts of convent life,' said Catharina. 'If the opportunity arises, I would be very grateful if you would speak to her and test her vocation. Naturally, we would not oppose service to the Lord, but I worry that she may have too romantic a view of nunnery life.'

Needless to say, I have no clue at all of nunnery life, but then I recollected that the mayor had suggested that I should call upon the sisters at the convent on Friday while the Civic Guard drilled, so I offered to take Aleydis with me so she could see it at close quarters, and on the way back I would point out the privations and discomforts she must expect.

'That is most generous of you,' said mevrouw Thins, before Catharina could say anything to the contrary.

It is as well that I have a good memory, because I seemed to be committing myself to appointments cluttering an already overfilled diary. It dawned on me that almost every time I wanted to do something in this investigation, somebody sidetracked me or a more urgent task appeared.

Catharina was speaking, and I realised to my shame that her remarks were addressed to me. I was obliged to ask her to repeat them.

'I know, she mumbles terribly,' said her mother. 'She always has. I have difficulty hearing her myself sometimes.'

Sensing an argument bubbling up, I quickly confessed that I had been distracted, and had the wit to blame a handsome painting on the wall opposite.

'It's one of Johannes's best,' agreed Catharina. 'Maybe he should have had a professional model, however.'

I realised — belatedly — that Catharina was the lady reading the letter in the picture. In my defence, her hair was now styled differently, and I had not seen her in profile, but I felt rather a dull fool as a result.

'Master,' Catharina continued, 'I was asking whether you think there is any risk to my girls. I have a mind to send them to my mother's family in Gouda if they will be safer there, but we would have to divide them, for it would be too much for any one household to take them all.'

You may be sure that I weighed my words very carefully.

'Mevrouw, I cannot say that we know exactly what goes through the abductor's mind. We know that the girls taken have all been around eight years of age, but otherwise there is no clue as to how he selects his victims, except that they were always alone. The best advice I can give is to counsel your daughters to go round in pairs and have a care for each other. If they will do that, they should be safe.'

'That is a comfort, Master,' Catharina replied.

'How very sensible,' mevrouw Thins added. 'I knew we could have faith in this young man to remove our affliction. It is surely only a matter of time before the miscreant is hanging from a gallows somewhere.'

I preferred not to think about that. The notion that I could bring a man to a public death did not sit comfortably with me. I am, of course, well aware that theological authorities differ on the propriety of capital punishment. Calvin was in favour of it, saying "let us remember that, while Christ forgives the sins of men, he does not overturn political order, or reverse the sentences and punishments appointed by the laws." Luther too thought that at least heretics and blasphemers should be put to death, so I suppose he must be said to have supported execution. Personally, I have qualms about ending a God-given life, and I am very glad that it is not my decision. Sensibly, I kept my opinions to myself.

Not so Vermeer, however.

'Do you not think that he may be deranged?' he asked nobody in particular.

'Deranged?' said his wife. 'In what way, deranged?'

'Not responsible for his actions. Mad, insane, use whatever word you want. It seems to me that if he is not in his right mind he can hardly have made a conscious choice to harm the children, and therefore it would be wrong to punish him when he should be pitied. Do you not agree, Master?'

'Well, I — erm...'

Fortunately I was spared the need to answer by Catharina, whose eyes blazed with rage.

'Not punish him? Not punish someone who has killed a young girl? I hope you would not be saying that if it were one of our daughters, Johannes Vermeer. A man can take being understanding too far, you know! If someone harmed our girls I would kick him off the ladder myself, aye, and fend off anyone who tried to pull on his legs to show mercy.' She wagged her finger at her husband. 'That's the kind of soft-headed thing you'd do. You'd poison him before he was hanged so he didn't feel himself choke. I know you. You're a good man, but you're too tender-hearted.'

Vermeer shrugged gently as if her opinion made no difference to him, and I thought I had escaped the inquisition, then I heard mevrouw Thins speaking to me. 'And you, Master, what think you?'

I hoped someone would come banging on the door to require my presence elsewhere urgently, but it never seems to happen when you need it.

'I think that if God has so ordered the life of a man that he lacks his senses, we must consider very carefully what the consequences of that may be. And though his reasoning be faulty, yet if he knows that his acts are wrong, then he must answer for them.'

A happy picture came into my head of my father's dog. 'When I was a boy, mevrouw, our family had a small black dog. I am not sure what variety of dog it was, for I have never seen another like it. It was an intelligent beast by the standards of dogs. One Christmas my mother left a piece of roast pork on the table while she attended to something else, and the dog stole it. My father, who had a great respect for the dog's abilities, solemnly questioned him as to its whereabouts, and as the dog whined gently and shuffled uncomfortably, it was quite clear that he knew he had done wrong, and was feeling guilty about it. We found the meat in the corner where the dog slept, but by then the animal had vanished. Now, it seems to me that since the dog obviously was aware he had transgressed, he was fit to be punished for it.'

'Well said!' proclaimed Maria Thins, clapping her hands delightedly. 'Johannes, if the murderer knew what he was doing, he must be hanged or he will do it again someday.'

'Perhaps,' Vermeer conceded, 'or perhaps not. Who can know? Was the dog punished?'

'Yes,' I said, 'when we finally found him. Father gave him a good thrashing.'

'And did he steal food again?'

'From time to time.'

'Then what was the point of the punishment?' Vermeer enquired.

'You may be sure,' mevrouw Thins interjected, 'that if the dog had been hanged he'd never have stolen again.'

This is an argument I have frequently heard advanced, but I cannot see how you can describe hanging as a deterrent. Not committing a sin because you are dead is no cause for pride. If the purpose of the punishment is solely to prevent a recurrence, you might achieve the same by casting the malefactor into a dungeon until he mends his ways. Of course, whenever I suggest that someone argues that if you keep a man locked up for many years you must feed him at public expense, so hanging them is a lot cheaper. On top of which, our medical schools need a ready supply of corpses for dissection. If we are successful in stamping out sin, how will we train our surgeons?

The remainder of the evening was very enjoyable. Johannes was very reticent about his painting, but Catharina was only too keen to show off his work, much to his discomfiture. Finally he deflected discussion from himself by drawing my attention to a particularly fine little piece by the late Carel Fabritius, who died in the explosion of 1654.

Mevrouw Thins stirred matters by comparing the prices earned by Fabritius and Bramer against those asked by Vermeer. Put bluntly, Vermeer was no businessman, and tended to accept the first offer made to him. As a result, some of his work was ludicrously under-priced. Against that, he argued that Fabritius and Bramer had national reputations, and there was therefore a market for their art farther afield, whereas his own fame was confined to the Delft area.

For all that people had told me that Vermeer had money troubles, I saw no evidence of that. Catharina referred to the old inn on the Markt that Vermeer inherited from his father and which he had just leased out at a good price. She confessed that she was much happier with the regular rental income and hoped that the difficult days of the past were now behind them. Had I the gift of prophecy, I would have known that their prosperity would not last, and within a year they would struggle as the country was invaded by Louis XIV and his allies. Maria Thins's land was among that flooded when the dykes were broken down, resulting in a catastrophic loss of rents.

I took my leave and walked back to the inn. It was a cold, clear night, and by the time I reached my lodgings the icy wind had made me very glad of my long cloak. I opened the door of my room and was delighted to see that Lucie had made up a fire in a small brazier, so the chamber was cosy, and although it was dying down now, the fire still threw some light across the room. There was a certain amount of smoke, requiring me to open the window briefly to let some escape.

I could not help but notice the familiar heap at the end of my bed where Lucie was sleeping on the floor. Having told her before that she could stay only on that single night, I ought to have woken her and thrown her out, but I was inhibited from doing so by a number of circumstances. First, she was sleeping soundly, and disturbing her seemed unduly cruel. Second, it was a cold February night, and the room was probably warmer than her own little attic chamber. Third, having drunk quite a quantity of Vermeer's excellent wine, I couldn't be bothered. And fourth, if she wanted to stay, at least this time she was not on the bed, so I occupied it myself and was soon soundly asleep.

CHAPTER SEVEN

For the benefit of those of my readers who are not Catholics, I should explain that many of us hold Friday as a day of penance and mortification in memory of the passion of Our Lord on Good Friday. This involves refraining from meat, for example, but also prayer, reflection and some sacrificial discomfort such as wearing a hair-shirt. I believe that I may possess a hair-shirt — I was given it by a well-meaning aunt — though goodness knows where it is. I have known priests who scourged themselves, fasted until sunset or took cold baths as acts of piety. This all strikes me as rather self-indulgent. I avoid red meat and shave in cold water, and that seems to me to be adequate for most occasions. Friday is also the day when I usually make confession, but on this particular Friday I had no plans to do so. This was partly because nobody in Delft was supposed to know that I was a Catholic, and attending confession might have given the game away, partly because I did not know any priests here, but mainly because I had not had time to put together my weekly list of sins.

I should stress that the list is necessary, not to enable me to marshal an abundance of sinful acts and thoughts but to help me to identify a bare few for confession. I hesitate to claim any special holiness of my own, but fortunately I have been prevented from sin by an almost total lack of opportunities: I have no need of money, and women have always found me immensely resistible, so occasions for sin do not often come my way. The result is that on the eve of confession it usually takes me quite a while to think of anything to confess, and I frequently find myself making things up, such as owning up to impure thoughts that I have not actually had. This is a good choice, because confessors, being priests (and men) themselves, sympathise and keep the penances to a minimum so that we will go on sharing our imaginary sexual fantasies with them in the confessional; and, frankly, when you have passed an hour or two on the other side of the grille hearing people's confessions, you can do with all the excitement you can get.

There was some irony in this, because on this Friday I actually had something to confess. Waking in the morning, I was rather disappointed to find that Lucie was gone, and I had a dim recollection of a dream which may have involved a measure of impropriety. I do not know that for sure, of course, but there were circumstances that led me to suppose that I had been in the middle of some carnal thoughts when I woke, and if they did not centre on Lucie, I do not know who else it might have been.

I gritted my teeth to shave in cold water, and was just stropping my razor when Lucie knocked and entered with a pitcher of hot water. I was about to send her away when it struck me that it would be uncharitable to do so, and it would be unfortunate if she got the idea that her labour had been in vain. It therefore seemed best to me to sacrifice my own wishes and shave in the hot water.

Things became rather more difficult when I came down to breakfast. Lucie had again concealed some meat in the bread, but I had to draw the line at eating meat just to please her. On the other hand, to refuse it might puzzle and upset her, so I hit on the idea of taking the meat and hiding it in my sleeve, with a view to giving it to a beggar as an act of charity later, but then it occurred to me that if I gave it to a Catholic beggar on a Friday I would be encouraging sin, so I must give it to a

Reformed beggar, though how I would know the difference was not clear to me then. However, God is good, and as I left the inn for the short walk to the town hall I was set upon by a dog who must have detected the meat, for he took a large bite out of my sleeve — and, unfortunately, my arm.

I was cradling the arm and hoping the dog was not rabid when I was helped by some good Samaritans passing by, one of whom belaboured the dog with his staff while two others helped me to the apothecary's shop at the sign of the salamander. The young man there dressed the wound, painting it with wine to clean it before wrapping it in fine muslin. I asked how much he wanted for his labours, but he refused to accept payment from a man of the cloth. If only others were as generous, particularly innkeepers.

Thus chastened, I returned to the town hall. Claes noticed my bandaged arm at once.

'Master! You've been attacked!'

'It's nothing, really,' I replied.

'Is it a knife wound?'

'No, just teeth marks.'

'Teeth marks? What kind of footpad leaves teeth marks?'

'It wasn't a footpad.'

'Not the murderer?'

'I doubt that, unless the murderer has four legs and a tail.'

'A wolf?'

'No, Claes, just a normal dog, albeit a particularly boisterous one. It waylaid me as I left the inn.'

'But why, Master? Did you annoy it?'

'No, Claes, it must have smelled the meat hidden in my sleeve.'

Claes opened his mouth as if to ask why I should have meat concealed in my clothing, but closed it again, no doubt reasoning that either it was a curious ritual associated with the university or that it was none of his business where a gentleman keeps his meat. I would have explained, but then I would have to disclose my Catholicism, and it would be more trouble than it was worth. Better to let Claes think that I was an eccentric.

'I have the woodcuts, Master,' Claes said, producing a package from a small chest that he carefully locked again. I assume it held the mayor's most private papers.

The picture was well produced, faithful to Vermeer's original and surprisingly delicate given the haste with which it had been prepared. The artist must have worked well into the night by the light of candles to have it ready so soon.

'I recognise her now, Master. That's the bucket girl.'

'The bucket girl?'

'I'd see her from time to time with a yoke over her shoulders and a bucket on each end as she followed her mother around the city selling fish and shellfish. I had no idea she was only eight. I hope no harm has befallen her.'

'So do I, Claes, but I grow less optimistic with each day that passes. I hope that whoever took her has somewhere warm to keep her.'

'Well, Master, so long as we find no body, there is hope.'

'Yes, I suppose so. But who knows what horrors she is facing each day until we track her down? At least we know she cannot have been taken for ransom. There can hardly be a poorer family in Delft.'

'But ransom would be better than carnal knowledge of so young a girl,' Claes answered, a crack in his voice.

'Let's get these handed out to the sergeant and his men. Where are they, by the way?'

'They have been watching the roads and canals for anyone attempting to leave with a girl.'

'Perhaps she was gone before they were in position.'

'Of course, that may be true, of the first two girls at least. But they were in place before Anna van Setten was taken. She, at least, must still be in the city.'

'Why didn't you tell me this before?' I cried.

'You didn't ask,' was the answer. At the time I was vexed, but now I see that there was some justice in the response.

'So if Anna is here, Magdalena must be here, or he will have had to leave her unattended.'

'Or she is already dead. But if he left her unattended, either she or Anna must still be so, for no man has left with a young girl and he cannot be in two places at once. The barges have been thoroughly searched.'

'How diligent are the sergeant and his men, Claes?'

'There are none better than the sergeant, Master.'

'But there must be many ways out of the town.'

'There are, but they are all watched. The land around is flat and a few men placed in the windmills can see very well. The gatekeepers can see everyone coming and going by land, and they have been stopping all the barges too.'

'I saw nobody when I arrived,' I protested.

'No, but wait till you try to leave. The canals have even been watched by night, and the Civic Guard dragged a large chain across the Zuidpoort to stop anyone leaving through the widest channel.'

I needed to think, and I could do without Claes chattering in my ear while I did so. We knew that the murderer must have been inside the city two Sundays ago, when he buried Gertruyd, and last Sunday, when he abducted Anna. It was unfortunate that the guards had not searched those entering the town, because it would be good to know that Gertruyd's body had been in Delft before she was buried, but even without that proof it seemed very likely, because the killer could have buried her in many more secluded places if he had been outside the walls. Why would he risk detection to bring a body to bury when he could do so in perfect secrecy outside the town? I was confident that he was close at hand, holed up somewhere in this small city, and if the girls were still alive, they were here too.

'I trust that you have not forgotten the Civic Guard is drilling this afternoon, Master. I have sent word to the Mother Superior at the convent that you will call upon her this afternoon at the mayor's request.'

'You still have convents?' I asked. In some cities Protestant sentiment had made it difficult for the sisters to continue and I knew that at least some of the convents of Delft had been put to other uses.

'There is still the Bagijnhof,' said Claes, a reference to a lay order of women who pursued the religious life for a fixed term of years and might then re-enter the world. Aleydis Vermeer could have become a bagijn but was, it seems, set on a full religious vocation, so this could not be what she had in mind.

'No other?'

'Yes, Master, there is an order who look after the almshouses. In Oranje Plantage there is a set of almshouses that are devoted to the care of unmarried and widowed Catholic women. The sisters who look after them live in a house near the Horse Market. I will show you the way. It's not far.'

We walked together to the Horse Market and Claes showed me the alley that led to the convent. While we were there I realised that we were quite close to the two windmills and the Pieterszoon smallholding.

'Claes, I believe a number of the older people would like to pay their respects to Gertruyd tomorrow but they are too infirm to walk there. Do you think there might be a cart or carriage that could bring them?'

I explained about Jan Pieterszoon and his wife Anna, but I was sure there would be others.

'I'm certain that the mayor would be keen to help. He is concerned that the family should be supported in their grief and has been encouraging as many as possible to attend. I will ask him to speak to the citizens before the Civic Guard drill to see how many can lend carts and carriages.' He nodded towards the alley. 'The good sisters will want to come for a start.'

'I thought they lived a secluded life?'

'They never miss a funeral, Master. But perhaps I'm being uncharitable. The sisters have a vocation to nurse the dying, and therefore they know many of those being buried.'

I understood that very well. When you have been ministering to someone in their last days it seems very natural to want to walk with them on their final journey on this earth. Apart from any other consideration, someone must comfort those left behind.

Suddenly I became aware that this idle chatter was doing nothing to take my task forward, and decided that I must do something. The difficulty was that I had no idea what that 'something' ought to be. It was easy to blame Claes's interruptions, but the fact was that my mind had gone completely blank. I needed an idea, and I had no notion where they were to be found.

'Claes,' I asked, 'if you were in my shoes, what would you be doing next?'

'Looking for new shoes, Master. Yours won't fit me.'

'It's a figure of speech, Claes. I'm asking what you would do if you were me.'

Now that this had been explained, Claes was prepared to give the matter the whole of his attention.

'Master, I think you need to meet mijnheer Lievens. When Gertruyd disappeared he organised some of the dock workers to search for her. If he told you where he searched it might help us to narrow down the area that we need to search ourselves.'

Claes was right, and I kicked myself (figure of speech again) for not having thought of it myself. Lievens had been able to call on a lot of friends and neighbours within a few minutes of Gertruyd's disappearance. Knowing where he had looked would be a great help, added to which he was likely to know of waterside places where the girls may still be hidden.

'They told me he works in a brickworks. Do you know which?'

'There are a great number, Master. But I'm sure his wife could tell you.'

Thus it was that I found myself heading to the south-west once again, having persuaded Claes that the best service he could do for me was to round up as many carts and carriages as he could to ensure that the church was full on Saturday.

I paused at the well and looked about me. The small gate that Adriaan had noticed was shut on that Sunday morning was firmly closed, and the court was deserted, except for a little fellow who sat in the doorway of a cottage on the north side. I waved to him, and he waved cheerily back, then returned to consideration of a crust that he was gnawing.

'Nico?' I called, but he started and ran inside. Within moments a woman appeared brandishing the paddle from her washing tub.

'Who are you, and what do you want?' she yelled.

'Forgive me, I am…' I began.

'Forgive you? What have you done that I must forgive? I warn you, if you've harmed my boy I'll open your skull though I swing for it.'

A little placating seemed to be called for.

'Mevrouw, I am here to find mijnheer Lievens, and I thought to ask his wife where he works. My name is Mercurius, and I am the mayor's agent in the search for the three missing girls.'

She seemed doubtful. 'And what does my Nico have to do with that?'

'When I was last here, Gertruyd's mother said that if anyone was here when Gertruyd was taken, it would be Nico. He may have been a witness.'

'He's but a child, and not yet two years old,' his mother protested.

'That may be, but it does no harm to ask. And,' I added, having recalled that every mother is moved when she hears her child praised, 'I am told that Nico is uncommonly forward for his age.'

The paddle was lowered.

'That's true,' his mother agreed.

'Then perhaps we can ask him. Does he remember the last time he saw Gertruyd?'

Nico's mother picked him up and hugged him close, then, in a soft voice, she asked if he knew Gertruyd. He nodded decisively.

'That's Clara's sister Gertruyd,' she expanded.

Nico nodded again. There was no doubt in his mind as to the identity of the Gertruyd we wanted.

'And you know that Gertruyd has gone to be with Jesus?' his mother asked. Nico was less sure about this, but nodded doubtfully as if averring that he knew that it had been said, but he had theological scruples about the concept.

'Now, my bright boy,' his mother continued, 'do you recall the last time you saw Gertruyd? It was the morning of the Lord's Day, before church.'

Nico sucked his thumb for a moment before deciding that it was unwholesome.

'When Gertruyd left, do you remember the man who came for her? What did he look like?'

Nico was extraordinarily decisive. Without hesitation he pointed at me.

To say that I was taken aback would be an understatement. If I had not been convinced of the truth of my own alibi, I might have been swayed into arresting myself.

'You mean he was a pastor?' I asked.

Nico had returned to a minute inspection of his troublesome thumb.

'Was it the dominie?' asked his mother.

Thankfully, Nico shook his head.

'A man like the dominie? A man with a big black hat?'

Nico cogitated, then shook his head once more.

'A man with black hair?'

Nico frowned. I suppose if the man wore a hat, Nico would not have seen his hair.

'Well, then, why don't you go with me to the dominie and you can show me what he has that is the same as the bad man?'

Nico shrank back as she approached, but when he realised that she obviously trusted me, he leaned forward in her arms and batted my shoulder before grabbing a handful of my cloak.

'He wore a black cloak?'

That seemed unlikely to get us very far. Almost every man in Delft would have a black cloak. My brainwave had fallen short, and I was about to tip my hat in salute and depart when Nico's mother drew attention to what her son was doing.

'He's trying to lift your cloak. I think he's feeling for an edge that isn't there. It's not a cloak, Master. It's a cape. The man wore a black cape.'

The women at the pump had mentioned a cape too. It was a large step from that coincidence to deciding that it was necessarily the same man, but it was encouraging that it could be. I had not seriously considered that three different men could be implicated, but now we had a measure of evidence — slight, and likely to be discounted by the magistrates, to be sure, but still evidence — that at least two of the appearances involved a man with a cape.

Jannetje Dircks paused in her work to invite me inside. I explained that I hoped to speak to her husband, and she gave me directions to the yard where he worked. I was sorry to see that she looked, if anything, older and more tired than she had when we spoke two days before.

'Pray for us, Master,' she implored. 'My husband has taken it very hard.'

'You look tired and distressed yourself, mevrouw Dircks,' I responded. 'Of course I will pray for you, but what do you want me to pray for?'

She covered her mouth with her hand as if she could not say precisely what troubled her. 'He is not the husband I love,' she said. 'He has become a different man. He weeps at night when he thinks I am sleeping.'

'You don't look as if you have slept for many nights,' I said thoughtlessly, causing Jannetje to brush some stray hairs under her cap and pinch her cheeks to redden them. 'You must understand your husband's grief. He is meant to be the strong one, the rock on which the family stands, and now he finds himself shaken by this catastrophe. He probably feels inadequate.'

'He need not,' she said, 'for I find no fault in him. He has ever been an attentive and loving husband, and I bless the day when we first met. But I suspect that he rages within to think of what happened to her. It is all he talks about, day and night.'

I took her hands in mine. 'I will talk to him and assure him that we will find out what happened to Gertruyd. He can help in that. Maybe if he can act he will not feel the need to talk. And meantime I will pray for you both, that God will be a comfort to you and you will be a strength to each other.'

For a brief moment, she smiled, and I glimpsed an angel far from Paradise.

The towpath by the canal was littered with clods of red earth, and I had to lift the skirt of my cloak to avoid trailing it in the filthy sludge that made walking there so treacherous. At length I came to the hut with the little steps outside that Jannetje had described, and entered, removing my hat and bowing to prevent my head scraping along the ceiling.

The man at the desk made to rise, but I begged him to remain seated. It was as well, for when my eyes became accustomed to the poor light I could see he had only one leg and his crutch was resting on the side of the small barrel that he was using as a stool. The top of the barrel was made more comfortable by a cushion in a bright green cloth that looked to my untutored eye rather like silk. It seemed a little incongruous to have such a luxurious item in so mean a hut, and my eyes must have betrayed my thoughts.

'A gift from my master's wife, dominie,' said the man. 'When I lost my leg in his service, the master kindly found me a position here, and the lady his wife sewed me this with her own hand.'

I made approving noises, though privately I doubted that a silk cushion, however elegant, was much of an exchange for a leg.

'I'm looking for a man called Lievens,' I said, 'the father of the murdered girl.'

'A shocking business,' said the man. 'I hear she is to be laid to rest tomorrow.'

'She is,' I agreed. 'Will you come to the Nieuwe Kerk?'

'It's a long way to walk, to be honest,' he said. 'I will if I can.'

'I believe the mayor is sending carts to collect those who find walking difficult.'

The man brightened at once. 'Then I shall ask the master for leave to go.'

'You work every day?'

'Aye, mijnheer, except the Lord's Day, of course. But the master is a God-fearing man and I'm sure he will allow us to attend. Unpaid, no doubt, but why should he pay us when we're not about his business?'

'Who is your master?' I asked, knowing that I probably would not know him, whoever he was.

'Why, Wilhelmus van Setten,' came the reply.

The crippled one pointed to a group of men, and it was easy to pick out Gerrit Lievens. He stood half a head taller than the others, and that half a head was crowned in a blaze of red hair.

Some men's hair fades in sunlight, but Lievens's mane gave him the look of a lion, and an angry lion at that. He worked methodically but silently, and I sensed something of an atmosphere as I came towards him and his colleagues. They did not dare to laugh and joke as normal, because life could not be normal given what had happened, and they were waiting for some sign from Lievens that the cloud was lifting before they returned to the banter and buffoonery that made their days pass quicker. They would have a long wait. Even today I can feel the oppressive weight of that silence in the cold February mist.

'Mijnheer Lievens?' I asked softly. He looked up, but did not answer. 'I am Master Mercurius, of the University of Leiden. The mayor has sent for me to help find the man who killed your daughter.'

Lievens stood upright. His legs were still splayed in the braced position he adopted to bend and fill the brick moulds with the clay mixture. It gave him an aggressive appearance. I am, as readers will recognise, a man of peace, but even if I were the wickedest thug I ever met I would take no liberties with Gerrit Lievens.

'You spoke with my wife,' he said. It was curiously toneless and flat, just an assertion that needed no confirming.

'I did. And I have been there again today, talking to little Nico.'

'Nico? He can barely talk. He's just a baby.'

'He talks enough. He told me he saw the man with whom Gertruyd left.'

'How did he describe him?' Lievens asked urgently.

'Nico can't tell us that, but he could say that the man wore a shoulder cape.'

'That doesn't help us much, Master,' Lievens said bitterly. 'There's many a man with a cape in Delft. I have one myself.'

'Come away, mijnheer, and let us talk.'

'We can talk here, in front of these men. They helped me search for Gertruyd. I have no secrets from them. They're good men, every one of them.'

I had the feeling that I was being omitted from that classification.

'As you please. I have no secrets either. And every man of goodwill can and should help me.'

There was general nodding.

'I see two of you are wearing capes.'

'Are you accusing...' one began.

'Not at all. I was going to ask whether you would wear your cape on a Sunday.'

'Of course not. Unless it were raining,' Lievens replied. 'They get smelly and dirty at work.'

'I am not too knowledgeable on this subject,' I confessed, 'but it seems to me that a cape is preferred to a cloak in wet weather because it leaves your arms free to work.'

'That's right. A man can hold his tools without tangling them in a heavy woollen cloak. And a cape, if it's leather, does not hold the water so much.'

'So if a man is wearing a cape on a Sunday, what do you think explains that?'

The men looked at each other for a moment before one answered me. 'Either he was working on that Sunday, or he was a man who does not go to church. A heretic or worse. That would explain the evil that he did.'

This sentiment provoked general agreement.

'But who would work on the Lord's Day?'

'Farmers must,' said Lievens, 'for cows need milking. And sailors are governed by the tides, not the days. But that Sunday was a fine day, cold but dry. No farmer would wear a cape then.'

'A sailor, perhaps?'

'Aye, because they wear their capes in all weathers to guard against the salt spray.'

I was convinced by the argument when one of the bystanders threw a damp cloth on my newly-kindled fire.

'Anyone who has a ship to unload wears a cape,' he said, 'and they would work on a Sunday. They're paid when there's a cargo, and if they do not work Sundays, by Monday the work is gone and they're left without a wage.'

'Mijnheer, I have to tell you something you may not wish to hear. I was with the surgeons when they examined your daughter.'

'Don't tell me she was interfered with,' Lievens exclaimed, his voice laden with anguish.

'No, far from it. It seems that the murderer may have tried to revive her. He gripped her by the arms and shook her.'

Lievens eyes were cast down as he muttered a response. 'Shook herself, more like.'

'Shook herself? I don't understand.'

Lievens flopped on a crate and began to wring his hands. 'She had the falling sickness. Sometimes she would fall into fits of shaking and know nothing of it afterwards, and other times she would just fall to the floor as if she had forgotten how to breathe.'

'Did this happen often?'

Lievens opened his hands in a gesture of uncertainty. 'Two or three times a year, perhaps. It's been getting worse as she grows.'

'And what provokes the swoons?'

'We don't know. Sometimes she complains if the house is stuffy, or it can happen if she has a fright. But she was a good girl.'

I laid a hand on his broad shoulder. 'I'm sure she was. And a child with such a malady is a great worry. But it may be that she had one of these attacks and the abductor shook her to try to revive her.'

'Whatever he did, she's dead,' Lievens wailed.

'I know, I know,' I answered. 'And I cannot bring her back. But we are taught that so innocent a child is surely in a happier place. However much we miss her, it would be no kindness to bring her back, even if we could.'

Tears ran freely down Lievens's cheeks. 'A father would always wish her back. We were a family, and now we're wrecked.'

'Gerrit, your wife and Clara need you to be the anchor of their family again. You must be strong for them. I cannot begin to feel your sorrow, but you have the prayers of every good person and we will find out what happened to Gertruyd.'

There I go again, making promises I can't keep.

CHAPTER EIGHT

Lievens and his colleagues had done a very thorough job of searching along the south side of the city, turning to follow the road to the west. They had run, so a man with a small girl, even with ten minutes' start, would surely have been seen. It led me to think that the killer had a place within, say, a thousand paces of the well where he could hide Gertruyd and where the cries of the searchers would not be heard — unless, of course, she had been killed at once. But the surgeons were agreed that she was not long dead when she was found, by no means three weeks after her death. Therefore, she must have been alive when the searchers were calling for her, so why did she not respond? Obviously, because she could not, I thought. She was bound or gagged, and the speed of this made me think the killer came prepared. It was true that there were no marks of bonds or chains on her wrists and ankles, but they may have healed by the time she died.

When I arrived at the town hall I found Claes receiving instructions from Van Leeuwenhoek. Knowing Van Leeuwenhoek to be a man of science, methodical and ingenious, I took him into my confidence and told him what I had discovered.

He listened attentively, and then displayed an aspect of his personality I had not seen before. 'Claes, a map of Delft! Quick, man! Any map will do, if it be accurate.'

Claes unrolled one he retrieved from a chest of drawers and weighted the corners with ink-wells and candlesticks.

'We must not deface this, but a good copy will serve us well.' Laying another piece of paper on the first, he pressed it down hard. 'No good,' he said, and picked up the two sheets together. To my astonishment he marched to a window and asked me to hold the two corners to the right while Claes held the two to the left. I realised then what craft he had in mind. The sun shone through the papers and the design on the rear one could be seen on the front. Taking a pen, Van Leeuwenhoek swiftly drew along the revealed lines to make a passable copy of the original.

'Claes, when we're done here, we must cut out the outline and make a pattern in wood in case such a chart is ever needed again.'

'I'll see to it, mijnheer Van Leeuwenhoek.'

'You needn't sit back down again. I have another task for you. I want you to go outside and count how many paces it is from the town hall to the Nieuwe Kerk. Well, don't sit there gawping! Off you go!'

While he was gone Van Leeuwenhoek measured some of the main landmarks on the map and reproduced them on his copy in the correct locations. Claes returned, having counted both to and fro and seemed disappointed that they were not the same numbers.

'No matter,' said Van Leeuwenhoek. 'You probably tired as you came back and your stride shortened. We'll use the bigger number so we draw the larger circle.'

What circle? I had not begun to see his cunning.

'Now, Master,' Van Leeuwenhoek explained, 'you tell me that these men believed that the girl must have been concealed within a thousand paces of the well, or they must surely have seen her in the streets. I'm not entirely convinced they're right, because there are many small alleys, but let us assume that the searchers reaching the larger streets would effectively make a cordon around the district. Given that we know the number of paces between the town hall and the Nieuwe Kerk on this map, we can work out its scale, and thus I can draw a circle one thousand paces from the well, which I now do.'

He drew, and stood back well satisfied. It seemed to me to take in a large part of Delft, but it was a start, I suppose.

'Now, how long was it before Magdalena Kuijper was missed, and how did her mother and neighbours search?' he asked.

'The mother had little help but they searched to the south and east where the canal sweeps round, then they walked up Oosteinde towards the centre of the town.'

'Excellent. So we may take it that they explored the small part of the town to the east of this circle and some of it within. And I know that Anna van Setten's family and servants searched in each direction along Molslaan as far as Oosteinde to the east and Oude Delft to the west. A circle of a thousand paces from the bridge at the west end of Molslaan seems reasonable.'

He drew again. The two circles overlapped by more than I would have liked.

'Thank you, mijnheer. This is very helpful,' I lied. 'But if the abductor wore a working man's leather cape, why did nobody express surprise to see him walking hand in hand with Anna van Setten?'

'I don't know,' Van Leeuwenhoek replied simply. 'But I'm not the man charged with the inquiry. It's your job to find out.'

He was right, of course, though he did not need to be so brutally direct in saying so.

'Could it be that they recognised him as one of Van Setten's workmen?' Claes suggested.

I was mulling over this possibility when Van Leeuwenhoek waved it away with a dismissive gesture. 'That can hardly be because nobody recognised him at all. If I see you in the street and recognise you as the mayor's clerk, then when I'm asked afterwards I'd be able to say who you were. Nobody noticed them. It's as if they seemed to belong together. Something united them more strongly than the difference in their apparel separated them.'

Fortunately Claes expressed my thoughts before I could articulate them. 'Eh?' he said.

'For some reason they looked more alike than they looked different,' Van Leeuwenhoek explained, 'though it's hard to imagine what that could be.'

'Perhaps the maid is lying and she delivered the child to another place.'

Van Leeuwenhoek had a horrible manner of discounting viciously with ideas he did not care for. He swatted the ideas away like flies that only troubled him briefly. 'No, no, Claes. That won't do. Either the other child would have known where they went, or she would have had to be taken home first before the maid returned for Anna, and we have the testimony of kitchen staff that the maid did not go out again after she brought the other girl home.'

I returned to the map. 'You know Delft better than I do. We've drawn these thousand pace circles but that's not what actually happened. The kidnapper can't have known that he would get this much start. He could only have expected a two or three minute lead. Maybe we can justify the circles being smaller. Suppose they were half this size, just five hundred paces.'

Van Leeuwenhoek obliged. Now there was much less overlap, broadly the area around the Armamentarium to the south, extending to the east as far as the Bastion, and then north to Molslaan. If we drew a similar circle from the site of

Magdalena's abduction, it reached as far as Molslaan — just — and to the Bastion, but not as far to the west as Gertruyd's home.

'So,' I said, 'is there anywhere in this area where a man could be sure that a child would not be heard or seen?'

'There is only one way to find out,' Van Leeuwenhoek said, and went to fetch his cane and his cloak.

Van Leeuwenhoek was born to stride. Ordinary walking was beneath him, as was any diversion from the shortest possible route. He barged his way across the Markt, booming 'Excuse me!' or 'If you please!' when people had the temerity to cross his path or stand talking in his way.

He obviously had somewhere in mind, but I was unsure what it might be. Eventually he paused at the bridge leading across to the weavers' cottages, turned, and looked back towards the city.

'So, we may assume that the killer — for such he was — and Gertruyd Lievens reached here. There is no other sensible and quick route from the well.'

'They may have headed out of the area to the west,' I said.

'But that proposition falls foul of the knowledge that the child must have been lodged in the city while the second girl was snatched,' Van Leeuwenhoek retorted. 'And I am familiar with that road. The absence of buildings means that a traveller on it can be seen from some distance. I should be very surprised if none of Lievens's neighbours thought to look that way.'

'I was told that an old sea-captain, the father of a woman called Trijntje, looked out of his window along the road.'

'Hah! Precisely,' Van Leeuwenhoek cried, making him one of the very few people I have ever heard to exclaim 'Hah!' in ordinary speech. 'The scientific method requires that we establish a working hypothesis, then test it to prove or disprove it.' In deference to my supposed learning he added, 'Though I use the word "prove" in a loose sense, since Almighty God is not constrained by any law of science. One day he may cause an apple to fly upwards from a tree to confound us.'

'What hypothesis had you in mind?' I asked.

'It seems to me, Master, that on reaching this point, the killer had three choices. He could continue along the canal on the west side of the city heading north; he could follow the south wall towards the Bastion, or he could head in broadly the direction we have just come from, to the north-east. On a Sunday morning, that last option would help him to mingle with the crowds, because people would be going to church, and there is anonymity in a crowd, but on the other hand the chance of recognition or discovery would be higher. If he followed the canal to the north, he would have been in plain view for some time, because it is so straight here. The south wall has a bend in it, and he could be gone from sight quite quickly. What do you think?'

I was still thinking when Claes piped up. 'Begging your leave, mijnheer, but I cannot see him risking going into a large crowd. Gertruyd might easily have slipped his hand and he could not recapture her without drawing attention to himself. If I were in his shoes, as I believe the expression is —' the blackguard glanced at me as if he were explaining this for my benefit, would you believe? — 'I would follow the south wall but I would turn into the first alley and follow the road parallel to this.'

Van Leeuwenhoek stroked his chin. 'Yes, I believe that works as an hypothesis. It reduces the risk of being seen, leads him to the area of town where his lair may be and would explain why the followers did not see him. Come, then, let us do likewise!'

I was obliged to trot to keep up, which is rather undignified for a cleric at any time and particularly difficult on slushy cobbles. When we came to the first turning to the left Van Leeuwenhoek held his cane out sideways to indicate the route, giving a porter a blow to the shoulder that caused a certain amount of local dialect to be used. Fortunately I did not understand it all, though I think I could catch the drift. We walked forward to the next turning to the right, where Van Leeuwenhoek paused.

'Too cluttered, I think. There is too much garbage on the ground and obstacles in the way to move quickly. Let us take the next turning instead.'

He declared this more promising, and so we turned to the right and cut our way through the local inhabitants until we arrived at the west side of the Bastion.

'And from here, he could go anywhere,' Van Leeuwenhoek announced. 'In the absence of evidence, we cannot take our hypothesis further.'

'But we cannot simply do nothing,' I protested.

'Science can do no more,' Van Leeuwenhoek claimed, 'but we can look for evidence. I suggest I look to the north, you to the east and Claes towards the south and along the wall, and we meet back at the town hall in an hour.'

Without waiting for our agreement, he marched off, so Claes and I mutely obeyed his command. Van Leeuwenhoek had a way of proclaiming his thoughts as if no argument were possible. I recall nothing like it in my experience, except, perhaps, an archbishop whom I once heard arguing that castrating small boys for service in the Papal Choir was somehow good for them. I thought that if this were such a boon then perhaps we should castrate potential archbishops too, a safe proposal since I never expected to be one.

I roamed through the streets and alleyways, comforted by the thought that so long as I did not cross any major canal I could not get lost. Near the bastion there were various types of shed, but I could see none that were good candidates, because the accessible ones were too near the streets and cries would be heard, whereas the less accessible ones were either derelict or too small. There were two shops that were shuttered, but when I put my ear to the boards I heard no sounds within, and there were several near derelict houses, but I could see no sign of a child when I looked around, though some showed signs of recent occupation. Empty genever flasks and chicken bones suggested that others had been living there.

The nip as the wind hit my cheeks reminded me of the urgency of finding these girls if they were still alive. They were poorly equipped to withstand this cold, and I felt rather ashamed of myself for enjoying my evening with the Vermeer household so much when I should have been out with a lantern searching for Magdalena and Anna.

Considering the physical hardships the girls faced reminded me, I am rather ashamed to say, that some refreshment was needed for my own mortal frame, so I paused at a small inn and ordered some beer and a plate of bread and cheese. As I sat I reflected on the irony that Wilhelmus van Setten was Gerrit Lievens's employer. No doubt Lievens would be docked a day's pay to attend his daughter's funeral. If I had never understood the parable of the talents before, I did now, because Van Setten was just the sort of employer who would expect his stewards to double his investment.

It occurred to me then that I had not yet spoken to mevrouw Van Setten. If her husband was a hard master, it seemed that the lady had a tender side. Although I had been uncharitable about the matter of the cushion, it remained the case that she had no obligation to offer one, still less to make it herself. And there remained that curious utterance of hers that she 'knew this would happen one day'. Knew what would happen? What was inevitable about it? Verelst's sister had passed it off as the kind of silly remark women made, but nobody had suggested to me that mevrouw Van Setten was a silly woman.

I drank up and walked on, and in a few minutes found myself gazing out over the basin by the Oostpoort. A flotilla of barges bobbed in the water, and one was slowly reversing away from its mooring to begin its voyage. I could see the sergeant's men waiting further down the channel to board and search it as it passed, so I could be confident that no barge could avoid scrutiny. This was a much more efficient method of oversight than trying to search every barge that was moored, when trying to keep track of the numerous small movements as barges were shifted to allow others to come and go would have taxed even the most organised constables.

The striking of the clock reminded me that I was going to be late for the rendezvous at the town hall, but since this would be attributed to my diligence rather than the beer and cheese I felt quite relaxed about keeping the others waiting. As it happened, I need not have given it a moment's thought, because Van Leeuwenhoek had gone about his duties, leaving word that in the unlikely event of my searches achieving anything Claes was to seek him out. Even if I had made progress I might have denied it just to annoy the supercilious so-and-so.

There is an etiquette to visiting a convent. It would be discourteous to disrupt the hours of prayer, so there would be roughly two and a half hours, between the end of *None* at about half past three and the beginning of *Vespers* at six o'clock, when a visit was appropriate. It meant we would not be offered supper, which was more likely to be between *Vespers* and *Compline*, but it allowed us to make our visit in daylight, so I had arranged to collect Aleydis at three o'clock.

On the way to Vermeer's house I passed the painter himself hurrying in the opposite direction. He wore a breastplate and carried a helmet and his pike. The pike, a fearsome spear about three times the height of a man, was a difficult thing to hold at the best of times, but attempting to run with one that was held in one hand was beyond Vermeer, who tripped himself up with the lower end and sprawled across the path. I bent to lift him up, and he let go of the pike to restore his helmet to its rightful place on his head.

'Oh, it's you, Master,' he said. I noticed a hint of being unhappy to see me which was explained by his next remark. 'I must apologise if you heard what I just said.'

'As a matter of fact, I didn't,' I answered.

'I am very relieved,' he said. 'Remind me to mention it at confession.'

'Consider yourself confessed,' I murmured. 'A couple of Hail Marys should meet the case.'

'I can manage that. Thank you, Father.'

I looked around to see if anyone had heard him say it, but there was no sign of it. 'Please don't call me that in public,' I hissed.

'Sorry — I forgot. I must run,' he said. 'The sergeant doesn't like being kept waiting.' He attempted to doff his helmet politely, but the pike spun from his grasp, so I grabbed it and restored it to him, wishing him Godspeed.

Aleydis was waiting in the front hall of the house on Oude Langendijk, a demure navy bonnet on her head and matching gloves cradling a missal. She spent so much time with her eyes lowered that she must have been an authority on the floors of Delft, but there was little sign of that submissive nature as we walked along.

'Eleven is a very young age to decide upon the religious life, Aleydis.'

'Forgive me, Father, but my mother misled you. I am nearly twelve.'

'Indeed? I suppose that makes quite a difference — when you're eleven. When you're as old as I am, Aleydis, the move from eleven to twelve seems like a twitch rather than a giant step. And please don't call me Father in the street. We Catholics must be discreet.'

'Father says that,' she replied. 'But are we not called to proclaim our faith, even to the point of martyrdom if need be?'

This was awkward. 'Ah, yes, on the matter of martyrdom, do you not think that God would prefer a live Catholic to a dead one? And there is such a thing as taking excessive pride in offering oneself for martyrdom.'

'Did not St Lucy have her eyes gouged out rather than deny her faith?' Aleydis continued fervently.

'Ah ... opinion is divided on that. Some later sources seem to suggest such a sacrifice on her part...'

'And St Agatha of Sicily had her breasts cut off rather than renounce her Christianity.'

'Yes, but that is no reason to court...'

'I would gladly give my breasts to God, Father, because if I take a vow of chastity I would have no need of them.'

I ran my finger inside my collar. It suddenly seemed much warmer. 'I begin to feel uncomfortable with the turn this conversation is taking, Aleydis. It is not right that a young lady should talk about such things with a man.'

'But you're not a man. You're a Father, Father.'

'I'm a man and a Father,' I corrected her, 'just as the sisters are nuns and women. And please remember what I said about calling me a Father.'

'Yes, Father. Sorry, Father.'

We walked on, further conversation being inhibited by my suggestion that we should each say three Hail Marys and three Pater Nosters silently in preparation for meeting the sisters. I was halfway through my second Pater Noster when Aleydis declared that she had completed her duty.

'It's not a race, Aleydis. There is no advantage in praying quickly.'

We arrived at the convent and I knocked on the door. The sister who opened it conducted us at once to the Mother Superior. Aleydis fell to her knees in front of the Reverend Mother.

'Please get up, child,' the nun said in a strong, deep voice. She must have been a wonderful contralto with a tone like that. She offered me a hand. 'You are welcome, dominie,' she said.

'But, Reverend Mother, he is not a dominie. He's a priest.'

The Mother Superior looked me up and down doubtfully. 'He is dressed as a dominie, child.'

'Forgive me, Reverend Mother,' I felt obliged to say lest Aleydis should be labelled a liar, 'I was ordained in France by the Bishop of Troyes, Malier du Houssay, who instructed me to remain discreet to maintain a church in being if persecution should return.'

'If persecution should return we will not need an alternative church,' came the reply.

I recalled a possible piece of evidence that might satisfy her. Turning my back, following a suitable apology, I reached through to my undershirt and retrieved my little breviary. Opening it I showed her the inscription on the fly-leaf, which read '+ Johannes, Namur, 1664', the signature of Johannes Wachtendonck, who was the bishop to whom I was assigned on my return to the Low Countries.

'I beg your pardon if I doubted you,' the Mother Superior said, making as if to kneel, but I restrained her. 'If you have a little time, perhaps you would hear confessions. Our own priest can only come on alternate Fridays.'

'Willingly,' I said, which was something of a distortion of the truth. All right, it was near to a downright lie. Hearing confession is one of my least favourite tasks.

'May I be heard too?' Aleydis asked, with altogether too much relish for my liking. What an eleven-year-old girl could have to confess, however pious she might be, was hard to imagine.

The Reverend Mother invited us to stay for supper. This also entailed an invitation to Vespers, which made me feel that the day was going from bad to worse. I could not help but notice Aleydis's countenance, which bore every trace of rapture at the thought of sitting through a service in a convent. I say Vespers, of course, whenever I can, but I do not make a fetish of it, and I take the view that Lauds at six in the morning and Vespers twelve hours later are best said privately, in your own room if possible. I also prefer to say Lauds horizontally, lying like a tomb effigy on my bed, and covered by a blanket as if by my shroud.

I must have feigned enthusiasm sufficiently convincingly, because the Reverend Mother suggested that Aleydis should talk to the novices for a while so they could share their experiences of religious life with her as being nearest to her own age. Aleydis duly wandered off with the mistress of novices, and I was left with the Reverend Mother while we waited for a queue to form for confession.

'What brings you to Delft?' she asked.

'I am here at the invitation of the mayor to discover what has happened to three young girls who have gone missing, though sadly one has been found dead. But you will not have heard of this.'

'We are secluded, Father, but not out of the world. We had heard something of this terrible series of events. The loss of a child is a pitiful event. We must pray for the parents.'

'If you would, Reverend Mother.'

'What are the girls' names so that we may pray for them too?'

'Gertruyd Lievens, Magdalena Kuijper and Anna van Setten.'

The elderly nun gasped and held her hand over her mouth. 'Anna van Setten? We did not hear that. She was not the girl found dead, I hope.'

'That was Gertruyd Lievens.'

'Forgive me, I must not rejoice that one dies rather than another.'

'Do you know the Van Setten girl?'

'No, Father, not well. But the family is well known. Indeed, this very house was a gift from the family about a century and a half ago.'

'They were Catholics then?'

'Indeed, and devout. Of course, that was before the so-called Reformation. Mijnheer Van Setten asked last year if he might see the deed of gift. I think he had a mind to try to reclaim it if we could not prove the donation, but, God be praised, the documents were safe in our care.'

'Were, Reverend Mother? Not are?'

'I have lodged them with the Diocesan Office for safe keeping. It may be suspicious of me, but I feared that a burglary might take place. And I regret to say that I was right. The window behind you was broken one night and this room was ransacked. But I had the papers safe under my mattress until I could find a trusted courier.'

A knock at the door interrupted us. It seemed that the nuns were itching to confess their sins, so I steeled myself for a grim hour or two and headed for the confessional.

It was every bit as awful as I expected. In fact, I had underestimated how vile an experience it would be. This group of young innocents, chaste and virtuous, accused themselves of a range of misdemeanours that could not have been bettered in a dockside tavern in Amsterdam.

Quite apart from missing services, having uncharitable thoughts, gluttony, envy, lying, gossiping and laziness, there had been an outbreak of carnal impulses, if that is the right expression, and at least one had succumbed to self-abuse. I had no idea how a woman did that, but I took her word for it. I listened patiently and doled out penances, though I must admit that there was no great logic behind the impositions. I simply had no idea of the going rate for some of these offences, and had issued penalties at random until I decided to try a different approach.

The nun in question had confessed to uncharitable thoughts, a lack of truthfulness, and having helped herself to a spoonful of honey in the kitchen, when she threw in a fantasy about being defiled by the gardener's son.

'What penance do you think would be appropriate?' I asked.

The answer shocked me. 'The usual priest normally requires me to pray a complete Rosary,' she said.

'I am more severe,' I replied, 'because you cannot have been sincere in your last confession if you have repeated the offences. You will pray *two* complete Rosaries. '

She seemed surprised that there had been such pastoral inflation but accepted my doubling of the sentence with due obedience.

I returned Aleydis to her family, regretting that she had enjoyed herself far too much but expressing the hope that I had persuaded her to think carefully upon her choice and to delay making it until her sixteenth birthday. I also reminded her that she was bound by her duty of obedience to seek her parents' consent before entering a convent. I subsequently discovered that the outing had tempered her enthusiasm to a certain degree, though it had less to do with my strictures than with her examination of the novices' underwear.

I walked back to the inn and decided that an early night was called for. My arm was aching and I wanted to pray privately to prepare myself for the funeral the following day. I wanted so much to be able to say some comforting words to Jannetje and Gerrit, though I had no idea what they might be.

Lucie must have seen me mount the stairs, because no sooner had I removed my boots than she knocked at my door and presented me with a tray. 'I saved you some supper, Master,' she said.

I lifted the inverted bowl that covered the platter and found some meat, peas and dumplings in a thick gravy, and a piece of bread. Ordinarily I would have wolfed the meat, but since it was Friday it was out of the question, though I confess that I heard a voice inside my head telling me nobody would know, and then a louder one telling me that God knows all things. I wish He would tell me where those girls are, I thought.

'Beg pardon, Master?'

'I didn't say anything.'

'You did, Master, you said something about girls.'

I must have voiced my thoughts aloud, which is a bad habit to fall into. 'I said I was tired after looking for the girls, Lucie.'

'Yes, Master. Very good, Master.'

I had a brainwave. 'Lucie, I'm too tired to eat much. I'll just eat the bread — why don't you eat the rest for me?'

'Master?'

'I wouldn't like the cook to think I didn't like her food by leaving it.'

I had expected her to take the tray away, but she entered my room and closed the door behind her.

'I can't be seen eating it, Master,' she whispered, and sat on the edge of the bed before tucking in.

I nibbled at the bread as she wiped the plate clean with the last of the meat.

'You've got gravy on your chin,' I told her.

She wiped her mouth with the back of her hand. 'I asked around about the girls, Master, but nobody could think of anything that connects them.'

'Never mind, Lucie,' I said wearily. 'Thank you for trying.'

'I feel really sorry for Anna van Setten, Master. People say she always seems so sad. She never has any fun.'

'I'm afraid that's the lot of a young lady in a grand house. They spend most of their lives inside and their only friends are girls of their own class.'

'She had no friends, though, Master. Even her own father doesn't seem to talk to her very much.'

'I suppose they don't have much in common,' I said. I recalled what Verelst's sister had said about the girl being so unlike her father.

'She doesn't look like him at all,' Lucie said artlessly as she licked the platter. 'But then, she doesn't look like her mother either.'

'I've never seen her mother,' I said. 'What does she look like?'

'Quite tall, but it's her eyes, Master. Anna's eyes are blue, but her parents are both very dark with brown eyes and black hair.'

I wanted time to think. 'Now, Lucie, I will pray for you tonight, but you must stay in your own room. I need to be alone this evening.'

'Very good, Master. Thank you for the dinner,' she said, and left me without complaint.

I settled down to read my bible and pass some time in meditation. Thus occupied, it was a surprise when my devotions were interrupted by a sudden realisation connected with the case, and a possible explanation for a gnomic comment began to crystallise before me.

CHAPTER NINE

Rain clattered against my window and dawn seemed unable to struggle through the black clouds. If ever there was a day fit for a funeral, this was it. Lucie brought my shaving water and a note that Claes had left. The mayor had experienced some success, and a goodly number of carts would be sent around the town to bring the infirm to the church. They had already been dispatched, and soon the Markt resounded to the clopping of hooves as the carts brought their human cargo to the Nieuwe Kerk.

The mayor had generously sent his own carriage to bring the Lievens family and allow them some privacy. He escorted them himself, and showed them every consideration as he led them to the front pew and introduced them to the minister who would conduct the funeral.

It struck me later that the family had played no part in the arranging of the obsequies. The city had taken it over, and while it was undoubtedly grand, dignified and sincere, it was also very formal. After a while we heard mourning music, and the sergeant and his men fired their muskets once in salute, coming to attention as the small coffin was borne into the church by four pall-bearers. Van Leeuwenhoek walked behind, carrying his staff of office, and supervised the placing of the coffin on the trestles set to receive it. Having done so, he bowed to the mayor, then to the parents, and retired. It was well done, but I felt that the parents had enough to cope with without all this pomp and ceremony.

The minister led prayers and launched into a lengthy address in which he reminded us that it is not for us to question the ways of Almighty God, whose objective in calling young Gertruyd to him would no doubt become clear in the fullness of time. Given how many children die each year, every preacher of any denomination has a little store of such addresses, and there was nothing particularly personal about this one.

The minister boomed an invocation to prayer, and we all knelt piously. If I expected some tender expressions I was immediately jolted by the intercession that begged God to deliver the murderer of this young girl to justice, where his sin would be publicly expiated by exemplary punishment. I did not feel that I could say a heartfelt amen to the petition that the murderer should be an acceptable sacrificial victim offered up to the Lord, and that we would all reflect upon the certainty of everlasting punishment for our sins which awaited us at the end of our own lives. I recognise that my somewhat unusual spiritual journey may have left me with an eclectic theology of my own, but I find eternal misery an unappealing doctrine. A loving God sent his Son to atone for our sins, and while I will not pretend that my own sins are trivial, I incline to the view that subjecting me to the fires of Hell for all time would be disproportionate. I just hope that God thinks so too.

Lost in my thoughts, I realised that everyone else had resumed their seats while I was still on my knees. Showing a delicate reverence for my cloth, the minister waited politely until I had raised myself up and deposited myself on the pew once more. He seemed to have taken the delay as proof of my unusual piety rather than daydreaming, and on shaking hands after the service he took care to tell me that he was minded to retire in a year or two, if God spared him so long, because he felt the cure of so large a congregation needed a young, vigorous man.

'Let us hope that God calls one,' I said, at which the pastor smiled knowingly and I added inaudibly, 'but it won't be me.'

I felt that I ought to say a few words to the family, but I was taken aback to see Jannetje coming towards me, with her husband a step behind.

'Thank you for coming, Master,' she said. 'My husband and I have faith that you will discover who killed our little Gertruyd.'

Until that moment I had not felt any particular pressure to succeed, beyond the fact that this was the task allotted to me and I wished to be diligent. But now it seemed imperative. I simply could not let these good people down. It also occurred to me that there is a world of difference between people expressing confidence in your ability to do what they could have done, as when the Rector asked me to address the graduates of the university, and those who are helpless asking you to do something for them. This was not "one of those things you say"; these people meant it.

'You may rest assured I will do all that lies in my poor powers,' I stammered.

'Your powers are not poor,' she said. 'We believe that the Almighty will guide you to the truth.'

As if that were not pressure enough, her husband said much the same thing in different words. 'It's good that a learned gentleman is willing to help us ordinary folk,' he said. 'May God bless you.'

May God help me would be a better prayer, I thought. They invited me to join them at the inn where, no doubt, there would be beer enough to help them forget their grief, but I declined, saying that I wanted to follow up a clue and there was no time to waste. This excuse had the added advantage of being true, because the germ of an idea had been forming in my head and I wanted to pursue it before I forgot what it was, but first I needed to find Claes.

The clerk was in the church retrieving the trestles, cushions and any other items that might have been lost.

'Claes,' I cried, 'where am I to sup tonight?'

'With mijnheer Van Ruijven.'

If it had been anyone else I might have asked to be excused, but I had already seen his temper in full spate. Moreover, it struck me that he might be willing to give me a little special help on Sunday without others knowing what I had asked. I had a suspicion that I might be about to turn over a rock that others wanted left in place for many years to come, so it would be as well if as few people as possible knew my intentions.

The Lievens family might have had great faith that the Lord would guide me to the truth, but I was beginning to feel that if God and Mercurius comprised an Inquisition, one of us (and I don't want to name names) was not pulling His weight. I knelt in prayer as the guests dispersed, hoping that an angel might tap me on the shoulder and give me a clue or two, but the only tap I had on the shoulder turned out to be from Jan Pieterszoon.

'My wife and I wanted to thank you for arranging the cart to bring us to town,' he said, respectfully removing his hat.

'You must thank the mayor,' I answered, 'for he organised the loan of them.'

'Yes, but it was your idea,' he said. 'It isn't always those who do the work as have the ideas.'

How true, I thought, how true. Maybe God had sent his angel in the shape of this elderly farmer with the bad hips, in which event it was a surprising shape for an angel to take. But could it be right? Could the abductor not be the mind behind the enterprise? Was someone telling him whom to befriend and snatch?

We spoke for a while until Claes came to tell us the cart had returned, when I helped them to mount the back and returned to the church. I wanted to catch the minister alone.

It seemed that he had gone off to accept someone's hospitality, but by good fortune the verger was still there, sweeping the floor free of the mud brought in on the mourners' boots. I introduced myself to the verger, whose name was Jacob. He was a man of forty years or so, broad in the shoulders and quiet in his demeanour. He was more like a household's chief steward than most vergers I have known.

I explained that I would esteem it a great favour if I could pass an hour or two in reading the parish registers.

'There's no harm in that, I'm sure,' Jacob replied. 'I'm sure the pastor would want to extend that courtesy to a brother minister.'

'I'm sure he would. He seems very hospitable.'

'That he is, that he is. Well, I'll lead you to them, if you'll follow me.'

We passed to the north-east corner where a small robing room nestled. The verger produced a large iron key from his belt, unlocked the chest, and invited me to pick such of the registers as appealed to me.

'Perhaps the most recent ones?' I offered. A subterfuge occurred to me by which I might disguise my real motives. 'You'll know that the mayor has asked me to investigate the disappearance of the three girls. I thought if I checked the baptism registers for eight years ago I might get some idea which other girls might be in danger.'

'A Christian thought, mijnheer, and I would gladly help you if I had the reading, which I have, but only for plain letters. Handwriting leaves me tangled.' He swiftly located a couple of books and opened them on the desk before me. 'This book ends in 1662, and that one continues thereafter.'

I knew it was a shot at hazard, but I hoped that if I could find the three register entries for the three girls it might confirm the idea that I had. Of course, they could have been baptized elsewhere, and in the case of Magdalena Kuijper it was possible that she had not been baptized at all. I confess that I have never understood those clergy who deny Christian baptism to innocent babes on account of their illegitimacy, a circumstance in which they have played no part and cannot influence, but I hoped that the minister of the Nieuwe Kerk was a kindlier man than his actions in banning the Kuijpers from his church would suggest.

It did not take too long. I found a baptism for Magdalena Kuijper first, performed on a Thursday morning, presumably when there were few around to see it, but at least it had been done. She was described as the bastard child of Liese Kuijper, of Oostpoort. The next one was Gertruyd Lievens, daughter of Gerrit Lievens, brickmaker, and Jannetje Dircks. Finally I found the baptism of Anna van Setten, daughter of Wilhelmus van Setten, merchant, and his wife Mathilde. I wrote down the three dates, and realised that, by the grace of God, I might be making some progress at last.

Mijnheer Van Ruijven kept a very fine house, elegant, understated, full of expensive items accumulated by a man of taste. Claes, an inexhaustible fund of information about the local worthies, had told me that Van Ruijven had married an independently wealthy woman, Maria de Knuijt, and since Van

Ruijven himself had bulging pockets, it was unclear whether he had ever had to work for a living. He was certainly busy about good works, and his name seemed to be attached to many of the charities around Delft.

By the good fortune of coming from a Remonstrant family, he had never been asked to waste a lot of time being an alderman, but he was acknowledged to be a shrewd man, if a firm believer in strict earthly punishment. I pondered briefly whether this severity had anything to do with his Remonstrant belief that God does not punish all sinners except the elect for all time; if you don't believe that God plans to pass all eternity allowing devils to insert hot coals into the anuses of the wicked, you might take a harder line on the stocks and pillory.

I handed my cloak to a servant and followed my host into a room with large windows and fine furniture. I was admiring a painting of a young girl with a pearl earring when I heard the door open behind me and, turning, came face to face with the loveliest specimen of young womanhood I had ever seen.

She curtsied and stood before me, a fair-skinned woman with brown ringlets clasped in a mother of pearl clip on each side of her head, a ruby red dress which was so neat at the waist that I would have believed that I might completely encircle it with one arm, and an exquisite lace collar, stunningly white and not quite meeting fully at the centre, where a small wedge of pale skin could be seen. Given what piece of pale skin that was, I could not stare, or her father would probably have run me through with his sword, for this was the daughter of Pieter van Ruijven, a sixteen-year-old delight called Magdalena. It would not be tactful, I thought, to comment on the coincidence that this was also the name of one of the victims.

'You'll have noticed that my daughter bears the same name as one of the missing girls,' Van Ruijven declaimed, saving me the need to trouble myself any further about tact.

Van Ruijven had two very different levels of converse. Most of the time he spoke quite softly, but firmly, in the manner of one who is used to being obeyed and does not need to raise his voice to be listened to, but at intervals he would speak like an open-air preacher.

During dinner he explained that it was a constant concern to him that unworthy young men might pay court to his daughter because of her wealth — on one occasion he described it as "her extreme wealth" — and not because they esteemed her for her many virtues. He hoped that he would find a young man whose gifts would assure his fortune without needing to diminish hers, a man of parts, of learning, a civilised man.

'That is my wish too,' his wife chimed in.

'Father, mother, you are embarrassing our guest,' Magdalena chirped prettily, dipping her head so I could not see her eyes, but her cheeks were reddened.

'Not at all, not at all,' Van Ruijven claimed. 'He is a man of the world and knows good sense when he hears it. A good wife is an adornment to any man and the foundation of a happy home, as I well know.'

He gripped his wife's hand lovingly and smiled. Such open affection astonished me — I had been told he was a libertine, one who took advantage of his maids. Glancing around the room at the two who were setting dishes on the table, I could only think this must happen at night, when he could not see their faces.

'In any walk of life, a handsome and educated wife is a great boon, do you not agree, Master Mercurius?'

Well, perhaps not for a Catholic priest, I thought, but I did not dare to say so, and was quick to agree. It was then that the whole ghastly truth dawned on me. Magdalena had been tricked out like this to impress me.

Was I naïve not to have seen it before? The repeated reminders that the minister of Nieuwe Kerk would be retiring and the setting of this honeyed trap were all of a piece. The burghers of Delft wanted me to settle down there. This was quick work indeed, because they had not met me until four days before, but maybe the local alternative candidates were poor competition for a university man.

I can admit now to this journal that juffrouw Van Ruijven was a considerable catch. Never mind the wealth, she had a smile that could melt marble, flawless skin and two of the cutest dimples I have ever seen. Had it not been for the small difficulty of my vow of chastity, I should have been down on one knee at once begging for her hand, and possibly dribbling over the exquisite Indian carpet. If I am frank, much of the conversation of the evening passed me by, because I was regarding the young lady opposite and ensuring that my next confession would be a lengthy affair.

At length the ladies retired, and I found myself alone with Van Ruijven, who suggested that we withdraw to a pair of fine silk-covered chairs near the window to catch the last light of the day.

'She is a fine girl, don't you think?'

'She is, mijnheer, very fine.'

'Are you betrothed back in Leiden?'

I was tempted to say yes, just to release the pressure on me, but it would have been untruthful and I was beginning to wonder whether there were any loopholes in the vow of chastity that a clever bit of casuistry could squeeze me through. I must find a Jesuit, I thought; they are always good at that kind of thing.

'No, I'm not. I must confess that with my studies and my duties...' I spread my hands helplessly.

'Of course.' Van Ruijven smiled benignly. He obviously felt that he had done enough to plant the seed, for he now changed the subject. 'How are your labours progressing?'

I recounted the events of the last few days, more or less as I have described them to you, but omitting any mention of Lucie. I hope I need not say that I did not think of Lucie in any improper way, and the idea of making her my wife was laughable, so I did not withhold her name for fear of introducing a conflict with Van Ruijven. I simply recognised that some things are better left unsaid, that's all.

I then broached the favour that I hoped to ask. 'I wonder, mijnheer, if you know of anyone who may be able to lend or hire me a horse?'

'A horse? A pack horse, a riding horse?'

'To ride. I must go to The Hague tomorrow.' Knowing Van Ruijven's views about observance of the Lord's Day I expanded my request. 'Of course, it's not too far to walk. But I should like to arrive in time for Divine Service if possible.'

Van Ruijven smiled that understanding smile of his once more. 'Naturally. And you will need to arrive as fresh as possible. I have a horse myself, but I have a better idea. Why don't I send my carriage to the inn and you may have it for the day?'

'That would be extremely generous of you,' I said — and I meant it. I just hoped he did not think he was doing a favour for his future son-in-law.

'That's settled then. If you'll excuse me, I'll just go and tell the coachman.'

Before I left I was ushered into the fragrant presence of Magdalena and her mother once more. Maria de Knuijt was sitting at her embroidery frame while her daughter was practising at the virginal. Was that entirely coincidental, I wondered, or an oblique testimony to her purity?

I made polite conversation for a brief time, when his wife suddenly recollected that she wanted her husband's opinion on some hangings for the hallway, and I was left alone with Magdalena. Since the door was open, she had no immediate need of a chaperone, nor did she seem to want one. This matchmaking may not have been her idea, but she knew what was expected of her.

'Are you musical, Master Mercurius?' she enquired.

'Only in the sense that a tomcat is musical,' I replied truthfully. I can chant a psalm, and music formed part of my training, but I play no instrument other than a drum.

'My parents tell me that music is an important accomplishment for a young woman.'

'I am sure they are right. Fortunately I am not a young woman, nor ever like to be.'

She giggled and then, suspecting that this was immodest in some way, suppressed her laughter with her hand across her lips. Let me not dwell on those lips; even now the thought of them moves me strangely. How curious our society is that, were I a shepherd's boy and she a milkmaid, we would have kissed at once with all the freedom of youth, but as it was we could only share a knowing glance. Careful, Mercurius, I told myself. Remember your vows.

I floundered, my conversational skills being unpractised, and finally said the first thing that came into my head. Well, the second actually, but you need not trouble yourselves about the thought that I suppressed. 'Do you know Anna van Setten?'

Magdalena became serious. 'Not well, Master. She is much younger than I am, but we met from time to time when our parents met. She seemed such an unhappy girl.'

'Unhappy? How so?'

'It is not my place to criticise my elders, but I think she found her father severe and slow to express his love. So unlike my own dear papa.'

Her own dear papa must have been listening outside, because he returned with a cheery, 'What's this? Did I hear my name?'

'Your daughter was speaking of the fine relationship that you have with her, mijnheer. I'm afraid I was asking her if she knew Anna van Setten.'

I expected his brow to cloud in disapproval, but instead he backed up his daughter, proof that he had not missed a word said while he was out of the room.

'Ah, a sad family. There is not the glow of warmth about it. Naturally, Mathilde is a fine mother and takes great care of her daughter, but — if I may speak candidly — Van Setten is not a man to whom kindly feelings come naturally. But you have met him, I think?'

'I have, mijnheer. And I am bound to say that he shows a very proper desire to see his daughter restored to him.'

Van Ruijven contemplated his glass of wine, tipping it gently and watching the colour of it changing as he did so. 'Did you notice a green jade statuette in the Chinese style on his desk?'

'Yes, I did. A seated man of some kind.'

'I believe it is called a Buddha. No matter; but I'll swear that if someone had stolen that figurine from him it would wound him more than the loss of Anna.'

I could not believe that, but nobody there was going to contradict him.

I lay on my bed, inspecting the ceiling of the chamber and the opportunity I saw before me. In the manner of an accountant, I made a list of debits and credits to balance them off.

Item, you, Mercurius, are an ordained priest. (An ordained minister too, but let's not quibble.)

Item, the Pope takes a dim view of priests marrying and thereby breaking their vows.

Item, excommunication is likely to follow, cutting me off from the Blessed Sacraments of the Church and assuring me of an eternity in Hell with all the hot coals et cetera *we mentioned earlier.*

Item, it would be worth it for a lifetime in the company of Magdalena van Ruijven.

Item, and that's not even touching on the joys of the bedchamber, about which we will draw a veil, largely because I cannot quite imagine them.

Item, she would come with a dowry of some magnificence.

Item, I could do a lot of good for others with that dowry.

Item, nobody knows that I am a priest, except a bishop (now dead), *the current bishop* (soon to be dead), *and God.*

Unfortunately, that was quite a stumbling block. God would not forget. And even if he did, Aleydis Vermeer would not, and I was fairly certain that she would be counselling me to castrate myself to avoid the temptation to lapse were she in the room now. After all, if she was prepared to forfeit her breasts for her faith because she did not plan to use them, I was sure that she would regard a priest's privities as mere decoration, fit to be removed if they became an inconvenience to his faith.

And so to bed.

CHAPTER TEN

Morning came, and I was awakened by a pounding on my door.

'Master, a grand carriage has come for you, and you still abed!'

I dressed quickly while Lucie brought shaving water and some bread and cheese. There was no hidden meat today. Perhaps she knew that I had forgotten to pray for her last night, so I quickly mumbled a prayer while she was out of the room.

Shaving and chewing are best done separately, but somehow I completed both tasks, gathered up my things and descended to the carriage. The coachman told me he was ordered to stand at my service the whole day, and asked me where I wished to go.

'To The Hague,' said I. 'Let's start at the Binnenhof.'

The Binnenhof is the seat of our government, a fine series of buildings around a neat courtyard and, to be honest, the only building in The Hague whose name came to me when I was asked for a destination, but it was probably the right starting point. I had a busy day ahead of me, but one that was likely to confirm or disprove my ideas completely.

We trotted along the road in the pleasant, crisp morning, the coachman chattering to his horses and I sitting in relative comfort in the carriage. This is the way to travel, I thought. Keeping warm and dry and expending no effort was very much to my taste, and it took no time at all for the seductive thought to occur to me that this could be my life if I married Magdalena van Ruijven. I conjured up a mental image of her sitting opposite, then reminded myself of something my dear late father once said to me about riding in a carriage.

'Always remember, lad, when you enter a carriage, a lady never sits facing the horse's arse.'

I swapped to the opposing bench so that my imaginary Magdalena would have her back to the offending view, and sighed with contentment. Then I remembered that I had work to do, and forced myself to concentrate on the task set before me.

Not much more than an hour had elapsed when we pulled up in front of the Binnenhof and I was forced to think of my next steps. Working on the principle that parliaments and universities probably have much in common, the key was to seek out the porter.

I was directed to his lodge and found him close to a pot-bellied stove. He sprang to his feet, but I bade him resume his place and explained who I was and what I was doing in Delft. I further explained that I was looking for the daughter of Wilhelmus van Setten who was at one time employed in government business.

'Aye, sir, I remember the young gentleman.'

'I think the child's disappearance may be connected to his time here. She may even be lodging here. Do you know where mijnheer Van Setten stayed in The Hague?'

'Aye, sir. It's a porter's job to know them all. But in this case, it's easy, for he had an apartment just along the street. If you will turn to the right outside, and look for a building with a dark red door, the apartment was on its upper floor. But he gave it up some time ago.'

'And when his lady came to live with him, did she live there too?'

'Lady, Master? I remember no lady.'

I had said that I would attend Divine Service and, on the suspicion that the coachman would be questioned on his return, that is where I headed next. I was delighted to see that the minister of the church was a man full in years, who gave an excellent sermon on our duty never to question the station we occupy in life or our status as one of the elect or one of the damned. He took his text from the parable of the Prodigal Son, which I can never read without feeling a deal of sympathy for the wastrel's brother. I do not have it in me to waste my substance on riotous living, but I could certainly stand by and tut over someone who was doing so.

I waited at the end of the service in the hope of a few private words with him. Sometimes the ministers' network is the best way of finding information. After a few pleasantries I broached the question of the Van Settens' time in The Hague.

'Wilhelmus van Setten? Yes, I remember him. Of course, I knew his father, now sadly taken from us.'

'You may recall then that Wilhelmus lived here while on government service eight or nine years ago.'

'Indeed I do. He was unhappy here, I'm afraid. He missed his home and he hadn't the patience for government work. I think he found many of the people he was dealing with to be doltish types.'

That was easy to imagine. I suspect Wilhelmus van Setten thought most people were doltish types.

'Do you recall his wife coming to join him for a short while?'

There was a hesitation that I thought betokened an unease in discussing the affairs of a former parishioner, so I explained that I was investigating the kidnapping of their daughter.

'Oh, dear me! How terrible!'

'The daughter was born here, and I wondered whether someone in The Hague would represent a refuge to her if she were able to escape, or, indeed, whether someone here might have remembered her and decided to seize her.'

'I think there is some mistake,' said the minister. 'I recall the lady's visit, though it was very brief. And while I am not well-versed in the ways of women, yet I saw no sign that a birth was likely soon.'

'This would have been late in 1662,' I said.

'Yes, I remember the time well, not long after the English king returned to his crown. Mijnheer van Setten was here for about a year and a half, and his wife came for about two months at the end of that time. But the child must have been born later.'

I thanked him for his information, congratulated him on an excellent sermon, and took my leave. Now, here's a pretty puzzle. Mathilde van Setten leaves Delft without a baby, spends some time away, and comes back with one, but she did not apparently fall pregnant while she was in the one place she is known to have visited.

I was still gnawing my thumb when I had an idea, and hunted out the verger to give me a start. After a moment's surprise at my question, he provided an answer and gave me directions, and so I marched off across the city.

I found Westeinde and soon spotted the old convent buildings. Children in immaculate white aprons or shirts were sitting outside, the older ones reading the bible to the younger children. I rang the bell, and before long a jolly woman with her hands covered in flour came to greet me. I explained who I was, and asked whether the person in charge could grant me a brief interview. She waddled off, and returned soon after to invite me to come inside and follow her to the apartment that the warden and his family had there.

The warden came out to greet me, and I apologised for disturbing him. I explained my mission and extended the mayor's compliments to him, which he took very kindly, though he must have been as baffled as me. I had no idea why I said it, but it seemed the kind of thing that might smooth my path, as indeed it did.

'Three girls, each eight years old, have disappeared from their homes in Delft,' I explained, 'and sadly one has been found dead. I am trying to trace the others. One is called Magdalena Kuijper and the other is Anna van Setten.'

'And you think there may be a connection with Westeinde?'

'The matter is one of some delicacy,' I continued. 'I have an idea that for reasons of their own Anna's parents are not being entirely straightforward with us.'

'Really? They would endanger their own daughter?'

'Obviously that is not their intention, but it is the effect of what they are doing.'

'Let us examine the records together,' he suggested, and led me to his office, detouring on the way to grab a bottle of wine and two glasses. When he heard that I had not eaten, he also sent for a dish of chicken and potatoes. It was a simple dinner, but an excellent one, still memorable now as I write.

The warden turned the pages, and we carefully read the names. Finally, on 6th December, 1662 I found what I wanted. A baby girl, eight weeks old, had been received into Westeinde, and within the week, she had been found a new home, in the household of Wilhelmus and Mathilde van Setten.

Anna van Setten was adopted. That was why she did not resemble either parent, and perhaps it explained her cool relationship with her father. The warden kindly brought another bottle, and I toasted his institution wishing it every success and all prosperity, and bestowing a donation from my pouch.

I finally returned to the carriage with a copy of the ledger entry and the makings of a profound headache. On the journey back to Delft I could piece something of the tale together. A woman who yearns for a baby, but has not been able to have one; a man who wants a child to continue his line (and therefore would prefer a son), a disinclination to let others know their business, and then an opportunity presents itself. The man is summoned to The Hague and an idea forms. If he adopts there, nobody will ever know, but to make it plausible he must bring his wife there and sequester her away from the public gaze for some time before she returns to Delft some months later with her new baby.

However, fortune is not with them, and in the short period that they have during which the story will be believable the only tiny baby offered for adoption is a little girl. The wife will not leave without her, so they take the child, perhaps intending that at some future date they will return to look for a boy. For the husband, this baby was unwanted and he has no interest in her, whereas his wife is devoted to her. For unknown reasons, the return to collect a boy is not possible, and as time passes it becomes increasingly less credible.

An awful thought struck me. If they are ever going to adopt a boy and pass him off as their own, the Van Settens would have to do so soon, given Mathilde's age. If the girl is keeping Mathilde in Delft, preventing the prolonged stay in The Hague that made the original adoption appear like a natural birth, then the girl will have to go. Was it possible that Wilhelmus van Setten's craving for a son had caused him to engineer the disappearance of his own daughter? If so, then the other two abductions would simply be designed to conceal the real purpose. The girls would be expendable once the object was achieved. If he were merciful, they could have been returned (had one not already died), but if, as I suspected, Wilhelmus van Setten had no concern for the harm done to others, he might have had the girls smothered.

It was a sobering thought, and after all that wine in The Hague I needed something to sober me before I had dinner with Van Leeuwenhoek.

Having spent too long in The Hague I just had time to drive directly to Van Leeuwenhoek's house. I tipped the coachman and told him I would thank Van Ruijven personally as soon as opportunity permitted. I brushed any visible mud from my shoes and hose and knocked on the door.

Van Leeuwenhoek's house was not as I had expected. I had envisaged something sterile and austere, perhaps with lots of scientific equipment and a small cot in one corner where he would snatch a little sleep now and then. In fact, it was elegant and well furnished. Certainly, there were a number of brass things whose purpose was completely unknown to me, but since many contained cog wheels or clamps I took them for scientific instruments. I had forgotten that mijnheer Van Leeuwenhoek was a draper, which explained the ready access to some beautiful cloth that was laid over furniture.

The other surprise was the presence of a family. I was not aware that he had married at the end of January, and his wife Cornelia Swalmius proved a very attentive hostess. I hope that when I was introduced to her I did not show how unexpected the presence of a wife was. I had formed the idea that Van Leeuwenhoek was undoubtedly a bachelor, unfamiliar with the little stings of Cupid. In fact, he had been married twice, as he readily explained on introducing his daughter Maria, a fine girl of about fourteen years, who was the surviving child of his first wife Barbara.

While Magdalena van Ruijven delighted my eye, Maria van Leeuwenhoek was a tonic for a man's brain. I would have expected that Van Leeuwenhoek would be a dogmatic father, brooking no naysaying, yet his scientific temperament made him willing to consider good arguments from any source. As a result, Maria was very willing to dispute with him in a spirited way that I might have thought unbecoming in another family.

He was a man of great contradictions. I looked in vain for any substantial library in the house. He was entirely self-taught, an ingenious mechanic capable of constructing his own devices, and utterly ignorant of the writings of others. He had, it seemed, picked up a smattering of information but he tested everything for himself, and while an excellent artist, as I shall explain shortly, he had perhaps the most abominable handwriting I have ever tried to decipher. This was due, I believe, to his tendency to scribble quickly using an abbreviated language of his own devising. Even when he told me how a sentence read, I was unable to construe it thus.

While we were waiting for dinner to be served mijnheer Van Leeuwenhoek had the kindness to show me some of his extraordinary scientific work. He began by inviting me to view the world through a tiny glass ball held in a pair of tweezers.

I jumped with alarm. 'What am I looking at?' I asked.

'Allow me to give you a more practical demonstration,' he said, and placed a small piece of glass on the windowsill. I could see that it bore a dead flea. 'Have the goodness to look at the flea through the glass sphere,' he continued.

It was extraordinary. The flea appeared as big as a cow, and I could make out many features quite invisible to the unaided eye.

'This is astonishing!' I cried. 'How is it done?'

Van Leeuwenhoek gave a contented smile, the first I think I had seen from him.

'When I was a boy, not much older than Maria, I was apprenticed to a draper in Amsterdam. He taught me to appraise the quality of cloth using a magnifying lens which allowed me to inspect the weave closely. The glass sphere functions as a tiny lens — but I have improved its quality until I am now able to see much more than just the threads in a cloth sample.'

I continued to inspect the flea. 'I am astounded to see how fearfully and wonderfully made this little creature is. We think a flea of little account, and yet it is as perfect in its own way as a thoroughbred horse.'

Van Leeuwenhoek opened a folder for me, and revealed some of the drawings that he had made of what he had seen.

'These are remarkable,' I goggled. 'You have seen things that no other man has seen, mijnheer.'

'I am blessed indeed. But this is not the most remarkable thing you will see today. I must ask you to be discreet about what I will show you now. I have found that others have been gravely disquieted by it.'

I agreed, of course. Whatever wonders this present-day Simon Magus could unfold, I was eager to see them.

He handed me a soft sliver of wood. I recognised it as a tooth-stick.

'I see you keep your teeth clean, Master, as do I. Please rub the stick around the base of your teeth for a moment or two.'

I did as he asked. He then took the stick and invited me to assure myself that the little dish he next handed me was clean. I was happy to agree that it was. Then he rolled the stick across the dish so that my spittle was thinly spread. Now he invited me to look again through his lens at the spittle.

I recoiled. Was it horror or surprise? 'What are they?' I gasped.

'They are little animals,' he replied. 'I call them animalcules. So far as I can tell there are many tribes of them, and they live in all sorts of places. There are few where they are not to be found. If you look in stagnant water, you will find many, perhaps millions in a small cupful.'

'It is a revelation to see them,' I said, 'but why do others express disquiet?'

Van Leeuwenhoek seemed pained by what he had to say. 'The bible does not mention them. Did Noah take a pair of each on the Ark? If he did, he need not have done, for many of these tribes seem able to produce children by simply dividing their own substance. One parent would have sufficed.'

'The bible does not mention them, but if it has pleased God not to reveal His handiwork until now, how could it? I hope, mijnheer, that you will publish your drawings and receive the credit your work deserves. You have opened our eyes to the smallest works of our Creator, and are therefore a benefactor to mankind.'

Van Leeuwenhoek appeared strongly moved by my words. I learned later that he had debated destroying his drawings after the first reactions he received to them, and when he published his work he was labelled a liar and a charlatan by many, before he was finally vindicated. There were those who judged him to be some sort of heretic and yet he denied it firmly, claiming that his experiments had deepened his faith.

'Consider, Master, what this shows us. You and I are each the dwelling-place, nay, the entire world of millions of little creatures. They know no other world than the surface of your tongue. It would take them many days to voyage from one side of your mouth across the ocean of saliva to the far shore. They have no perception of the wonderful world outside your mouth. Does this not prefigure our own elevation to glory? We think this world is everything and yet one day we will be lifted out of it and shown a world of infinitely more pleasures and delights. We cannot imagine what the Almighty may have in store for us, any more than these tiny animals have any notion of an eyeball, or a hand. If they were transported to the outside of your cheek, they would discover a world of wonders beyond their imagining.'

Many of the little animals seemed to lack any organs of sense. They resembled little worms or seeds drifting back and forth in my spittle and yet they moved where they chose.

'Now consider this also,' said Van Leeuwenhoek. 'When we clean our mouths, we kill many thousands of these small creatures. I have observed that if we rub salt upon our gums to clean our teeth, many of them shrivel and die. I have never known that I was doing that. I am a murderer on an unimaginable scale, without ever having intended them any harm. Should I repent for what I never meant to do? And I am as mighty and powerful, from the perspective of these little creatures, as God is for us. It is thus proof of God's love for us that He is able to have a care for every man and woman on earth. He knows all of us by name, which we could never do for all these animalcules, even supposing that they had names. Master, does that not fill you with awe? As King David says in the Psalms, "What is Man, that thou are mindful of him?" And yet God provides for us all.'

It was heady stuff, even for a Sunday, but I gave thanks that I had seen it with my own eyes. That psalm, Psalm 8, goes on to tell us that God made us to have dominion over all his other works, sheep, oxen, the beasts of the field, the fowl of the air and the fish of the sea. Now we would have to add Van Leeuwenhoek's little animals of our mouths to that list.

A servant came to tell us that dinner was ready, and we returned to the dining room. To my surprise the table was laid for just two.

'The ladies are dining separately,' Van Leeuwenhoek explained. 'I thought it best, so that we can discuss your enquiries freely, without causing them distress. We will join them again later.'

'That is most considerate,' I said, 'particularly as I have discovered matters of some delicacy I would hesitate to open in front of ladies.'

That was a flagrant untruth. I would probably have blurted out whatever came into my head and regretted it later, but I must own that I was keen to have a feminine perspective on the state of mind of Mathilde van Setten. It is hard to imagine the yearning for a child — any child! — that might make a woman fall in with a deceitful scheme. But if she had acquiesced in a deception to gain a child, surely she would have no part in a stratagem that would now deprive her of that child to gain another?

'I may begin my explanation yesterday,' I suggested. 'Following the funeral, I searched the church registers and found the baptisms of all three girls. But while Magdalena and Gertruyd were baptised within a few days of their birth, Anna was not.'

'That is not unusual,' Van Leeuwenhoek objected. 'Those in higher social positions may need some time to issue invitations.'

'Indeed so,' I agreed, 'but I have rarely known that to exceed an extra fortnight, and more commonly a week will suffice.

Anna van Setten was not baptised until Christmas Eve. That struck me as odd for a child whose birthday, we were told, was 12th October.'

'I grant the oddity,' Van Leeuwenhoek conceded.

'It then occurred to me that a child born then would have been conceived around the previous New Year. It is not far from The Hague to Delft, about an hour's ride as I have seen today, but I can understand why Van Setten would need apartments at The Hague. And yet he does not seem to have returned to Delft at all during his time in government service, and his wife only journeyed to The Hague in the summer. The porter at the Binnenhof did not know of her existence. I suspect that Mathilde Van Setten was lodged out of the public gaze so that nobody in The Hague would see that she was not pregnant. She returned thence with a small baby, but that baby was not her own — it had been adopted on Monday, 11th December, five days after being delivered to the care of the orphanage at Westeinde.'

Other men might have expressed surprise at this revelation. But Van Leeuwenhoek was made of sterner (and drier) stuff. His sole response was a question. 'Why not a son?'

'No male babies were received between the middle of September and the end of January. Presumably they could not wait any longer.'

'I have only a dim recollection of the precise circumstances,' said Van Leeuwenhoek, 'but I recall that Van Setten fulminated against the treaty signed with the English in the last months of 1662. He believed, and was proved right, that the English were using it to buy time to arm themselves. Having been unable to convince others, his account was that he withdrew from service. However, I should not be surprised if his hostility to the treaty made him unpopular in The Hague and he was told that his services were no longer required. Without the recovery of his expenses, he would be unwilling to run two houses. So, son or no son — back to Delft,' he added tartly.

'I am thus satisfied that Anna van Setten is not the natural child of the Van Settens; but whereas the accounts I have heard make it plain that her mother accepted her fully and treated her as her own child, her father appears never to have done so. I further suspect that Anna does not know the circumstances of her arrival.'

'She has no need to know it,' said Van Leeuwenhoek. 'I would not tell her either.'

'Perhaps not. It may be that she is better off not knowing, and when, please God, we find her, there is no reason why she should be told.'

'This is all very well, Master Mercurius, and I admire your resourcefulness and tenacity in uncovering it, but are you any nearer tracing the whereabouts of these poor children?'

'I am puzzled by words that the Van Settens' gardener heard when the child went missing. Something like "I knew this would happen one day". Did she perhaps think that the child she loved so much would one day be taken from her?'

'The sense of unwarranted happiness comes to us all from time to time, Master. I have myself known the pain of losing children. Maria is my last remaining child. I have lost three sons and a daughter.'

'I am sorry for it, mijnheer. It is unimaginable to those who have not felt it.'

Van Leeuwenhoek fingered his glass awkwardly. There was something he wanted to say but he was struggling to let it escape. 'How did you find the Vermeer household when you visited?' he asked.

Obviously he had decided to change the subject rather than broach whatever it was that was moving him so strangely.

'It is … noisy,' I answered.

'I know,' he replied. 'There seem to be children everywhere. I cannot abide to go there. All those children.'

I could imagine that this serious man would find the bustle and chaos of the Vermeer home uncongenial. And then I realised that he had not changed the subject at all. Van Leeuwenhoek did not go to Oude Langendijk because he could not bear to be surrounded by the happiness of so many children. He stared into the fire, and his eyes moistened, and I saw a lonely man who had lost so much joy from his life. Four children, and then a wife; and I remembered what the Psalms also say: *Sicut sagittae in manu potentis ita filii excussorum. Beatus vir qui implebit desiderium suum ex ipsis.* As arrows are in the hand of a mighty man; so are children of the youth. Happy is the man that hath his quiver full of them.

And unhappy the man whose quiver has been emptied.

We sat peacefully before the cosy fire. Maria would have sung for me, but it being the Sabbath her father would not permit it, so we made desultory conversation, until we were interrupted by a hammering at the door. The maids made shift to answer, and a tangled, disorderly figure rushed in, breathless, discomposed, one of his stockings hanging limply about his calf. 'They told me you were here!' gasped Vermeer. 'Forgive me for intruding — but I think I know what the girls have in common.'

Van Leeuwenhoek suggested that the ladies should withdraw, and gave Vermeer a restorative glass of claret wine. Vermeer gulped it down and reached into his pocket to produce three sheets of paper. 'These are the pictures of the three girls that have been circulated,' he explained. 'This is Gertruyd, as I drew her body, this is Magdalena, as I drew from her mother's instructions, and this is the copy of the miniature that was made at the mayor's order by some other artist.'

Even at this moment of high excitement Vermeer could not resist the inflection in his voice that conveyed just a little doubt about the accuracy of the word "artist". 'A sketch, another sketch, and a woodcut made from a miniature. These are fine so far as they go, but they lack life, and it came into my head that I could improve upon them in one particular. You will recall, Master, that Liese Kuijper asked if she could have a copy of the sketch as a keepsake?'

I nodded my agreement.

'So, this afternoon I walked down to that quarter of town to deliver her drawing, but I took the opportunity to ask her how I should colour the drawing for her. And that's when it came to me.'

'Get on with it, man!' Van Leeuwenhoek growled. 'What came to you?'

'They all have red hair. We all saw the body of Gertruyd Lievens, who had the brightest orange hair under that little cap of hers.'

'It's true,' I said. 'When De Graaf released it I was too busy sniffing the wine in it to have any regard for its colour.'

'Then I have seen, as you have not, the original painting by Bramer of Anna van Setten. The miniaturist flattened the colour and made it appear a normal blonde, if you can see it at all under her cap. But actually her hair as Bramer painted it was a light coppery colour.'

Van Leeuwenhoek concurred. 'I have seen the girl leaving church with her hair trailing down her back. It was as Vermeer describes.'

'Then the only one remaining, whom none of us have seen, was Magdalena Kuijper, and her mother assures me that her hair too was a bright orange. I believe, Master, mijnheer, that the killer is looking for a red-headed eight-year-old, but he doesn't know what she looks like.'

'Red-headed girls of that age cannot be numerous,' mused Van Leeuwenhoek.

'I have been looking about me all afternoon,' Vermeer added, 'and I have seen no others of the right age. But if I'm right, then no other girls are in danger, except red-headed eight-year-olds. Guard them, and we will trap the man.'

I was unsure what our response should be, but Van Leeuwenhoek suffered from no such doubts. Scooping up the papers and lobbing Vermeer's cloak into his arms he strode towards the door.

'Let us share this with the mayor at once,' he announced.

The mayor listened carefully. We had caught him in a state of undress, which much embarrassed him, wearing only his shirt, breeches and hose which he quickly supplemented with a fur cloak.

'What do you recommend?' he asked.

'We can set people's minds at rest,' urged Vermeer. 'Tell them that only redheads are at risk.'

'But if you are wrong, what a responsibility would lie on our heads then! Suppose we tell the citizens that and then a dark-haired girl goes missing?'

Van Leeuwenhoek intervened. 'Let us gather the facts, without which we cannot make a rational decision. We need to know how many red-headed girls of eight or nine years we have here. If they are few, we can set a man to privily observe each and keep them safe.'

The mayor liked this idea better. 'Let us do that. Let's make a proclamation in the morning to require all parents of such girls to bring them to the town hall.'

I coughed gently. 'Forgive me, but will not such a proclamation alert the killer to the fact that we are closing on him? Might he not decide that his safest course of action is to kill the other girls, if he has not already done so?'

The mayor blanched. 'Ah. That puts things in a different light.'

'If I may say so, even if we were to make such a proclamation, the general public will only rest easily when the killer is on the gallows,' Vermeer added.

'The problem lies with a public notice, then,' Van Leeuwenhoek suggested. 'Could we not convey this information to the sergeant and his men so that they can keep watch over such girls as they see them? With their co-operation, by this time tomorrow we may have some idea how many girls are at risk and we can come together again to consider our options.'

This was assented to, and we dispersed. As we left, I thanked Van Leeuwenhoek for his hospitality and asked him to apologise to his wife and daughter for disturbing the tranquillity of their home.

'The tranquillity of their home was disturbed by the murderer, not you,' he replied. 'They have rarely been calm since they first heard of all this. But I sense that an end is in sight, and I shall pray tonight that the darkness in our lives is soon dispelled.' He inclined his head in a small bow and turned for home.

Vermeer removed his hat and scratched his head. 'I don't know whether I'm excited or appalled,' he said. 'Did you notice that I'm invited back tomorrow evening? That's a first. Usually

I'm only there because I'm a leader of the painters' guild. A straw man in a smock would serve their purposes just as well. But now, thanks to your willingness to treat me equally and take me into your confidence, they are finally showing me some respect. I don't want riches or titles, just to feel that I count for something in my home town. When I'm gone who's going to remember me?'

'Your many children for a start. People listen to you because you're a man of good sense who has held back for too long, Johannes. I have nothing to do with it. You use your eyes to observe, and you saw what we did not, that the killer is only interested in red-headed girls. Your artist's eyes have served us well.'

He seemed mightily content with the compliment, clapped his hat back on his head, tipped it to a more rakish angle, and took his leave of me.

I walked back to the inn at the end of a long day, tired, dishevelled, having drunk more than I should, and facing very much the same of sort of day in the morning. It would start early, but by God's grace it might well end in success. I had a theory to test, and I had some names in my pocket that would give me a start.

I saw Lucie serving drinks and told her not to worry about breakfast for me, because I would be leaving at first light to return to The Hague, and it was a long walk. I climbed the stairs wearily, removed my shoes and splashed my face with cold water. That was a mistake; the water was icy and it was all too invigorating an experience for that time of night. I brushed and folded my clothes and climbed into bed, began my prayers, and I suspect I was asleep before I reached 'Hallowed be Thy name'.

CHAPTER ELEVEN

It was still dark when I sensed rustling close at hand. Someone was moving my belongings laid out on the nightstand by my bed. Fortunately, I had no weapon concealed within them, but I was aware that in my tiredness the night before I had left my pouch in my pile of clothes, and I would not want to have to explain to the Rector that I had lost the university's money.

In the very faint glimmers of moonlight entering at the window I could see a hand sweeping my things aside, and decided to act while I had surprise on my side. I grabbed the arm and leaped from my bed.

The trespasser screamed.

'Lucie?'

'Master?'

'You will waken the house. What are you about, girl?'

'I brought you a little parcel of breakfast, since you must leave early.'

'That was very kind,' I began, but then was interrupted by a light from the doorway. The innkeeper was standing there holding a candle, and by its light I could see that I was holding the arm of a young girl wearing only a thin shift, while I was sitting on the edge of my bed in my shirt. It could easily be misinterpreted.

'What's going on here, then?' asked the innkeeper.

The innkeeper lost no time in suggesting that the whole thing could be forgotten if I made a small payment to compensate for the "disturbance to other guests". Since there were no other guests, it was an obvious attempt at extortion, and I resisted.

'I will, of course, have to report this to the mayor,' he said.

'Please do. I am happy to explain to him.'

'And the Rector.'

This was substantially more serious. The Rector had the power to dismiss me for gross misconduct, though I was fairly confident that I could provide an adequate explanation to him, and he was a fair man.

'I am content for you to do so,' I bluffed. 'In fact, I may do it myself. While I'm at it, perhaps the mayor would like to investigate the common gossip that you lend your wife to male travellers.'

'That's a filthy lie! Who says so?'

'Just about everyone,' I said. 'In fact, people have been curious about why I have been overlooked.'

'My wife is a good and chaste woman.'

'No, she isn't,' Lucie interrupted. 'What about the time those visitors from Hamburg were here and she sang the song about the girl with the scarlet cloak?'

The innkeeper looked discomfited, but Lucie was just warming to her theme.

'Then she sang the one about the nun's little hen and the big cock…'

'Rooster. It's a rooster,' he protested.

'And she sat on their laps with her skirts lifted up…'

'Yes, well, we'll talk about this in the morning,' he said. 'Now go about your business.'

Lucie left, and I flopped back on the bed. That was a poor start to the day.

Since I was awake, I might as well set out, I thought, and dressed quickly. There was no water to shave but I rinsed my face and stepped out into the frosty morning. The cobbles glinted with the watery light of the moon, and I tried to recall the road that we had followed the previous day in the carriage. If I walked briskly, I would take no more than three hours, I judged, and I wanted to arrive as the city set about its day.

I crossed to the east side of the canal and headed north. The road was straight and level and I made good progress. The chilliness of the morning was a stimulus to walk briskly. I came to the town of Rijswijk and reminded myself that Jannetje Dircks came from there and had sent her younger daughter to her mother for safe keeping. It was not a great distance, but it would have been quite a march for a six-year-old girl.

Shortly after I left Rijswijk I came upon a pleasant resting place where a stream joined the canal and I sat to eat my breakfast. Thus invigorated, I rose and stepped out once more, giving thanks to the Almighty that it was not raining.

That continued to be the case, but only because it snowed instead. As I entered The Hague large flakes began to drift across my view and melt at once as they reached the ground. Soon my cloak was damp about my shoulders and I was very glad to step inside a hostelry decorated with a gaudy nameboard that announced it to be The Green Parrot. I have never seen a live parrot, though I understand them to be uncommonly intelligent birds — and talkative too, for they can speak like a man. The eponymous green parrot did not, for he had been stuffed these many years and stood looking markedly disconsolate, as anyone might whose feet have been nailed to a perch.

He provided a talking point even in his inanimate state, and mine host assured me that in his prime he was a great attraction whose antics amused many a customer. It appeared that he was particularly skilful in the learning of sea shanties, snatches of which he had by heart, and that it was as well that he had passed over, since he had a marked disregard for the clergy. The sight of clerical garb was sufficient to bring out his saltiest language and the most improper suggestions. I should have liked to have seen the little fellow, even at the expense of being abused thus, because it would have been amusing to take him to a clergy convocation and see how animated he might become in a roomful of ministers.

I paid for my mulled ale and continued on my way, the snow having abated somewhat, and passed through The Hague on the westward road to the little village of Scheveningen. Scheveningen lies about half an hour's walk beyond The Hague, on the coast of the North Sea, and is a fashionable place for the well-to-do to take the sea air. Carriages passed me from time to time as they headed for the promenade, there to complete a small loop before heading home. I had no clear idea where to start but for a clergyman there is always one option that surpasses any other. Look for a steeple.

The minister of the church at Scheveningen had not been there in 1662, but when I produced my slip of paper he willingly brought his own registers.

'Here we are,' he declared. 'Jantje van Schip, died 4th December 1662 in the twenty-third year of her age.'

I checked against the entry I had copied from the orphanage register. *An infant girl, eight weeks of age, the daughter of Hendrik Maria Brielle and Jantje van Schip (now deceased).*

'It seems that the father died first and the baby was brought to the orphanage when her mother followed,' I murmured.

'Perhaps so,' said the young, fresh-faced minister. 'I suspect that the father's middle name hints at a Catholic birth.'

'Yet the mother was buried here?'

'There is no Catholic church and we have always been accommodating towards anyone who professes a Christian faith, Master.'

A fine ecumenical example, I thought. Whatever the disputes at synods and councils between the different sorts of Christian, here, where ordinary people worshipped, nobody seemed too interested in the divisions.

An idea presented itself to me. 'If the mother lingered for a while, she could not have fed her baby. I wonder whether she had other children.'

'They would surely have been taken to the orphanage in The Hague too if they had existed. We haven't such an institution here.'

'So if she cannot feed, she would need a wet nurse. Where might I find such a person? Is it possible the woman who nursed the baby Brielle is still alive in Scheveningen?'

'I cannot tell, but I know who may be able to answer your question.'

He gave me the address of a woman who acted as local midwife. Riek was a jolly woman who had borne five children of her own and who welcomed me sitting in the back yard of her house as she laundered their linen.

'I remember Jantje. It was so sad. She gave birth to her first girl, and never really recovered. A fever grabbed her about a month after the birth, and she declined. I can't remember who fed her baby for her, but there are plenty of women who lose a child yet have milk.'

'Is there no family? Is Jantje's mother still living?'

'No, Master, she was alone in the world, except for her husband, of course.'

'And when was he taken?'

'Taken, Master? No, he lives yet.'

'Hendrik Maria Brielle is still alive?'

'Aye, sir, he is. He is a deep sea sailor who was far from home when his daughter was born. He came home after a couple of years, and the news nearly broke him. I have not seen him for many months now, because he sails to the East Indies.'

'Where does he live when he comes home?'

'I cannot say, sir. His house was cleared when Jantje died and rented to another couple. I should try the seaman's chapel. They may know there.'

I trudged along to the headland where a small chapel stood facing the sea. A sailor landing could hardly miss it, and it would be a natural place to go for help and succour. The minister was just a young fellow, but after hearing my request he took me to the home of an old man who had previously been the verger. He announced himself as Franciscus Stoemp, and repeatedly told me that he was eighty-two. I bit my tongue, or I might have said that if he did not stop repeating that fact his chances of reaching eighty-three were diminishing by the second.

Stoemp remembered Brielle well.

'It was a shocking thing, your worship, shocking. A young man comes home after a long voyage to Africa and races to his home, to find to his joy that his wife is still with child. She is delivered of it, and he can hold it for a while before he has to return to his ship to earn his living. This time he is gone for eighteen months, because he is bound for the East Indies, and when he returns he runs to the house, only to find another family living there who know nothing of his wife and daughter. I recall tales of him distractedly stopping complete strangers in the street, asking them if they know anything of it. At length, someone tells him his wife has sickened and died not long after he left, and the baby has been taken to The Hague where there is an orphanage to care well for it.'

'This Brielle — how can I find out if he is at sea now?'

'I don't think he can be, your honour, because I saw him arrive not a month ago. He used to doss down in the chapel hall, but he's not there this time. I know, because when it's bitter cold I go there to keep warm because coal and wood are expensive. He stayed just the first night then said he had a job to do.'

'And how will I know him if I see him?'

'Oh, that's easy, your mastership. He has a big shock of red hair.'

Scheveningen is a small place, not much more than a village, and it did not take long to seek out all the people whom Stoemp thought Brielle might turn to for help, and to hear them all say that they did not know where he was and that they had not seen him for more than a month.

I was confident that I now knew the man we were looking for, but I had no idea where to look for him. Delft, obviously, but where? He could not be at the seafarers' usual haunts because they had been searched thoroughly by the sergeant and his men. I started on the weary trudge back to Delft, and it was good fortune that my way took me through The Hague, for it provoked an idea that I needed to follow.

I found my way back to the orphanage and sought out the warden.

'These little children must need a wet nurse,' I said, 'and so must the Van Setten baby, who was only two months old.'

'I see that,' said the warden, 'but why do you want to know?'

'Because if my theory is right, someone told Hendrik Maria Brielle where his baby had gone.'

The warden was outraged. 'That is highly confidential. I keep the records locked away at all times and we generally refuse requests to inspect the ledger. You were a privileged exception, mijnheer, in view of the gravity of the circumstances.'

'You misunderstand me. I do not suggest that anyone saw the register, only that they discovered what town was involved. He does not appear to have known which family had his daughter, just that they lived in Delft. Now, it seems to me that if the Van Settens were determined to keep the adoption secret, they could not employ a Delft wet nurse.'

'Such women gossip terribly,' the warden agreed. 'Their secret would have been known before long.'

'Precisely. But these things cannot be left to chance. They must have engaged a wet nurse before they collected the baby, and therefore I suspect she must have been a local woman here in The Hague. Of course, I can ask the Van Settens, but I suspect they will uselessly deny the whole story is true. Surely the only person who could have told Hendrik Brielle where his daughter was would have been her wet nurse, or a member of the staff here.'

'As you observed yesterday, Master, we go to great lengths to keep these things secret, to the extent that we have two books. Arrivals are kept in one, and adoptions in the other. Without both books, the child cannot be followed. It is a necessary safeguard. Some mothers regret giving the child up and attempt to find them again. We cannot permit that. It would be unsettling for the child.'

'But in this case Jantje did not give the child up; she died. And her husband did not give her up either, because he was at sea. Perhaps someone felt that his story was so sad that he was in some way entitled to see his daughter again.'

'I have no objection to asking the question, but I do not know whom to ask.'

'Brielle must have come here within the past month or so.'

'How do you know that?'

'Given the urgency of his search, he can only just have found the trail. If he knew it led to Delft, he would have done all this during his last shore leave. Good heavens, man, surely he must have been terrified that if she ever moved again he would lose all hope of finding her!'

'Yes, yes, I can see that,' the warden mumbled. 'I will bring the staff together so you can speak to them.'

It was a strange gathering, tense, silent, watchful. If anyone guessed why we were there, and knew themselves to be innocent, they must have been watching the others keenly to see who had done this terrible thing. Or, perhaps, they may have seen it as an act of compassion. But we needed to know what had been said, and we needed to know quickly.

I explained the events in Delft and that I suspected that Hendrik Brielle was implicated. I described our belief that he was snatching red-haired girls at random in the hope of finding his daughter. If I was right, then he had finally found the right girl, though whether he knew that was unclear. But if we were to rescue the girls we must know what he knew. Only thus could I hope to think as he thought. And, I added, if they had any ideas where he would hide out in Delft it would be a kindness to share them.

I finished speaking and looked hopefully at the clutch of servants and staff. Nobody moved, nobody spoke. I had the option of trying to extract the name of the wet nurse from Mathilde van Setten, but she may not even have known it.

'Master?'

One of the youngest maids had her hand raised.

'Yes, juffrouw?'

'A man such as you speak of, a big man with red hair and a foul-smelling sailor's cape, I've seen him.'

'Where? When?'

'He came here soon after the new year. He asked at the kitchen door if anyone could help him find his daughter.'

'Is this true?' said the warden.

There was a sullen silence.

'I said is this true?' he roared.

The cook stepped forward, kneading her apron in her hands. 'It was a pitiful sight, warden. He asked again and again, and told us a heart-rending tale of his beloved young wife dying and his baby being taken away.'

'And you betrayed our trust? You shared a secret which must ever remain so?'

The cook's eyes blazed with defiance. 'I did not! I could not, because I didn't know anything. But if I had, I would have told him, because my conscience told me it was the right thing to do.'

The warden drew close to her and attempted to cow her into submission. 'Your conscience! And is your conscience clear now that a young girl lies in the ground and two more likely to follow her?'

'He won't harm his daughter. He would die first. I saw the pleading look in his eye, and it was not that of a murderer.'

'So now you are a judge too? A girl died at his hands, and when he is caught, he will hang. And what good will that do his daughter?'

It was at that second that I lost the will to find this man. I just wanted to slink back to Leiden and forget I was ever sent to Delft, because this was a story that could never have a happy ending. If we missed him, people lived in fear and a dead girl went unavenged. If we trapped him, he hanged and another young girl lost her father. The pointlessness of it disgusted me at that moment.

Nobody else wanted to speak, so I shrugged and thanked them. I turned to leave, when I heard a man's voice. It came from the man who worked in the kitchen garden. He was gaunt and weathered, tanned and with piercing blue eyes. He wore a leather jerkin and a tatty straw hat.

'Warden, if I have done wrong, I must pay for it.'

'You, Marinus? You, of all people?'

'I had nothing to tell him, but my heart wept for him. So when he left, I followed him. I was careful not to speak to him on the property here, warden. I trailed him to the inn near the school, and there I said that we knew nothing, but that if he could find old Beatrix she assigned the wet nurses then, and might be of service to him.'

The warden plainly knew nothing of old Beatrix, whoever she was.

'Who is this Beatrix woman? Where does she live?' he asked.

'I don't know exactly, but in one of the hofjes at the back of the Oude Hof.'

I asked the warden publicly not to punish them, but to accept that we all make mistakes and that it had taken a high disregard for their own self-interest to make them come forward. Reluctantly, he agreed that there would be no action taken.

Marinus told me how to find the hofjes, the little rows of almshouses that nestled at the back of the Oude Hof, which is a grand house where the daughter-in-law of William of Orange was living after she was widowed. I walked there and found Beatrix to be a bright, buxom old lady.

'Yes, Master, such a man came here,' she conceded. 'He offered me money to tell him where his girl had been taken, but I refused it. I could have taken his silver and spun him a yarn, but if the truth be told, I did not know where she had gone. All I could tell him was that I had been asked to find a wet nurse who would be well rewarded but who would have to live a while in Delft.'

'Did he ask who she was?'

'He did, but it did him no good, because she ran off with a tinker to Rotterdam and there's no telling where she is now. At the bottom of a canal, I shouldn't wonder. Low company, you see, Master. Fall into it, and it's a devil of a climb back out.'

In other circumstances I could have passed a happy hour or two listening to this spirited old lady, who reminded me somewhat of my own grandmother, whom God had so far preserved, though if she ever finds out I have become a Catholic she is likely to drop dead on the spot of a fit of apoplexy. My grandmother is a tiny woman whom I never remember seeing in any colour but black, with a little black rosette bonnet tied under her chin with a piece of black ribbon. She is absurdly proud of me, though she seems to think the high point of my learning was to master the alphabet, which she bids me recite when I see her. She claps her hands with joy throughout and then invariably tells anyone who will listen: 'What about that? The whole alphabet, mark you, not just parts of it. And in the correct order too!' As if she knows what the correct order of letters is.

I gathered up my hat and cloak and made to leave, but Beatrix stopped me.

'If I've been a service to you, Master, will you be one to me?'

Having already been caught with one woman in compromising circumstances that day I dreaded to think what she might be about to propose, but all she wanted was someone to fetch her a bucket of dried peat from the yard behind, which I gladly did.

Well wrapped against the biting wind, I set off again to return to Delft. It was already growing gloomy, or I would gladly have passed a little time in the Green Parrot once more, but I left it behind me and stepped out on the high road.

I had asked Lucie to walk over to the town hall and give Claes a note saying that I would not be back for dinner, so I needed to find somewhere to eat. At Rijswijk I found a very clean eating-place and was surprised to see it not better frequented, but discovered when the bill of fare was discussed that the owner eats no flesh meat, but subsists only on vegetables and fruit. I tried to explain to him that all modern medical knowledge is agreed that he will surely die within months on such a diet, as the vital force within his veins ebbs away if the blood is not replaced in his victuals, but he told me he had lived without meat for ten years and meant to live twice ten more. He persuaded me to try a dish of eggs and spinach, which I found very fine and occasionally make for myself even now.

It was now growing quite dark, but in an hour or so I was back in Delft with time to clean myself in my room before meeting the mayor, Van Leeuwenhoek and Vermeer for our appointed council, so I asked if Lucie could be sent up with some hot water from the kitchen.

'Lucie has been put out of her place,' said one of the other maids, 'for her immodest behaviour.'

I was scandalized. First, because it was unjust, but also because there was no woman who less deserved to have her chastity called into question. 'Where will I find her?' I asked.

'Her parents live in one of the damaged houses near the explosion.'

I donned my cloak once more, and found her sitting on the step outside the house. Nobody should have been living in such a place. In the explosion seventeen years before the blast had driven a great rift in its side, and I had no idea how long the front would remain attached to the back. Inside, the staircase had been replaced with a ladder. I was familiar with poverty, of course — I am a university lecturer, when all is said and done — but this shocked me.

'I heard about the injustice done to you,' I began. 'What will you do now?'

She looked at me with innocent eyes. 'I don't know, Master. Perhaps I'll take to whoring.'

'I beg your pardon?'

'Whoring. You know, when a woman sells…'

'Yes, I know what it is, Lucie. How can you think of such a thing?'

'My friend says it pays well. A few hours on her back and she earns more than I earn in a fortnight.'

'Yes, but…'

'And you don't need any letters or sums for it. You can make a tidy living.'

'But, Lucie…'

'My friend makes four guilders a day some days. That's if she can get eight men. Of course, where she goes wrong is she gives discounts to clergy.'

'Discounts to clergy?'

'Now don't you go getting ideas, Master, for she has the Spanish disease and I wouldn't wish that on any man. Except the innkeeper, I suppose.'

Lucie's mother crept up on us from behind, giving me quite a start.

'Now,' she said, 'what are you young people up to?'

Leaving aside the appropriateness of that appellation, I was too much in heat to think what I was saying. 'Your daughter has been telling me she proposes to sell herself to men,' I expostulated.

'Well, it's steady work,' her mother said. 'And there's not much else around.'

'You approve?'

'It isn't a matter of approving or disapproving. The girl has to eat.'

'But she has never been with a man.'

'They tell me men will pay extra for that,' Lucie interrupted.

'That's true,' said her mother. 'But you can only charge that once, so you make sure you get a good price for it, my girl.'

Those who know me will tell you that from time to time my mouth runs ahead of my brain, especially when I am in a passion. And I was certainly in a passion listening to this welter of nonsense, so it was not surprising that I said what I did next.

'If the only reason for this immorality is need, then I will find Lucie a job.'

Lucie looked up at me as if she had been struck by lightning. 'You will?'

'If that's the only way to keep you off the streets.'

Lucie got up and put an arm around her mother. 'Didn't I tell you he was a nice man? I never fancied whoring anyway.'

'Who would?' agreed her mother. 'It's bad enough having to do it with your father, and I'm married to him. The thought of letting complete strangers climb…'

'Could we stop this conversation now?' I exploded.

A silence ensued.

'I have work to do today and tomorrow, but I will not leave Delft without seeing your daughter in a position. You have my word. And now, goodnight to you both.'

I judged it best to walk the long way round to reach the mayor's house so that my anger might dissipate. A cat approached me as I crossed the Markt as if it proposed to rub against my leg, but must have sensed my hostility and slinked off into an alley where its green eyes watched me intently.

We gathered in the mayor's parlour, the mayor himself being fully dressed this time, including the collarette that carried the arms of Delft. Van Leeuwenhoek and I were invited to sit in the chairs at either side, and Vermeer arrived shortly afterwards, late as usual, and eased into the remaining seat. There was a child's dirty handprint on the seat of his breeches which he seemed not to have noticed.

I explained what I had learned during the day.

'If you had asked, I would gladly have lent you a carriage,' the mayor said.

'Thank you, but I only resolved to go to Scheveningen during the night. I left at first light, and it was a pleasant enough walk.'

Van Leeuwenhoek had been listening intently. 'It seems, Master, that the likely culprit is this fellow Brielle. I can well understand his grief upon discovering the loss of both his wife and his daughter. It might have been kinder if the authorities at The Hague had told him both were dead.'

I have often reflected since upon this idea. Can it ever be better to lie to someone than to be truthful? This notion of a little "white lie" is widely approved, and yet it seems to me that the ends can never be more moral than the means. You might as well say that a physician is justified in running his patients

206

through with his sword if he cannot cure them, because it will ultimately save them a lot of pain.

St Augustine of Hippo wrote two books on lying, and was clear that all lies are sinful and therefore impermissible to believers, for they misuse our God-given gift of speech. Moreover, when we discover someone has lied to us, the breach of trust feels greater if we have reason to trust them more; thus, if we are lied to by a drunken blackguard, we expect no different, but if a priest lied to us to spare our feelings, that would be a much greater breach of trust. How could it be better for Brielle to think his daughter dead than to know that she may be living happily somewhere being cared for by good people?

'This is all very well,' the mayor responded, 'but what are we going to do about it?'

'We should announce that we know who he is and invite him to give himself up,' said Van Leeuwenhoek.

I was framing a reasoned response in my head when Vermeer anticipated me somewhat.

'With respect,' he said (always a sign that the interlocutor is about to be highly disrespectful), 'if Brielle hears this announcement, as we would hope he would, what reason has he to give himself up? He has his daughter with him, and now he will hang and thus lose his daughter. He may feel that with one girl he has a chance of escape, whereas with two he will be encumbered, which would seal Magdalena Kuijper's fate.'

This logic inspired me. I could see a possible stratagem, one involving a degree of risk, but which might work. 'I think mijnheer Vermeer is right,' I said, 'but that is precisely the line of thought we must encourage.'

'What?' stammered Van Leeuwenhoek.

'I mean, that Brielle must be brought to think that he can escape if he only has one child with him.'

'You would sacrifice Anna van Setten?' asked Van Leeuwenhoek.

'You were prepared to sacrifice Magdalena Kuijper,' Vermeer interrupted.

'Please, please!' cried the mayor, waving his arms energetically. 'Let us be composed and dignified. This is too serious for petty squabbles. Let us at least hear the master defend his thesis.'

I paused to say a quick silent prayer and collect my thoughts.

'I propose that we should say that we now know that the culprit has left town, and therefore there is no point in maintaining the security cordon around it that has previously existed. We should ostentatiously withdraw the men guarding the roads and canals, and watch covertly from secure vantage points. I am convinced that if Brielle thinks he can escape, he will not lose a minute in trying to do so, probably by night. Tonight is the full moon. The next day or two would be the best possible time to slip away.'

'But if he achieves it...' gasped the mayor.

'I agree it is risky, but we have not found him so far despite the cordon. At least this will smoke him out of cover. And if I have understood this man's make-up correctly, he is not a killer. I believe that he would use Magdalena kindly. He has no reason to keep her, nor any to harm her. He holds her at present only to stop her telling us where he is hiding.'

'I see,' said Vermeer. 'You are suggesting that we use beaters to drive the prey out of the thickets so we may hunt it.'

'I see only failure in this,' said the mayor. 'If we are wrong, Van Setten will have my head.'

'He'll have all our heads,' Van Leeuwenhoek coldly observed, 'but I like the plan. I can think of no better idea. We cannot go on as we are.'

The mayor was still unwilling to approve it. All he could see was the prospect of earning the implacable hatred of Van Setten if the scheme miscarried.

It was Vermeer who came up with a plan to manage this. 'Then let us get his approval in advance. And if he wishes, let him join us in staking out the roads. Van Setten is many things, but he is not a stupid man. If your scheme has the merits that we think we see in it, then he will see it too. And if he has approved it, then he cannot call for our heads if it miscarries.'

'But if he disapproves, then we are hamstrung,' I moaned.

'Not necessarily,' smiled Vermeer, 'but at least we'll know what we're staking on our success.'

The mayor asked Claes to go to the Van Setten house and ask if Wilhelmus van Setten would join us at once. Within half an hour he entered the room, a fierce glint to his eye, and inspected us all in turn.

'Mijnheer Mayor, I have come in response to your invitation.'

'Please be seated. Master Mercurius will expound his discoveries and lay out a plan for your consideration. Of course, it is for us to determine the best course of action, but we are anxious that you should have the opportunity to make any observations you wish that will guide our judgement.'

A nice touch, I thought. The mayor is making plain that this remains our decision; Van Setten's role is limited to offering comments.

I described my work over the week. 'As you know, mijnheer, we have been looking for something that unites the three girls and helps to explain their abduction. Thanks to mijnheer Vermeer, we think we have found it. The kidnapper takes eight-year-old redhaired girls because those are the only things he knows for sure about his prey. He is looking for an eight-year-old redhead, but he knows no more about her.'

'And why would he be doing that?' sneered Van Setten, as if he had wandered into a home for lunatics.

'Because those are the only things he knows about his daughter. Hendrik Maria Brielle is the father of your daughter Anna, and he wants her back.'

Van Setten was visibly disturbed by this revelation. He sat silently as I continued.

'I have traced Anna back to the orphanage in The Hague, and from there to the little church in Scheveningen where she was baptised for the first time, before you had her rebaptised in the Nieuwe Kerk here. I thought that, like me, you misunderstood the note from Scheveningen to imply that both parents were dead, whereas one was only at sea, but now I understand what your wife said while you were searching for Anna. She said that she knew this would happen one day; that the natural father would eventually return and come for his daughter.'

It fell to the mayor to state the obvious. 'The inquiry would have been expedited if you had shared this information voluntarily at the outset, mijnheer Van Setten.'

Van Setten nipped his lip with his upper teeth. 'I... I did not deliberately conceal it. But you must understand that these are not easy things to speak of. We had gone to great lengths to hide the fact that Anna was adopted. Why throw all that away now, unless we could be convinced that a great good required it?'

'We understand,' said the mayor. As far as I was concerned, he was speaking for himself.

'But you may be of good cheer,' Van Leeuwenhoek told Van Setten, 'because we now know that he means Anna no harm.'

'Nor can he be expecting a ransom,' Vermeer added. Did I detect a hint in Vermeer's voice that suggested that this would be a greater comfort to Van Setten?

Van Setten composed himself. 'What do you propose to do?' he asked.

The others looked at me significantly.

'I suggest that we have two alternatives. We continue as we are, in which event we risk your daughter sickening, for Brielle could hardly send for help, even if he can afford it; and I need not point out the obvious, that this has not been crowned with success so far. The other option, which I favour, is to give him the impression that we believe that he has already left, to withdraw the guards on the roads and canals, and thus encourage him to try to leave with your daughter. He is on foot, and cannot travel fast. We will, of course, continue to watch the roads and canals, but secretly, using men in ordinary day clothes, discreetly placed.'

'Can we not leave only one road open?' Van Setten suggested.

'Then he will surely suspect a trap. The only story that will convince him is if he sees all the roads apparently open. And tomorrow is a good day for it, because it is the full moon tonight.'

'And if he breaks cover, how will we hear about it?'

By great good fortune, or possibly divine intervention, the answer to this had come into my head just before he asked it. 'We will have observers with a large lantern in the uppermost part of the Nieuwe Kerk tower. It can be seen from all parts of Delft. When the message reaches the church, the observers will swing their lantern in accordance with a code, so onlookers will know in which direction to run.'

There was a pause as Van Setten considered. The mayor was growing decidedly uneasy.

'I approve the plan,' Van Setten said at length. 'At least we will be able to get on with our lives one way or the other.'

The mayor jumped up and shook his hand warmly. 'Be assured, mijnheer, we will all do everything we can to restore your daughter to you. Do you wish to stay while we discuss the details?'

'No,' Van Setten answered, 'I shall return to my wife. And so, goodnight.'

And he was gone. There was a shocked silence as the door closed, and finally Van Leeuwenhoek broke it. 'I had thought he might have wanted to help recover his daughter safely.'

Vermeer shook his head sadly. 'He wants to enjoy the fish without doing the fishing,' said he.

By the time I left, we had crafted our plan. The mayor would have the announcement made in the Markt and at other prominent places in the town during the morning. At noon the sergeant would collect all his men amid a cacophony of trumpets and drums and they would parade in the Markt so nobody could miss it.

At sunset the men, together with the Civic Guard members, would gather in the town hall, wearing their drabbest clothes with no white about them. Each would be issued with a dark lantern and assigned a vantage point. These positions would be drawn up by the sergeant during the day. The mayor would also find some fleet-footed boys to act as messengers and Claes and Lucie would be stationed in the tower of the church. Eyebrows were raised when I proposed her name, but I explained that she was used to carrying out orders to the letter and, being unemployed, would be able to rest during the day and thus be alert all night if need be.

'Are we all clear, then?' asked the mayor.

'Thank goodness we don't have to carry those damned pikes,' muttered Vermeer, earning a glower from Van Leeuwenhoek. The mayor had diplomatically chosen not to hear it.

We dispersed to our homes, and I lay on the bed musing that only a week before I had been enjoying my beer and my book in the inn on the Langebrug. Such a lot had happened since; but much more was to happen on the next day.

CHAPTER TWELVE

I slept late and took my time over breakfast. Returning to my room I gathered my things and then impulsively decided I needed to visit the convent. I hoped to use their little chapel for some prayer. Since I needed the Lord's help this day, I had better go through my devotions properly.

I would not want to give the impression that God and I had only a passing acquaintance. My ordination was important to me; so much so that I had gone through it twice. And while I may have been flippant in these pages, a man's journal is not a systematic exposition of his faith.

I dipped my fingers in the holy water, crossed myself, genuflected at the top of the aisle, and knelt humbly in prayer. I remembered a prayer that I was told was used by an English soldier during their Civil War: "Lord, thou knowest how busy I must be today. If I do forget Thee, do not Thou forget me." I knew exactly how he felt.

Having fulminated against lying the night before, the thought came to me that my whole plan was based upon a lie. We were deceiving Hendrik Brielle into believing that the roads were unguarded. If we were successful, he would pay with his life. Whatever happened, Anna van Setten's life would never return to its previous state.

But then, I thought, that life did not seem to have been a happy one. Was it even conceivable that she was happier now, living in a shuttered room with a father who loved her, than she had been in the silk-cushioned nest on the Molslaan? If we were right, she even had a girl of her own age to play with, for the first time in her life; and from all we heard of Magdalena, anything she had to share with Anna was bound to be educational for her. I'd wager Anna had no idea how to prick out a cockle or clean a scallop.

What about my own life? Here I was, neither fish nor fowl, a Catholic masquerading as a Protestant, concealing what should be open. I had faith, but not the all-encompassing generous faith of Aleydis Vermeer. And it was idle to say that she was like that because she was just a young girl. We all start in that fashion, but we lose that freshness, that unquestioning belief, that clarity of what is expected of us. We trim our faith to fit the world, when actually we should change the world to accommodate our faith.

We academics sat in our studies day by day writing intricate works to explain why the other side was wrong. I do not know that anyone has seriously debated how many angels can sit on the head of a pin — to which my answer is seventy-six: I have no evidence for this, but it's as good an answer as any I have seen — but there have been plenty of questions almost as ludicrous about which men have fallen out. Would it be so terrible if Protestants and Catholics agreed that it does not much matter what exactly happens at the consecration of the bread and wine, but that it matters a lot that it should happen as often as possible? Occasionally lecturers from Leiden dispute with colleagues from the Catholic University at Leuven (or Louvain, if you prefer the French name). There is much heat and not much light generated. I am almost minded to stand up at the next and suggest we call in a Mohammedan as a referee.

My mind was wandering. It does that too often. I forced myself to say the Matins prayers as a discipline to prevent digression, rose, bowed, and left the chapel. The Mother Superior was sitting patiently on the bench outside.

215

'I hoped to speak to you,' she said simply.

'I'm sorry. I hope you haven't been waiting long,' I answered.

'My time has not been wasted,' she said gently, indicating the rosary in her hand.

We walked together in the garden, cold as it was.

'I have been praying and reflecting on the young girl who came with you.'

'Aleydis Vermeer?'

'Yes. She has quite a zeal for the faith, and I would not want to discourage it, but she is still very young. May I ask what advice you have given her about her vocation?'

'As yet, I have given none,' I replied. 'I have tried to explain to her that the world is rarely as black and white as young people see it, and that if she does not learn to accommodate herself to that fact, her faith will be challenged too often on too many points.'

The Mother Superior nodded. 'That is a common view. For myself, I rejoice in someone who forces us back to the black and white choices because sometimes there is no grey area in which we may shelter. Don't you agree, Master?'

I could hardly not. I had just been thinking much the same in the chapel.

'To have her here would be a challenge to myself and the other sisters. In time, it will be good for us all; but for now, I would prefer her to stay within her family as a beacon for them. She has many brothers and sisters and her help will be a great support to her mother. Let her be an example to them all. Let her show her faith in the world rather than withdrawing from it. Then, when she reaches the age at which it is natural to leave home, we will welcome her here, if she still wishes it.'

'I will convey your wise words, Reverend Mother.'

And I meant it. She was much wiser than I was. Lest I forget them, I went at once and passed them on to Aleydis and her mother. Both seemed content, Catharina because she would keep her daughter by her a few more years, Aleydis because she would be the acknowledged star of the Catholic faith in that house until she entered the convent to sort them out too.

I sometimes wonder where she is now. Our paths do not cross. It is likely that as I sit here in Leiden writing this, she is somewhere near at hand and yet so far away, behind a cloister wall. But if God wills, I shall discover her one day.

This waiting was deeply uncongenial to me. Let night fall soon, I thought, and then let us see what happens. About four o'clock it darkened and I watched from the side of the square as the town's activity slowed. I bought a small porcelain tile as a souvenir of my stay in Delft, beautifully painted in deepest blue. My eye was caught by a printer's shop, The Golden ABC, wherein were some fine books, clean of line and sharp of print. As I looked in the window, a handsome young man of about eighteen dangled a lantern on a hook to give me light. He smiled and dipped his head in salute. I learned sometime later that I had just seen Jacob Dissius for the first time, but not the last. He was to be important in my life.

I did not know exactly what I was waiting for, but I had a keen presentiment that something was about to change. I walked down by the Oostpoort and watched the little barges shifting position once more, and was strolling along the Zuidwal when I experienced one of those moments that leaves a man slapping his head in frustration. How could I have been so stupid?

I ran along the wall to the southern gate, then continued on towards the well where Gertruyd Lievens had been snatched. I had concentrated on the road, but a few paces further away from the little gate there was the canal bank. The kidnapper could disappear so quickly because he had used a barge. Nowhere in Delft is far from water. Magdalena Kuijper was taken from a street that ended in a canal. Anna van Setten was standing on a bridge overlooking a canal when she was seized. The reason nobody saw her walking off hand in hand with her attacker was that she did not do so. She could have stepped down into the barge with him. But where would Brielle get a barge?

It was possible to row a barge in the calm waters of Delft. He could have steered one all the way from Scheveningen, but it would be much slower and harder work than walking. Perhaps he stole one, but then he had no hope of a getaway. Perhaps he bought one. Or possibly he took a chance on the owner not looking at it over the winter. But I was convinced he had one. Trying to walk with a young girl would slow him down, but he could sail quite quickly with her.

I wanted to find the sergeant to share this information with him, but before I could do so I spotted Lucie on the church tower, waving a large flag. She was making the sign of the Cross with it, a signal that she wanted me. For completeness sake, let me explain that for Vermeer she would make sweeping brush strokes, for Van Leeuwenhoek the circular shape of a lens, for the mayor she would dip three times in salute, and for the sergeant she would hold it upright and swing it from side to side. I ran to the Markt and met Claes coming the other way.

'To Oostpoort!' he gasped. 'They've found Magdalena!'

And so they had. She was cold but well, clutched in her mother's grasp. She would say nothing about her ordeal, resolutely clamping her mouth shut.

'Do you think she has been damaged, Master?' asked Liese.

'No, she looks well and is not distressed. I have a notion why she remains quiet, though.'

I brought Magdalena to the fireside and lifted her face gently so her eyes met mine.

'Don't worry, you can keep your promise. Did the man tell you that if you said anything before morning Anna might get hurt?'

She shook her head. So much for that idea, Mercurius.

'He doesn't call her Anna. He calls her Juliana.'

Of course he would! I had not found her baptism record in Scheveningen, but if they were Catholics she would have been baptised in some backstreet chapel.

'But he told you not to speak to us for her sake?'

Magdalena nodded, then returned her attention to the hot milk she had been given.

'I must go, Claes,' I said. 'He's taken the bait.'

I ran to the south gate. Pray God I was in time. He had at least half an hour's start on me, but I could run faster than he could row. Probably. On a good day.

I crossed to the west bank of the canal leading to the south towards Rotterdam. This was not as strange as it may seem. It would enable him to turn west and then north to follow the coast round to Scheveningen, even if there were no canals between. There were plenty of waterways around Schiedam and Rotterdam where he could hide. It was even possible that once he was clear he would leave the barge and proceed on foot, or even by coastal barge, a more robust ship that would return him to his home town or his ship.

I had stationed some men on either side of the canal, so it was unlikely that he could slip past, and since they had not raised the alarm, I began to take comfort from the realisation that he was still within our invisible net. But then I realised my mistake. There was a small channel from the basin where the barges could moor that led into the Westsingel, the great canal to the west of the town, and from there another branch headed west again. We had stationed people on the road, but not on the canal, because it had been in poor repair and was generally considered impassable. However, a lightly-laden boat with a strong rower could negotiate it. We had assumed that his first move would be away from the town; it did not cross our mind that he might go round the town before striking out for his haven. It was impossible that he had not reached any of our checkpoints by now, so I had to consider that he might have given us the slip.

Racing as fast as might be, I re-crossed the bridge and ran along the path, cutting the corner so far as I could to head north-west rather than north, then west as the barge would be obliged to do. After about five minutes I was feeling an ache in my side and leaned against a tree to recover myself, and then I heard it.

Plop, swish, pause, plop, swish, pause.

Someone was rowing in the dark. And the rhythm led me to think that he had abandoned the barge and acquired a smaller rowing boat. That was how he had manoeuvred past the debris in the Westsingel.

Wherever he was, he was rowing without any light but that of the moon. It was a cold, clear night. The air was still, so it felt pleasantly bracing rather than chilly, but once we were free of the lights of the town, you could see perfectly well in the silver-blue moonlight.

I paused and listened again. Plop, swish, pause. Plop, swish, pause. It was to my right, but not too far away. I dared not let myself be heard, so I came off the path and ran on the grass so my shoes would not clatter.

It was at this juncture, I think, that I wished I had left my clerical robe off. As I ran along I tripped on its hem and hit the ground with a thud. I lay perfectly still in the hope that I had not been noticed, but it was forlorn. Brielle stopped rowing and listened intently.

'Who's there?' I heard him growl. On balance, it seemed better not to answer. 'I said, who's there?'

I covered my face with my black sleeve which had the advantage of preventing the moon glinting on my pale skin, but the extreme disadvantage that I could no longer see anyone approaching. I have made many stupid decisions in my life, but that ranks very near the top of the list.

I heard no footsteps, but then a very welcome sound. A little girl whined.

'Keep rowing, Daddy, I'm getting cold.'

Once more I heard the comforting plop, swish, pause. I let him row a few strokes and then cautiously climbed to my feet and followed. The canal was extremely straight, but by good fortune someone had moored a couple of boats beside each other on the south bank, where I stood. Brielle would have to steer very carefully round them. He was also hampered because he could not trust Anna to act as his coxswain, so he was having to look about him at intervals to guard against hitting moored boats.

As his concentration was fully employed in working a passage round the boats, one of which was very loosely tied up, I raced past and ahead of him, and soon I was a full hundred paces ahead of him.

And then I saw exactly what I wanted. Some bushes, perhaps once part of a hedge, stood hard against the canal bank. I nipped behind them and discovered another boat moored there. The channel was not too wide, but there was nowhere narrower in sight. This was where I needed to be.

I crouched in the boat and waited my moment. The oars came nearer and nearer, and soon I could see the first ripples preceding the boat and disturbing the surface of the water. Next came the prow, and then the bench where Brielle sat. And so I pounced.

Springing from my place like a cat I executed a perfect jump, landing in the middle of the boat between Brielle and Anna. If I had stopped there, all would have been well, but my motion would not stop, and I found myself grasping at the far gunwale to stop myself falling in the water. I failed.

But by holding fast to the boat, I managed to tip it over, and Brielle fell in with me. Anna rocked and slithered, and finally fell, but she grabbed my arm as she hit the water and held tight to it. It hurt like a vice, but she was safe so long as she held on.

I am no swimmer, but I hauled the boat round so it was between me and Brielle, and paddled with my free arm for the shore. Predictably, I suppose, I travelled in an arc rather than a straight line, but I came to the bank and thrust Anna ashore. I was just clambering out of the water when Brielle seized me and tried to pull me back in. We tugged at each other until finally I shouted at him, 'For goodness sake, climb out of the water and let's talk!'

Stunned by this suggestion, Brielle did so. I pointed to a tree stump and held both hands up to show that I was not armed.

'I mean you no harm. Let Juliana sit there, and we can talk. I will not hurt you.' Then I thought that was rather a one-sided commitment on my part, and added: 'If you don't hurt me.'

Brielle was cautious, but he too held his hands up, palms facing me and we both sat on the grass.

'We should get out of these wet clothes,' I started.

'They wouldn't be wet if you hadn't pulled me in,' he protested.

'Well, we have no others. Juliana's dress is looking grubby.'

'I'm not well equipped with girls' clothes. I have money. I can buy some when we escape.'

'You won't escape. That's what I'm here for. And there are others following me. We have very little time before they arrive. And when they get here they'll arrest you for murder.'

'Then we should leave at once,' he growled, and made to get up.

'They will hang you, man! What good will that do your daughter then?'

'They have to catch me first,' Brielle said doubtfully.

'I doubt you would escape the district, but even if you did, this is a small country, and Juliana is not fitted for a life at sea. She had a comfortable life here. Her new mother loved her. She has more than you or I could ever give her. It's not what should have happened, but it has. I know you mean well, I know you love her, but it is kinder to her to let her go back. I'm sure if you did that I can argue that you should not be hanged.'

'Forgive me, but I don't have that much confidence in your powers. Are you a lawyer?'

'Well, no, I'm a priest. But if you admit what you did and lay it before the court, they may be merciful. The authorities know that the first girl died accidentally, and the other two will have been returned unharmed. I will swear that you were co-operative. They must listen to me: I am the man charged by the mayor of Delft with finding you.'

'So you found me. But if I just hold your scrawny little neck under the water there, they won't hear what you have to say, and we'll be away.'

'But not for long. All the municipalities in South Holland will know your name and description by the morning. It is being drawn up now. There is nowhere you can go except to a foreign land.'

'I will not give up my daughter,' Brielle growled. 'I have been without her these eight years. I cannot turn my back on her now.'

I thought quickly. 'It may not come to that if you will just trust me.'

'Why should I?'

'Ah! Inspiration! Thank you, God!' I whispered. 'Your name — Hendrik Maria Brielle. You're a Catholic, I believe.'

'What of it?'

'I'm a Catholic priest. If you tell me what happened under the seal of the confessional, I cannot speak of it in court.'

'You might,' he said doubtfully.

'And earn myself everlasting damnation? It's not worth that, Hendrik. Look, I'll tell you, and you can correct me where I'm wrong. Then I'll go to the mayor and say you made a full confession but I can't tell them what it was.'

'This is madness. They'll still hang me.'

'Not if you're not there.'

'Not there?'

'Let me have the girl and a confession and I'll leave you here to go where you please. My instructions were to return the girl and find out what happened. I'll have fulfilled the letter of my task. I have no interest in fitting you with a rope collar.'

'I'm not leaving my girl forever,' Brielle obstinately persisted.

'I don't want you to leave her. I want her to decide what she wants when she is older.'

'How so?'

'Let her stay where she is until she is of age. I know it's a lot to ask but it's in her best interests. Juliana — or Anna, whichever name you prefer — listen to me! You'll have to keep this a secret to keep your daddy safe. Will you do that?'

She nodded.

'What I have to suggest is this. Do you know your birthday, Juliana?'

'Twelfth of October,' she said. 'Six days before Saint Luke's Day.'

'That's right. So you will be twenty-one on the twelfth of October, 1683. That day will be busy with parties and so on. But on the next day, at the striking of noon, your father will be at the door of the Nieuwe Kerk. He will wait for you that day. If you want to see him, you can meet him there. And you will be an adult, so if you want to go with him, nobody can stop you. Or you can arrange to meet on another day later. Hendrik, you will have to stay away from Delft till then. Can you write?'

'A little.'

'Then remember this. I am Master Mercurius of the University of Leiden. If you need to contact her before then, send word to me and I will get it to her. But we can only do that in the most extreme circumstances — if you are mortally ill, for instance.'

Brielle looked at me uncertainly, but finally nodded.

'The Van Settens know now that you are still alive. Perhaps one day they will bend, but that is the best I can do for the moment. Juliana can decide for herself, and they will not influence her because none bar us will ever know that arrangement was made.'

Brielle pointed at the child. 'She's shivering. Can I hold her?'

'Hold her while you tell me all that happened. I'll come close too to add to her warmth.'

I remembered my Delft blue tile. God be praised it was still in my pouch. Like the rest of the contents, it was a bit wet, but it was undamaged. I handed it to Brielle. 'Kiss it,' I instructed.

'Kiss it? Why?'

'Just do it.' He obeyed, and I handed it to Juliana. 'You must treasure this. It will remind you that one day your father will return to kiss you again. Will you do that?'

She smiled, and tucked it in her bodice.

'Now, I know the story, but Juliana doesn't.'

Brielle began to tell the tale. He described how he had left for a voyage just after her birth, and on his return had discovered that his wife and child were gone. He eventually discovered that his wife had sickened and died after his departure, and the concerned authorities had taken Juliana somewhere for safe keeping. He had searched for her after every voyage, but nobody would tell him what had happened. And then, finally, the odd job man at the orphanage in The Hague had suggested that the wet nurses might know where she had gone. The old woman could only say that the baby had been adopted by a family in Delft. Thus, Brielle had walked to Delft. He had not seen his daughter for eight years. All he knew was that she had bright red hair like his.

'I walked the town, looking for red haired girls of the right age. My plan was to persuade her to leave with me, and I bought a second-hand barge to sail away. I lived there.'

'And that's how you escaped the searches. I saw the barges shifting mooring and it never occurred to me that a clever man could keep moving as the searchers approached.'

'Then I found the first girl. I spoke with her and told her I was her father. I thought that if I said that and I was wrong, they would protest, but she seemed so trusting. She came willingly, and I said we would go for a sail together. But when we spoke it was clear she was not the one. What was I to do now? I could not return her, or there would be a watch set for me and I would never find my daughter. I had to imprison her. I kept her drugged by day and moored the barge in the basin too far from the shore for her to escape at night.'

He appeared highly moved by the story he had to tell, and paused to wipe his eyes before continuing. 'Then I was around the Oostpoort and I saw this strapping young girl, broad-shouldered, strong for her age, red-haired. Surely this was my Juliana! I lay in wait near the pump, told her I was her daddy, and she came voluntarily.'

'She never knew who her father was. You answered a question in her life.'

'I didn't know that. But again it didn't seem right. I remembered my baby had a brown mark on the outside of one elbow. I didn't know if those things lasted, but neither of these girls had one. Then the Sunday before last I ventured into Delft and as we passed under a bridge I saw a girl feeding ducks. She rolled her sleeve up to throw her bread in the water, and I saw exactly the mark I recalled.'

He rolled up Juliana's sleeve to show it to me. Since it was dark, I had to take his word for it.

'I had my girl, and as soon as I could, I would flee Delft, but by then I was trapped inside. It was only when the mayor announced that the sergeant's men were being moved that I felt I could make the attempt. I returned the second girl unharmed, changed to that little boat that was easier to row in the dark, and the rest you know.'

'One thing you haven't explained. What happened to Gertruyd?'

'When she became agitated she swooned and began shaking. It seemed that she must have roused herself while I was off the boat and panicked to find she was alone. I was only a short distance away buying bread, but when I came below she was thrashing and kicking, and then she stopped breathing. I had no brandy, but I gave her wine and shook her … and she just died before me. I never intended her any harm.'

'I believe you. But she wasn't alone, was she? Magdalena was there.'

'Magdalena was asleep in the corner and could not be woken. I had given her a sleeping draught and perhaps gave her too much. When she finally stirred I had to explain to her that Gertruyd had died. We had to keep the body with us for two days until I could take her to be buried. I found a quiet spot and I laid her to rest decently. I whittled a cross from a twig and some wood I found here, and went back later to mark the grave.'

I sat reflecting on the account I had just heard. Juliana was still shivering and I needed to get her home. 'I'm content,' I said. 'Do we have a bargain?'

'I go free so long as I keep out of her life until she is twenty-one? It's the best I can hope for. At least I've finally seen her and spoken to her. And she knows where I'll be on that day.' He cradled the girl one last time and kissed her forehead. 'You know I'm not deserting you, don't you? I'd never do that. And I'm not afraid of a hanging either, only I'm not leaving you without your proper father.' She hugged him tightly and kissed him on the cheek.

'Now go,' I said, 'before anyone else comes along here.' I offered him my hand, and he shook it, then he righted the rowing boat and pulled away with long, clean strokes. I had no idea of the time, but I was weary, and I had a fractious girl to take home. And then I would have a lot of explaining to do.

CHAPTER THIRTEEN

I will not recount the scene at the Van Setten house in detail. Some moments are too private even for a memoir. The mother cried, the girl cried, the servants cried, I felt a certain dampness on the cheek. The only person who seemed untouched by the emotion was Wilhelmus van Setten. He thanked me curtly and bundled me out of the door.

The mayor came jogging along the street as I stood at the foot of the steps.

'She is home safe! Both girls restored to their families. Master, I salute you!' He removed his hat and performed an elaborate, if rather comical, bow.

'How did you know?' I asked.

'The young girl in the tower. She saw you run down by the Westsingel and when you were gone a long time, she signalled us to follow. We could not find you, but when you reappeared she waved the lantern again, and when we congregated at the church she told us she had seen you lead Anna home. Now, Master, come to the town hall, where we have beer, bread and meats to restore ourselves. But what happened to Brielle?'

I am told that when some people tell an untruth, they display some small sign, a twitch or gesture, that betrays that they are lying. I hope I have no such tic.

'I was alone. I could either rescue Anna or seize Brielle — and in truth, he was a big man and I could not have detained him. But I was able to lay hold of Anna and keep her from him. I think he might have tried to take her back but I reasoned with him — that I could not stop him but I would delay him long enough to ensure his capture, now or later. He knows now that his daughter is healthy and well cared for. That is what any father wants for his child. He cannot take her to sea with him, nor can he leave her alone when he goes. He did not want her to see him hang — so he has sworn not to return.'

'And you believe him?' This was said in the tone that one might adopt with a gullible country lad.

'I do. Not because he swore it to me, but because he swore it to Anna.'

The mayor thought a moment, then wrapped an arm around me. 'I concur. Now, let's have some refreshment.'

In the town hall, there was a festive air. Exhausted men, and one or two women, used the last of their energy in reliving their part in the recovery of the two young girls. I felt weary, but someone pushed a tankard of ale in my hand and gave me a chicken leg, and soon I felt more animated. I had done what I set out to do and could return to Leiden with my reputation intact. Granted, Brielle had escaped, but I had a confession from him and an undertaking not to return.

Then the flaw in my idea came to me. I had intended to announce that I had a confession but that as it had been given to me under the seal of the confessional, I was not at liberty to discuss it. But that would require me to admit publicly to being a Catholic priest, and if I did that I would lose my place at the university. And if I did not own up to being a priest, what reason had I for not disclosing the confession and breaking my promise to Brielle?

It was true that I had deduced large parts of the tale prior to hearing the confession, but I had taken a big chance in letting Brielle go (inasmuch as I could have stopped him) because I wanted to spare him the punishment that awaited him. It seemed so cruel to separate a father and daughter so soon after they found each other, but undoubtedly that was my duty. I could not pretend otherwise. There was, I suppose, just a chance that nobody would raise the issue. That comfort was denied me when I saw Van Leeuwenhoek crossing the room.

'My felicitations, Master Mercurius. But perhaps you would explain the whole circumstances to us while they are still fresh in your mind?'

'Excellent idea,' agreed the mayor. 'Silence, please, everyone! Master Mercurius is going to tell us what transpired.'

They sat around the room in eager anticipation, wondering what I was going to say to them. I was thinking exactly the same thing.

With the help of Van Leeuwenhoek and Vermeer, I explained how we had concluded that the kidnapper was looking for a girl whose exact appearance he did not know. I recounted the story much as I have in these pages, though in a more condensed form. I described the deception that we perpetrated on Brielle, and how we knew that it was successful when he released Magdalena Kuijper. I set out our plan to maintain a watch on all the routes out of Delft, but that we had overlooked one. When I realised it, there was no time to send for help. On foot, I had outpaced the boat, and capsized it. I did not describe exactly how.

It was at this juncture that my account necessarily became a little imprecise. I told how I had secured Anna and had persuaded Brielle that it was for the best to let her return to her family.

'He gave me his word that he would not return to trouble her childhood,' I concluded, choosing my words very carefully.

'There is the matter of the death of Gertruyd Lievens,' said Van Ruijven. 'Or do the murders of poor children not require an accounting?'

'She died in his absence as a result of a convulsion. Dr De Graaf gave his opinion that she was not murdered.'

'That's true,' Van Leeuwenhoek declared. 'De Graaf told me so.'

'And where did this villain obtain all the sleeping draught he needed to keep two girls subdued?' Van Ruijven demanded.

'I suspect he augmented it with genever,' I said, 'to which these young girls were not accustomed. But he said he bought it at an apothecary's shop in the town.'

There were several that might have been implicated, but for some reason everyone looked at Lieftingh.

'He bought one bottle! One! He told me he needed it for a mare in labour.'

'It must have been a large bottle,' Van Leeuwenhoek observed drily.

'Well, a mare is a large animal.'

'I cannot approve your actions,' said Van Ruijven. 'A man should pay for his sins on earth to expiate them before he faces judgement. By allowing him to walk free, you have endangered his immortal soul.'

I had not thought of it like that. In years to come I would set that topic to my brighter students — "mercy is not merciful: discuss" — and very few ever produced an answer that would have been graded well by Van Ruijven. He took his hat, bowed to the mayor, ignored me completely, and left.

Needless to say, I never saw Magdalena Van Ruijven again. I heard many years later that she had married the boy from the bookshop, whose fortune was made by it. When Van Ruijven and his wife were dead, his daughter inherited his fabulous art collection which, of course, passed into her husband's keeping. I might have been rich as Croesus.

There was an awkward silence as Van Ruijven's footsteps echoed on the stairs and the outer door slammed shut. I felt wretched, such a fool had I been not to see that I had no right to let Brielle slip away.

Van Leeuwenhoek rose to his considerable height, and eyed me gravely. 'I have no appetite to see a man choked to death,' he said. 'Either Brielle or you, Master. And I consider that your attempting to have stopped him would have led to one or the other of those outcomes.'

I had some suspicion that his scientific mind was quite satisfied that I would have been the one who choked. He flourished his hat in a courtly bow, and announced that it was late enough for him.

'Let's to our beds,' said the mayor. 'Master, tomorrow you must write your account and tender your expenses for reimbursement. I will arrange your transport back to Leiden. We are all indebted to you.'

If they were all indebted, I thought, then there could be no objection to my desiring that the debt be paid by helping another.

And that is how Lucie came to be employed to clean the town hall.

EPILOGUE

I slept late. Exceedingly late, to be honest. I think many of Delft's leading citizens did the same. Following a good breakfast, I repaired to the town hall and wrote a brief report which I gave to Claes. I was told that the mayor's carriage was to take me to Leiden when I was ready, so I wrapped my belongings in a parcel and glanced round the room at the inn for the last time. I hoped never to see it, the landlord or his appalling wife ever again. I kept that resolution.

I took my leave of the mayor, modestly accepting his thanks and giving what I believe was a suitably ambiguous answer when asked about the minister's position in the Nieuwe Kerk. I am inclined to think that the mayor interpreted my response rather in the vein of a clergyman giving the impression he did not want preferment because it is not the done thing to want it too obviously, whereas my feeling would more accurately have been described by the phrase "over my dead body". If Van Ruijven had been an orthodox Protestant, I should have been lucky to get past the front door, but he had no vote. In the event, and as I had suspected, the incumbent stayed on a year or two longer than anticipated, and by the time he came to be replaced, I had been forgotten.

Van Leeuwenhoek and Vermeer did me the courtesy of coming to bid me farewell. Van Leeuwenhoek was all politeness. I said that I hoped his little animals would bring him fame, as indeed they did, and his work with lenses made him known throughout Europe. He made some kind and completely inaccurate remarks about my work as a vindication of systematic method, which is the foundation of all science.

For my own part, I think my poor efforts illustrate how God, being perfect, has a sense of humour, and looked to my japes for some ready diversion from the business of running the universe, occasionally rewarding me for some especially ludicrous action by providentially pointing me in the right direction.

As I was climbing into the carriage Vermeer came running across the Markt, shouting to the driver to hold. 'I wanted to say goodbye in person and offer you my hand,' he said. 'I am grateful to you for making use of my gifts and helping me to feel useful. And, it goes without saying, for being so kind to Aleydis. She is a good child; indeed, they all are. I am blessed.' He clasped my hand warmly, and this benevolent, loving man opened his heart. 'Sometimes, Master, I consider how fortunate, how happy I am, and marvel at my fortune. I cannot imagine that a man can be so lucky for long.' He helped me into the coach. 'My wife and mother-in-law send their regards. You have made quite a conquest with Maria. I cannot remember her being so taken with a man.'

'I hope,' I said in a low voice, 'that I may rely upon your discretion.'

'About what?' said Vermeer. 'Oh, that! My dear fellow, who would believe me if I told them you were a Catholic?'

I never saw him again. Nearly four years later I heard that he had dropped dead suddenly at the age of forty-three. The war with the French had led to the deliberate flooding of Maria Thins's lands. Without her income, his family were in desperate straits. When he died, there was almost nothing left in the house, and Van Leeuwenhoek, who was appointed executor of his will, tried to sell the remaining paintings. It was said that Vermeer died of anxiety at being unable to keep his family supplied with the necessities of life. He owed the baker for nearly three years' bread.

Catharina kept her dignity. She argued with Van Leeuwenhoek over the sale of the pictures, and though he won the court case, yet he seems not to have forced the issue. Vermeer's kindly and honest nature had won him many friends, and some of them paid more than a fair price for his assets rather than embarrass his widow by offering charity.

Vermeer never had a formal student, but he taught his daughter Maria, who was able to earn a few guilders as an artist. She painted very few pictures that I have ever heard of, but I am told she specialised in painting decorations on doors and walls.

Aleydis never became a nun, but she did live in a convent as a sort of lay sister. I met her just once in later life when she was about thirty. I asked if she still craved martyrdom, and she told me that the pain of her father's early death had taught her not to seek it for herself, which could only distress those she cared for most.

'Your zeal worried me,' I admitted. 'I didn't feel it, and I thought I should. You challenged my faith, and thus changed my ways, and I will always be grateful to you.'

'And your caution changed mine,' she said. She bent towards me so she could speak without being overheard. 'When I said I was prepared to sacrifice my breasts, I didn't actually have any,' she told me, and then tossed her head back and laughed at my embarrassment. 'Aren't I wicked?' she asked.

I returned to Delft as soon as word of Vermeer's death reached Leiden. I paid my respects to his widow and mother-in-law and asked them to let me know if I could perform any service for them.

'You can,' said Maria Thins. 'Please pray with us. I am an old woman, doubtless a silly one, but I have tried to be a faithful servant of the Lord. In my life I have known a failed and violent marriage, a disrespectful son who needs to be confined for his own good, financial ruin and the loss of four grandchildren, and through it all I have sung the Lord's praises and continue to do so. God's ways are a mystery, and I do not complain about them. Even a minute of life on this earth is a great blessing, and we have no right to more. But, Master Mercurius, I need to know that there is some point to this suffering. I am the Lord's servant, and whatever His plan is for me, let it be so. Only let me believe that there is a plan.'

I hate such moments. The doubts of the faithful can be harder to cope with than the taunts of the unbelievers. But if my ordination meant anything, it was to comfort old, faithful women like Maria Thins.

'Let us pray an hour together,' I said, 'and God will ease your heart.'

We knelt, and we prayed, and then I brought to mind the psalmist's awestruck attestation of Divine Love for us: what is man, that Thou art mindful of him? Why does God care for each of us? And I further recalled that Sunday evening in Van Leeuwenhoek's study when he introduced me to a new world, a world of little animals, scooting to and fro busily and apparently unaware of my oversight. I told her what I had seen, and often meditated upon, and that I had concluded that if God has placed even these miniscule creatures in a congenial home, how can we doubt that He has a care for us?

She thanked me, and declared that her soul was comforted to hear it. 'You are a good man,' she said.

'No, I'm not,' I replied. 'I know many reasons why that is not true.'

'Oh, you university types,' she sighed, 'you think you know everything, but you don't know yourselves.'

Before I left Delft I walked across the town and found my way to the weavers' cottages. I hesitated before knocking, but what was the point of coming so far and not taking the opportunity to meet?

The door was opened by a tall, slim girl.

'Clara?' I guessed.

'Yes. Who are you?'

'I am Master Mercurius. I wondered if your parents were at home.'

'Father is at work, but Mother is here. I'll call her to you.'

A few moments later, Jannetje Dircks ran down the narrow stairs and stood before me. She had lost a little weight, but her colour was better and she had learned to sleep again.

'I didn't know if you'd be prepared to see me,' I began, 'after I failed to capture the man who abducted Gertruyd.'

'But you found out what happened to her. And the learned doctor was clear that she would have died anyway. I wish I could have been there to hold her as it happened, but God's will be done. Come, you can't stand outside. Please come in. I'm sorry that the house is a mess,' she said.

Every Dutch woman says that, and it is hardly ever true. It was well swept and scrubbed, and a little posy of wild flowers stood in a pot on the table, brightening the room. But the biggest surprise was on the wall, right where the window's light was strongest. It was a portrait of a young girl in a silvery shawl, smiling an enigmatic smile and containing so much life and energy you might think she would explode from it. I had a vague feeling of having seen it before, but I could not at first recall where.

'This is pretty,' I said.

Jannetje beamed, a luminous smile suffusing her features. 'It is my Gertruyd to the life,' she said. 'Mijnheer Vermeer brought it to me. He said that he felt I ought always to have her likeness by me, and it is a great comfort. In the evenings I gaze upon it and it is as if she were in the room with us and we are a family again.'

The power of art, I thought, to preserve the life of the dead and freeze them in our hearts; and now I knew where I had seen it. Vermeer had painted his daughter Beatrix, but he had never intended to paint her face. That is why that good-hearted man had kept it from his wife, and finally been compelled to promise to paint all the children when in reality his aim had been to paint the dead child of a poor woman. To have a great gift is wonderful, but to use that great gift in a great way is to be all that mortal man can be. I am not ashamed to say that my eyes filled with tears as I gazed upon it.

This child, whom I never saw alive, was there before me, impish, keen to be about her business, urgent with naughtiness, a living, breathing daughter captured for all time. I thought of her bruised and naked body as we examined it in the Armamentarium, but there was no sign of it here. Within that frame she was robust, rosy-cheeked, and possessed of flaming orange hair, the same hair that had led her to her fate.

'It has a title, Master, but I cannot read it well. Mijnheer Vermeer wrote it on the back. You may lift it down to see if you wish.'

I reverently eased the painting off its peg, turned it round, and moved to the light to see it better. Vermeer's handwriting was not good, but after a while I deciphered it fully, and choked back an unbecoming tear.

This little girl had brought me to Delft and had thus been the agent who allowed me to meet two of the greatest men of my day, who lived a stone's throw apart in a sleepy little Dutch town and yet illuminated the globe. As a result of working together to investigate her death they became closer and demonstrated what their respective fields could offer. And it was all summed up in the title of her painting.

She was, indeed, *The Allegory of Art and Science.*

A NOTE TO THE READER

Dear Reader,

Thanks for giving your time (and money) to read this story. I hope you enjoyed it.

It had its birth on a very precise day, 29 April 2011. It was also the day that Prince William and Kate Middleton (as she then was) were married, and my wife and I were in Delft. I had not realised until then that Vermeer and Van Leeuwenhoek were born within a few days and a few hundred metres of each other; so here we had, in one small town, one of the leading scientists and one of the finest artists of their day. At first I contemplated letting them be competing detectives, but it was more satisfying to introduce another detective whom they try to help.

Mercurius is a novice detective and needs all the help he can get, but then in 1671 everyone who detected was new to the job. I made him a university lecturer because asking for help from clever men seemed to me to make sense, and there was no need to disturb the common stereotype of the unworldly university don. Making him a secret Catholic added some internal conflict, particularly when he meets an attractive woman, and casting him as the narrator gives the story a different approach to my Slonský stories.

The Slonský stories are in the third person which means things can be described that Slonský does not yet know. That is not available to me for Mercurius, who can only tell us what he knows or has heard. That means, of course, that he can be wrong and mislead the reader, so long as he does not do it intentionally. The intelligent reader has to decide for themselves whether what he has just said is likely to be true. As a normal human being, his view of the truth of testimony is coloured by his assessment of the person giving it.

As a cleric, Mercurius has a strong moral compass. Some things, like capital punishment, worry him in a way that they might not worry another man of his time. On the other hand, if torture produces a confession, that is good for the victim's prospects in the next life and therefore to be encouraged; just don't expect Mercurius to do any torturing, because he does not have a strong stomach.

He wants a quiet life, reading when he can and lecturing when he must; unfortunately for him, he is too good at discovering answers to be left alone for long. In the next book, *Untrue Till Death*, his assistance is demanded by William of Orange. And you don't say no to him.

The painting in this book does not exist, but so few of Vermeer's paintings survive that it is easy to believe that some must have been lost. On the other hand, that offers up the tantalising hope that one day someone will find one in an attic.

If you have enjoyed this novel I'd be really grateful if you would leave a review on **Amazon** and **Goodreads**. I love to hear from readers, so please keep in touch through **Facebook** or **Twitter**, or leave a message on my **website**.

Dank je wel!

Graham Brack

Sapere Books is an exciting new publisher of brilliant fiction and popular history.

To find out more about our latest releases and our monthly bargain books visit our website:
saperebooks.com

Printed in Great Britain
by Amazon